MISSION DOSSIER

Agents

Vicky Mabrey, aka Snake: Chief Warrant Officer 2, Black Jaguar Squadron. Skilled in covert ops and hand-to-hand combat. Seasoned combat-mission pilot.

Griff Hutchinson: Chief Warrant Officer 1. U.S. Army Apache helicopter pilot. Decorated for bravery during combat in Afghanistan.

Location

Jungles of Peru

Task

To recover a stolen artifact of the Eastern Cherokee tribe—a seven pointed crystal star prophesied to have magical qualities.

Enemies

Felipe Balcazar: Owner of Balcazar Imports, a suspected front for stolen goods. Notoriously ruthless excavator of Native American artifacts. Rumored to force young men to help him dig up burial sites. Armed and dangerous.

Robert Marston: Billionaire businessman. Renowned collector of archaeological and present-day Native American sacred artifacts. Flagged by both Interpol and the FBI for criminal activity. Presently, insufficient data for his arrest.

Dear Reader,

Like the fast-paced holiday season, Silhouette Bombshell is charged with energy, and we're thrilled to bring you an unforgettable December reading experience. Our strong, sexy, savvy women will have you cheering, gasping and turning pages to see what happens next!

Let *USA TODAY* bestselling author Lindsay McKenna sweep you away to Peru in *Sister of Fortune,* part of the SISTERS OF THE ARK miniseries. This military heroine must retrieve a sacred artifact from dangerous hands. The last thing she needs is a sexy man she can't trust—too bad she has to work with one!

Check out Debra Webb's *Justice*, the latest in the ATHENA FORCE continuity series. Police lieutenant Kayla Ryan will risk everything to find her murdered friend's long-lost child and bring down an enemy who is closer than she ever suspected....

In *Night Life,* by Katherine Garbera, a former spy turned mother and wife finds herself drawn back into clandestine games when her former agency calls her in to catch a rogue agent—her estranged husband.

And don't miss Patricia Rosemoor's *Hot Case,* the story of a detective who enters her twin sister's dark world of wannabe vampires—and maybe the real thing—to find out why dead bodies are disappearing almost before her eyes.

As an editor, I am often asked what I'm looking for in a Bombshell novel. Well, *I* want to know what *you're* looking for as a reader. Please send your comments to me, c/o Silhouette Books, 233 Broadway Suite 1001, New York, NY 10279.

Best wishes,

Natashya Wilson
Associate Senior Editor, Silhouette Bombshell

Please address questions and book requests to:
Silhouette Reader Service
U.S.: 3010 Walden Ave., P.O. Box 1325, Buffalo, NY 14269
Canadian: P.O. Box 609, Fort Erie, Ont. L2A 5X3

LINDSAY
McKENNA

SISTER OF FORTUNE

Published by Silhouette Books
America's Publisher of Contemporary Romance

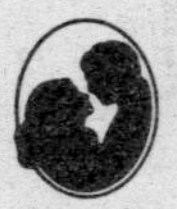

SILHOUETTE BOOKS

ISBN 0-373-51335-6

SISTER OF FORTUNE

This edition published by arrangement with Harlequin Books S.A.

Visit Silhouette Books at www.eHarlequin.com

Printed in U.S.A.

LINDSAY McKENNA

served in the U.S. Navy as an aerographer's mate 3rd class, a weather forecaster. She's no stranger to flying and got her student pilot license at age seventeen! The military is in her family and in her blood. Her family has a U.S. Naval history, and she was proud to serve her country. She has ridden in a T-38 "chase plane" during an actual test flight at Edwards Air Force Base and has flown in a B-52 on a day-and-night mission. She goes where the action is to get the sights, sounds and experiences to put into her books. Known as "The Top Gun of Military Romance," Lindsay created the first military romance in 1983 for Silhouette Special Edition. She's pioneered the field in many ways and continues to be a leader, just like her heroines.

To all my readers who love the chief warrant officer
helicopter pilots of the Black Jaguar Squadron.
I appreciate your support and enthusiasm. Thank you.

Chapter 1

Chief Warrant Officer Vickey Mabrey woke up screaming. She threw off the light U.S. Army green cotton blanket and sheet, and her sweaty bare feet landed on the cool surface of the wooden floor. Breathing hard, with her hair falling in disarray around her face, she groaned and leaned forward. Her elbows dug into her thighs.

Dammit! The same dream! A friggin' nightmare, actually. Her hands covered her perspiring face as she took huge, gulping breaths. Vickey felt the sweat trickling down her temples and following her rigid jawline. Trying to unclench her teeth, she kept repeating, "It's just a dream…just a dream…."

She slept naked, wanting to be one with the earth.

Not that a U.S. Army bunk was the earth, but it was as close as she was going to get under the circumstances.

Breathing raggedly through her mouth, she hoped her screams hadn't woken anyone in Black Jaguar Squadron barracks.

The two-story structure stood at the rear of a huge natural cave in a loaf-shaped mountain roughly fifty miles south of the famed archeological wonder Machu Picchu, Peru. Only the nearly all-woman combat squadron wasn't here for archeology. They hunted, all right: drug dealers flying cocaine out of Peru to Bolivia's border in order to sell it to the rest of the world. The buck stopped with her squadron.

Right now, Vickey wished she was anywhere but here, sitting in her own pooling sweat.

"Damn…" she muttered, lifting her head. After wiping the perspiration from her upper lip with a trembling finger, she turned and reached blindly for the pitcher of water and glass on her bed stand. Water. A mirthful grin cut across her tense features as she found the glass. It was automatic: wake up in the middle of the night with this dream, pour herself a glass of tepid water and then fall back into an exhausted sleep.

As she chugged the water, rivulets ran from the corners of her mouth. Vickey relished the feel of cooling water spilling onto her chest and trickling down between her small breasts. She would have loved to take a shower to get rid of the fear sweat clinging to her skin, but needed sleep even more desperately.

The BJS squadron flew 24/7. They were short on pilots, so everyone flew for more missions than they should. Vickey had heard that Major Maya Stevenson, the commanding officer of their four-year venture, was getting in new Apache combat pilots to help relieve the murderous flight schedule. That was something they all prayed for. Working a twenty-four-hour shift every other day was a killer in more than one way. Pilots without adequate rest between grueling and dangerous missions upped the ante on them getting killed.

Setting the yellow plastic glass back on the bed stand, Vickey eyed the dull light leaking from beneath the closed door of her cubical. All things considered, the place was relatively quiet. She heard some snoring and someone down the hall muttering in her sleep. The sounds were typical and soothing to her frayed nerves. Sleep was precious. Had she awakened her dorm mates on either side of her? It wasn't unusual for a pilot to have a nightmare and wake up shrieking. Why not? They put their asses on the line every day out there, flying the Peruvian skies in the battle to halt drug shipments.

The planes carrying millions of dollars' worth of cocaine might not have the arsenal to knock Vickey and her colleagues out of the sky, but the drug lords had hired Russian mercenary pilots, who flew deadly Black Shark helicopters. Those state-of-the-art machines were more than able to take on a U.S. Army Apache. And of late, Maya's team had lost two helos and two crews to the bastards.

Looking at her watch, Vickey saw it was 0300. That was when this nightmare always came. Why? Wiping her face savagely, Vickey groaned and lifted her feet off the cool floor, tucking them beneath the blanket once more. Snuggling her nearly six foot frame down in the cot, she pressed her face into the pillow, wanting to escape the dream. Lying on her stomach, she shut her eyes tightly. She had to get up at 0530 to be ready for another twenty-four hours of flight duty. She prayed to the Great Spirit for sleep to quickly return to her.

"Hey, Snake! Get your sorry butt outta that bunk!" Wild Woman gave the wooden leg of the bed a deliberate kick.

Vickey Mabrey, known to everyone as Snake, was sleeping. The green wool blanket was pulled up over her head and strands of her dark brown hair peeked out the top.

"Uhh..." Snake moaned as she stirred beneath the blanket.

"Come on, Snake! Rise and shine, girlfriend. We got duty in two hours! It's 0530, sweet thing. Up and at 'em..." Wild Woman grinned and nudged the cot leg again with the tip of her polished black flight boot.

"Get outta here," Snake mumbled.

Chuckling, Wild Woman went to the desk where Snake kept her automatic coffeemaker. It was the one luxury she insisted on having here at the Black Jaguar Base, hidden deep within the jungle-clad mountain.

"Ohh, I know that groan," she said, flipping the switch. Snake always prepared the coffee beans and set up the machine when she got off a twenty-four-hour duty in her Apache. That way, she could flounder blindly out of her bunk the next morning or night, depending on the schedule, and hit the switch. Turning, Wild Woman watched as Snake groaned again.

"Get the hell outta here…."

"No can do, Chief."

Vickey was half Navajo, so her colleagues called her "Chief"—her real title as a warrant officer—as often as they called her "Snake." Chief was a common title for warrant officers. Every Apache pilot had a nickname, and Vickey had earned hers the hard way. One day, shortly after being assigned to the black ops unit, she had climbed into the cockpit of her helo and found a young anaconda constrictor curled up on her seat. Of course, she had let out a shriek that could be heard throughout the massive cavern that housed the operation, including the two-story H.Q. building. In the Navajo religion, snakes were considered evil. Seeing one show up on the seat of the copter one was about to pilot wasn't exactly a dream come true.

The fragrance of perking coffee began to waft through the tiny plywood cubicle. Outside the thin walls, Vickey could hear other pilots waking up and moving around. Grumbling softly, she threw off the cover and sat up. Giving her friend a bleary look, she pushed her straight, shoulder-length brown hair off her face.

"You look like hell," Wild Woman said, grinning. "What did you do? Have that nightmare again?"

Wrinkling her nose, Vickey looked at the coffeemaker. The smell was enticing. Invigorating. "Yeah. I don't know why I'm getting it. It used to come once a month. I've had the damn thing for over a year now...." Vickey gave her blond friend a frown. Wild Woman, whose real name was Jessica Merrill, was already suited up in her one-piece black uniform with its mandarin collar. She leaned against the door, one booted foot crossed over the other, her hands propped on her hips.

Rubbing her eyes, Vickey stood up and padded to the coffeemaker. It was ready. *Good.* She poured some of the strong, black brew into a white ceramic mug. Sipping it, she looked over the rim at Wild Woman, who continued giving her an evil-looking grin.

"What's so damn funny this time of morning?"

"You." Wild Woman pulled a fresh flight uniform from Vickey's wooden dresser and tossed it on her cot. "You've got purple circles under your eyes, Snake. Standing there in the altogether, coffee in hand, hair uncombed, you look more like a wild woman than me." She tittered. Leaning down, she pulled Vickey's polished black leather flight boots from beneath her bunk.

"Go to hell, Miss Cheery Face... I need my coffee."

"Yeah, and a hot shower." Wild Woman's smile widened. "I'll meet you down at mess in twenty minutes, Snake."

"Yeah. Thanks..." Vickey watched her friend saunter out of her cube. Around her, she could hear the rest of the squadron getting ready for another day of duty. *Time to go after the bad guys.* Setting her coffee on the dresser, she opened her metal locker and pulled out a light blue cotton bathrobe, a towel and washcloth.

Time to get her act together and take a shower. At least the sweat from that damn nightmare would finally be washed off. As she opened the door to the hallway, a sour smile twisted her lips. She'd experience the fear all over again in the next twenty-four hours, flying combat duty. But at least she'd be starting out clean.

"You still look like shit," Wild Woman noted, sitting across from Snake as they ate breakfast in the mess, the U.S. Army kitchen facility. The space was filled with rows upon rows of picnic-style tables with benches. Ground crews, mechanics and pilots all mingled together—those going off duty, who wanted a meal before they hit the sack, as well as those going on duty, who were trying to wake up enough to be coherent on the job.

"That friggin' nightmare used to come once a month," Vickey griped. She slathered butter on her whole wheat toast. "Now I'm gettin' it once a week. It sucks, lemme tell you...."

Frowning, Wild Woman looked up from her aluminum tray filled with eggs, bacon and fruit. "Refresh me on it. You said it started over a year ago. And it's the *same* dream again and again?"

Shrugging, Vickey growled, "Yeah. It starts out with me standing in the dark. My heart is pounding." She gave her friend a cutting smile. "You know how your pulse starts racing when you sense Black Sharks hanging around behind those mountains, but you can't locate them on your equipment?"

"Know it too well," Wild Woman murmured. "Okay. Go on…"

Vickey picked up a piece of toast and munched on it. All around them, the laughter and soft chatter of women embraced them. It was a comforting sound. She saw a few men, but there weren't that many down here. Major Stevenson had started BJS as an all-woman squadron. Over time, she'd been forced to take on some men, but women still outnumbered them ten to one. Vickey liked it that way. She liked the company of women. Men sucked—or at least her experience with them had.

"Snake? The dream?"

Grinning, Vickey said, "Yeah…anyway, I'm in the dark. I feel something stalking me, but I can't see it. I can only feel it."

"You have great instincts," Wild Woman murmured. "Must be that Navajo blood of yours kicking in."

Nodding, Vickey said, "Maybe it is. Anyway, I feel this monster, this shadow in the dark, coming for me. I have an urgent sense that I have to save something. I'm hiding. I feel fear so bad that I wake up stinking from it."

She saw Wild Woman's large blue eyes go soft with compassion. "Don't give me that look," Vickey growled. "I don't want your pity."

"Of course not. I wouldn't *think* of pitying you, Snake."

"Liar…"

They both laughed and sipped their coffee.

Vickey felt a kinship with Wild Woman. They'd

gone to hell and back together, and Vickey had learned one important thing about her partner. Though short for a pilot, only five feet six inches tall, Wild Woman more than made up for her lack of height with sheer in-your-face bravado. That's how she'd gotten her own nickname; she would do wild, crazy things in the cockpit and in combat and walk away whole from the confrontations.

"Okay, you're looking for something while this goon is stalking you," Wild Woman prodded.

"Right," Vickey muttered. She stabbed at the last of her omelet with her aluminum fork. "I know it's near. I can sense it. And this dark figure is tracking me. It's a race for me to find it before he finds me. I go running around in what looks like a huge, dark warehouse. There are all kinds of boxes, all sizes, and I'm looking, looking, looking." Sighing, Vickey put her fork and plate aside. "Then I see this glimmer of light. I run toward it. The light gets brighter as I run like hell to get to it. Behind me, I can hear the footsteps of this goon. He's runnin' hard, and he's catching up to me. I'm not sure if I can reach the thing before he gets me. There's a lot of dust, and I'm choking on it as I run. The boxes are all old and covered in dust and cobwebs. I can barely see. But I spot this light."

Vickey picked up her coffee cup and took a gulp, burning her tongue. Muttering a soft curse, she put the mug down. "Finally, I find it. There's a glow coming out of this dusty old box. I screech to a halt, make a left turn and race down an aisle. This goon's nearly upon me. I know I have to get what's in the box before he does. I know if he gets it, we're all dead."

"That's kind of disturbing."

"Tell me about it. I reach the box. I tear the lid open. And there, floating in the air, is a seven-pointed star made out of what looks like glass or quartz crystal. It's just floating there in the box, and it's beautiful. I recognize this star, but I don't know how I know it. I touch it. And just as I do, the goon grabs my shoulder." Grimacing, Vickey said, "And that's when I wake up screaming. I'm sure I wake up our squad mates, too...."

"Hey, Snake," Wild Woman counseled gently, "we all have screamin' nightmares here. We're in combat 24/7. What the hell do you expect? We're human." She grinned recklessly. "Besides, being stuck in this mountain all the time, we don't get R & R like most army dudes do. We have to pop our cork in some way and let off steam from our daily travails."

Wasn't *that* the truth. Vickey glumly nodded. "I don't know what I'm going to do, Wild Woman. This dream is happening more and more often. I wish my father were here. He's a Navajo medicine man, and he might help me understand it. I sure can't figure it out myself."

"Is there a star like that in your Navajo culture?"

Shaking her head, Vickey said, "Not that I know of. That's what's got me goin' on this. What the hell does it mean?" She opened her hands in frustration, and stared at her friend across the table.

"Don't ask me. I'm a hodgepodge from the gene

pool." Wild Woman chuckled. "I got some Cheyenne in me, but a quartz crystal star isn't something I remember my parents talking about."

"I don't know *what* I'm going to do. I'm losing a lot of shut-eye over this damn thing. I can't afford all this sleep deprivation, Wild Woman." Rubbing her wrinkled brow, Vickey said darkly, "I think I need to talk to a shrink or something."

Tittering, Wild Woman said, "No shrinks here. Maybe talk to Elizabeth? Our medical doc?"

Vickey shook her head and said, "No. But my gut's been tellin' me to go talk to the major. You know, she's from the Jaguar Clan, a mystical, mysterious group. My sense is that she might know something, or maybe be able to give me a clue about this dream. I hate to bother her with something so trivial, because we're all under the gun here. We're short of pilots, short on time, short on helicopters. And everyone is expecting us to keep stopping these drug flights like we did before we hit this current crunch, with so many Apaches needed in Afghanistan and Iraq."

"I know...." Wild Woman moved one glossy, pale pink fingernail around on the redwood table. "We're in the hurt locker right now, there's no doubt."

"I heard the other day from Dallas Klein, the executive officer, that Major Stevenson is trying like hell to get a few Apache pilots who just spent a year in Afghanistan to be sent down here. That should give us some relief."

"Wouldn't *that* be great?" Wild Woman sat up and smiled. "Instead of always having to potty train male

Apache pilots who haven't seen combat? That would be a godsend."

"I hope she can pull it off," Vickey muttered. "We need some downtime. We can't keep going like this."

"Maybe that's why you're having this dream so much," Wild Woman said soothingly. She looked at her watch. "Well, time to boogie, Snake. We have to be at the squadron room in ten minutes for our briefing with Lieutenant Klein."

"Yeah…right." Snake unwound her tall frame from the bench. She felt tired. Exhausted, actually, but she wasn't about to let her sister pilot know that. BJS wasn't a place for bitching about what hurt inside of you. It was a combat squadron, and the women took care of one another. They were a tight, nearly inseparable group that had flown together for four years. Their loyalty had been fused in blood, sweat and tears—quite literally.

After Vickey dropped off her aluminum tray to the mess sergeant, she followed Wild Woman out the screen door into the huge cave that housed the operation. Walking with her black canvas helmet bag in her left hand, she looked out the mouth of the cave. It was a good quarter mile to the flat lip where the Apaches took off and landed. The usual white clouds surrounded the entrance, even now at daybreak.

Foggy conditions occurred with great regularity at this altitude. The base was situated at eight thousand feet, and built deep inside the mountain—the perfect hiding place. In front of the cave was a huge black lava wall nearly a hundred feet high and over five feet thick.

In the center was a hole they called the Eye. It was a rotor and a half wide—just big enough for an Apache to fly through, with a few feet to spare. One wrong move and a pilot could crash into the rock eye, killing all on board and destroying the twenty-million-dollar bird.

The black, gleaming wall gave them protection from the bad guys. No helo could come in over the top of it, although if a Black Shark merc was crazy enough to try and fire a rocket, he might succeed. But that pilot would be killed and everyone knew it. Black Shark mercenary pilots weren't given to suicide missions and their facility had never been attacked as a result.

As Vickey walked at Wild Woman's side, they dodged several electric golf carts whizzing by carrying personnel and supplies. This place was a beehive of activity.

"I've got an idea," Wild Woman said as they approached the two-story headquarters building, which sat off to one side. She halted at the aluminum stairs leading to the mission briefing room.

"Uh-oh." Vickey raised one eyebrow skeptically. "I get nervous when you think."

Chortling, Wild Woman grinned, showing her even white teeth. "How about after our briefing with Dallas, you amble down the hall to Major Stevenson's office? Her door is always open. If you happen to peek in and she doesn't look harried, pop in and tell her about your dream."

Mouth quirking, Snake said, "I really hate to bother her…."

"She'd want to know," Wild Woman said, jogging up the stairs, her hand on the rail. "No one cares about us more than she does. If you're losing that much sleep, Snake, the major would want to know." At the top of the stairs, Wild Woman pulled the door open and allowed Vickey to walk by her. Catching up quickly, she added, "You know the major is Indian, like you. Brazilian Indian. Who better to tell your dream to? I'll bet you a shot of pisco that she can help."

Smiling wryly, Vickey said, "A shot of pisco?" It was a popular alcoholic beverage in Peru, a kick-ass drink that looked like vodka but hit the drinker like an enraged bull running full steam ahead. Vickey liked to sit at the bar of her favorite restaurant in Cuzco and sip all night on one shot of the fiery drink. It was one of the few ways for her to relax. Music, dancing with the local Latin boys and a shot of pisco made her forget the danger of her job, if only for a few hours.

"Yeah." Wild Woman halted at the open door to the mission room. Inside, she could see Dallas, the X.O., up at the front preparing her notes. Many of their sister pilots were already seated. Sticking out her hand, Wild Woman said, "Game on, Snake? I'd like to win this one."

"You're betting a pisco that Major Stevenson can unravel this dream for me, right?"

"That's right, girlfriend. Shake on it?"

"And if she can, I'm buying you the pisco?"

"You got it."

Gripping Wild Woman's small hand, Vickey said,

"You've got yourself a bet. Now come on. The lieutenant is giving us the evil eye for not getting our butts in there…."

Chapter 2

As soon as Vickey entered the mission room to get her orders for the next twenty-four hours, Lieutenant Dallas Klein lifted her head from the papers she was studying at the podium.

"Snake, you're going up to Major Stevenson's office pronto. Wild Woman's your copilot today, so she'll take the mission briefing and fill you in later. Take off."

"Yes, ma'am," Vickey murmured, stunned over the order. What was going down here? It was unusual for an X.O. to ask one of the pilots to leave the ready room before a briefing. Vickey gave Wild Woman a questioning look, and she shrugged in response. She didn't seem to know what was going on, either.

Turning around, helmet bag in her left hand, Vickey left the room and moved quickly down the busy corridor to Major Stevenson's office, where she knocked on the door. Looking inside, she saw her commanding officer behind her desk—and two people sitting to her right on one side of the small office. Vickey didn't know them.

"Come in, Snake," Maya murmured, lifting her hand and gesturing for her to enter. "Shut the door, will you?"

Hmm, bad news. Major Stevenson had had an open-door policy ever since she'd started the BJS four years ago. Any person—enlisted, warrant officer or officer—could walk in and talk to her at any time about anything. It was a leadership style Vickey heartily approved of.

"Yes, ma'am," she murmured. After closing the door, Vickey came to attention in front of her superior's desk. Maya wore her one-piece black uniform with the Black Jaguar Squadron patch on her left arm—the only identification any of them carried. No flag identified them as citizens of the United States, so if they got shot down, no one could verify their origin.

"At ease, Snake. Have a seat."

Vickey took a chair slightly left of center of Maya's desk. She looked curiously at the man and woman in civilian clothes sitting rather tensely nearby. The woman was definitely of Native American origin, her skin copper-colored, her fierce gold eyes pinned on Maya. The man next to her was probably Native American, too, but Vickey couldn't be sure. He had copper-colored skin like the woman.

Pulling her attention back to her C.O., Vickey put the helmet on her lap and rested her hands on top of it.

Maya Stevenson was a Brazilian Indian with shoulder-length, straight black hair and emerald-green eyes. She had been adopted by a North American couple when she was a baby.

Vickey felt the power around Maya. It was no secret that the woman was a member of the mystical Jaguar Clan. Even growing up in the Navajo tradition, Vickey recalled times her father, a full-blood, would talk of when the jaguar had walked the mountains and valleys of the Southwest, where their people had a reservation.

"Snake, I want you to meet Kai Alseoun and Jake Stands Alone Carter. This is Chief Warrant Officer 2, Vickey Mabrey." She pursed her lips. "Say hello to them."

Vickey turned her head and met Kai's inquiring gaze. "Howdy," she said. Her gut instinct told her that while these two were dressed in civilian clothes, they reeked of the military. CIA? Maybe. FBI? No. The Bureau only operated within the U.S. The CIA had responsibility for the rest of the world.

"Nice to meet you, Chief Mabrey," Kai said in a low, husky tone.

Maya leaned back in her creaky chair, one hand on a desk overflowing with paperwork. "Well, Kai? Is she the one?"

The one what? Vickey frowned. Giving Kai and then Maya a curious look, she felt suddenly vulnerable. What the hell was going on here?

Kai nodded. "Yes, Major, she is."

That sure as hell sounded ominous to Vickey. Her frown deepened. "The one what?" she growled, swinging her gaze to Maya. She trusted her C.O. with her life. Maya would never lie to her. And Vickey wasn't that trusting of these two birds who sat like wolves in sheep's clothing two feet away from her.

Maya's mouth thinned. "Snake, you had any interesting dreams of late?"

Startled, Vickey's brows shot upward. "Ma'am?" Why should she be surprised Maya would know this? It was whispered that the woman was clairvoyant and could hear and see things others could not. Vickey's hands tightened on the black canvas bag.

"Dreams. You know…." Maya grinned and held Vickey's uncomfortable gaze.

"Well yes, ma'am. I have." Gulping, she glanced at the two strangers, who kept their intent gazes fixed on her. Right now she felt like one of her mother's specimens beneath a microscope. A biologist, her mom was fascinated by everything that lived. Now Vickey knew how a bug felt beneath her inquiring eyes. Not good. Definitely not good.

"Can you tell us about it? Or them?"

Vickey's mouth pulled in wryly. "Ma'am, I don't mind sharing them with you, but I really don't want to talk about them…here." As she waved her hand vaguely, she saw Maya's green eyes fill with amusement.

"Humor me, Snake, will you? These people are here because of a dream that Kai herself had. She's looking to corroborate it."

Stymied, Vickey studied Kai assessingly. Slowly turning her head, she nodded at Maya. "Okay..." And she launched into the dream about the quartz crystal star. As she spoke, Vickey noted Kai's responses. The woman seemed as if she could barely sit still. Vickey saw Maya's mouth pull into a sour smile of approval when she finished relaying the recurring dream.

"So that's it in a nutshell," Vickey said.

Maya lifted her chin and looked at Kai Alseoun. "Well? Is she the one?" she asked again.

The one? That sounded like Neo from *The Matrix.* Vickey had seen the three movies at least twenty times and loved them and their cryptic, symbolic message.

Kai nodded. "Yes, Major, she is. No question."

Gulping warily, Vickey shifted her position to look more closely at Kai. She was tall, at least six feet, with her hair in two thick, black braids that emphasized her Native American heritage. She wore casual clothing: jeans, hiking boots and a dark green, short-sleeved tank top. Who *was* she? Vickey sensed she was undercover, and her gut was never wrong about these things.

"The one what?" Vickey said defensively, giving her superior a look that said *Come clean and tell me the rest of this little secret.*

Maya picked up her coffee and took a sip from the white ceramic mug. Setting it down, she said, "Kai and Jake are here to verify something, Snake. Kai is Eastern Cherokee. She comes from a medicine family, like you do. Until recently she was in the U.S. Navy as an F-14 combat pilot. When she came home from the service, her grandmother, one of the elders of her nation, sent her out on a vision quest."

"Yeah, the hill," Vickey said. "I'm familiar with vision quests."

Nodding, Maya murmured, "I figured you were. Being a Navajo medicine man, your father would have trained you in many aspects of your culture."

"Yes, ma'am, he did." Vickey did not want to become a medicine person, however. She saw the hell her father went through—the pressures, the expectations of others—and she wanted no part of it.

"You're familiar with dreams being a message," Maya said.

"Yes, ma'am, I am."

"And how long have you had this dream about this star?"

"Over a year."

Maya looked at Kai. "Does that sound about right?"

Kai nodded. "It does. She would have started having the dream shortly after the clan totems were stolen from the Ark of Crystals."

Vickey frowned at Kai. "What the hell are you talkin' about?"

"My warrant officers are allowed to speak freely, as you can see." Maya grinned at Kai.

"No problem." A slight smile touched Kai's lips, before she turned her attention to Vickey. "I have a story to share with you, Chief."

Chief was a common title for warrant officers, who weren't true officers, but weren't enlisted, either, filling a gap between the two hierarchies. Vickey nodded. "Yeah, I'd like to hear it. Right now I feel like I'm looking through a plate-glass window, with you three on the other side."

Kai's mouth twitched again. "I'll try and remedy that situation right now, Chief Mabrey."

"Call me Snake."

Kai nodded. "Okay." She opened her hands and focused on the woman who sat tensely before her. "A little over a year ago, the Yam Clan, which takes care of our Ark of Crystals, had thieves break into the caretaker's home. They stole three of the seven totems that belong to the seven clans of our people."

"Yes, I'm aware of your ark. My father has worked with your medicine people in the past."

Kai seemed pleased by the news and continued, "This is better than I'd hoped. Of course you would know about us if your father is practicing medicine. Each of our clans has a quartz crystal totem. These crystals, it is said, were made in the stars and brought down to us. They are powerful. In the hands of a good-hearted medicine person, they help the clan remain healthy and positive. In the hands of a two-heart—a bad person—the crystals can be used to harm or even kill."

"Okay," Vickey said. "How do I fit into this picture?" She didn't see how she could. She was, after all, Navajo and not Eastern Cherokee. Each nation's sacred ceremonial tools were unique.

"I don't know why you were given your dream about the star crystal, Snake. I would have thought an Eastern Cherokee would have been chosen, but that's not how it has gone. The Great Spirit works in mysterious ways." Kai shrugged and gave her an apologetic look. "I was shown that three women, myself among them, were to retrieve the crystal totems and bring them back to my nation. We—" she turned to her partner "—have just returned from finding the Paint Clan crystal, which is now back with the keeper of the ark on our reservation. The next one to be found is the star crystal."

"I follow you so far. You think I'm having a dream about the Yam Clan's totem?" Vickey was trying to figure out this convoluted scenario. She was no stranger to dream interpretation, but while her father was very good at it, she wasn't.

"In my vision quest I saw the star totem coming to Peru after it was stolen," Kai stated.

"It's here? Where? Do you know?"

Kai shook her head. "No, the trail begins in Lima. I have no idea where in the city."

Maya sat up in her creaking chair and rested her elbows on her desk. "That's where you come in, Snake. You're the one who had the dream of the crystal star. Kai knows, without a doubt, that you're the woman to go after it and bring it back to her people."

"Excuse me?" Vickey said. "I'm not Cherokee. I'm half Navajo and half German."

Jake Stands Alone Carter spoke for the first time. "Snake, it doesn't matter whether you have Cherokee blood or not. You are part Native American, and the Great Spirit is asking this service of you. For whatever reason, it's you who were chosen, because you're the one getting this dream." His mouth curved in a rueful smile. "I'm half Cherokee myself. In our language we have no word for *why.* So we're accepting the fact that the Great Spirit has assigned other people to find our totems for us. It is the way it is."

Vickey knew that philosophy very well; she'd been raised with it. "Okay, I can understand the premise. Of late, I've been having the dream once a week, and it sure has played hell on my getting a decent night's sleep."

Chuckling, Maya said, "I would think it would."

"I can't tell the location of the star from the dream," Vickey told them. "I just see a typical Peruvian neighborhood with buildings one or two stories high."

"And you're being stalked," Kai murmured.

"Yeah, for sure. I don't know by who, but I can definitely feel the dude behind me, and he wants to kill me."

Jake looked at Maya. "She needs to know the rest of this story."

"Go for it."

Jake gave Vickey his full attention. "We know that a billionaire by the name of Robert Marston is collecting archeological and present day sacred items of indigenous people worldwide. He has collected pipes, for example, from many Native American nations. He also has pipe bags, rattles, feathers and other things that we use in ceremony."

Vickey's nostrils flared. "My father has a term for bastards like that—*power stalkers*. They want our people's sacred tools—the ones we use to help our nation remain spiritually healthy."

Kai smiled tightly. "You nailed it, Snake. That's exactly what Marston is. We haven't been able to prove that he hired men to steal our clan totems. We've got some evidence, but not enough to convict him. Yet. There is no clear trail back to this man, but Interpol as well as the FBI know that he's been in collusion with others to steal such things. He collects items of power for power's sake. He's known to have several personal collections at his homes around the world. His base of operation is in Toronto, Canada, but he has homes in Hong Kong and in Glastonbury, England."

"We feel he keeps all of the pieces outside the U.S., because if we gather enough evidence, we could go into his estate with a search warrant and try to find them," Jake explained. "And he's not about to let that happen. The FBI suspects he keeps his most important items in Hong Kong and England."

Kai continued, "We think one of the thieves he hired, a Giles Rowland, decided to keep the Paint Clan mask for himself. All evidence suggests that he was supposed to take the crystal totem to Marston in Hong Kong, but decided to try and hide it in a cave at the Red Center of Australia." She smiled wryly. "Rowland chose the wrong cave and fell to his death. Through a series of dreams and help by an Aboriginal medicine woman, Jake and I were led to it. We found it, found Rowland dead, along with evidence that the Paint Clan mask was supposed to go to Marston. He's got the money and the smarts not to be tied directly to anything. He's not going to tell police authorities that his man, Rowland, absconded with the Paint Clan mask. We know he had other men looking for Rowland in the Red Center because they discovered us and almost shot us out of the air." Kai shook her head. "Robert Marston is wily, like a coyote."

"A trickster," Vickey murmured. "Yeah, I know the type." One came to mind when she remembered her training at Fort Rucker, the U.S. Army base in Alabama where she'd learned to fly the deadly Apache helicopter. Griff Hutchinson, from the class ahead of hers, had been implicated in a plot to see her become AWOL—absent without leave—and get kicked out of the Army as a result. The men in his class wanted no females flying Apache helos. Hutchinson and his pack of coyotes had wanted to see the women of her group fail, even if they had to plot to do so.

"Marston is slick and sly. A global coyote," Kai said, frowning. "We were attacked a number of times by his men."

"And barely survived," Jake added, giving Kai a worried look.

"Marston has the money and the modus operandi," she muttered, anger leaking into her husky tone. "Without our clan totems, my people are suffering, Snake. The crystal objects are more than simple heirlooms. If your father is a medicine man, then you understand that such articles are infused with powers beyond what most people comprehend."

Nodding, Vickey said, "I carry a little blue stone that my father gave me." She pulled an old, worn deerskin pouch out of a pocket and held it up for them to see. "I'm no stranger to medicine and the fact that it can be used to help us or hurt us. I won't part with this stone when I'm flying. I know it helps to protect me."

"Then you do understand," Kai murmured.

Vickey heard the gratefulness in the woman's voice. "Yeah, I do." She tucked the pouch back into her pocket. "But I don't know how I can help you with this." She gave Maya a searching look. "Do you, ma'am?"

"I've got a few ideas, Snake." Tapping her fingers on the surface of her desk, Maya seemed to collect her thoughts. "But none of them are going to make any of you happy." She turned to Kai and Jake. "I can't lend Snake to a black ops in Lima or wherever. I'm too short of pilots right now. If I turn her over to you, like a dog going on a hunt, I'll be out a key pilot in my own operation. I realize the importance of this mission for you, Kai, but my hands are tied.

"There's a group of Apache helicopter pilots being assigned to us who were seasoned in Afghanistan. They should arrive tomorrow. But even at that, there's a month-long indoctrination. These pilots must train with my experienced team before I can cut them loose to fly their own missions against the druggies."

Vickey started in surprise. "We've got replacements coming, ma'am?" Her spirits soared. Replacements meant that eventually their grueling hours of duty would be reduced and they'd get more time off from flying. It meant more sleep, more rest and being more alert when they did fly combat missions. Joy threaded through her.

"Don't look so relieved, Snake," Maya said. "There's only three of them. All men, of course. But at least they're seasoned combat vets who have seen plenty of wartime action."

Only three. Vickey sagged back in her chair. With the U.S. Army strung out around the world, Maya wasn't getting the relief she'd anticipated. Vickey had spent four years, nonstop, down here. While she loved what she did, she would prefer a lessening of her flight hours. Three new pilots would help, but a lot more were needed.

"And," Maya said unhappily to Kai and Jake, "that means that even though Snake is supposed to go find this crystal star totem, I can't really allow her to do it full-time. I'll give her time off between her combat flying schedule here at BJS when I can. That's as good as it gets under the circumstances."

Kai shrugged and smiled in gratitude. "That's better than nothing, Major. And we appreciate your understanding how important this is to our people. Major Mike Houston, the head of Medusa, a branch of Perseus, is going to give you whatever Snake needs for her to search."

"What I need is more pilots," Maya growled. "Houston can't give me that, as much as I wish he could."

"Understood, Major. Mike will be in touch with you on the details to help Snake look for this crystal star. Lima is obviously a very good place to start."

"No disagreement there," Maya said. She gave Vickey a dark look. "But you won't be handling this mission alone, Snake. You need a partner—someone to cover your back while you snoop around and try and find this crystal."

"I don't have a problem with that," Vickey said, hoping Wild Woman would be assigned to go with her. She would make a good teammate, for sure.

Moving papers around on her desk, Maya sat up and pulled one from a pile. "This is a list of the pilots coming to us tomorrow. Of the three, one has a touch of Native American blood, and I chose him to go with you."

Frowning, Vickey said, "Why can't I have one of the women pilots I fly with, ma'am?"

"Because I need all of them here, to fly with these new pilots and get them up to speed, that's why. Matter of fact, the best way I can see to make ends meet is for you and this dude not only to fly together here at BJS, but work on the mission of finding the crystal as well." She dropped the paper back on her desk and gave Vickey a flat look. "So he's your partner both in the cockpit and on the ground, hunting for the star."

Trying to not show her disappointment, Snake said, "Yes, ma'am. Can I ask who it is?"

Maya's black brows knitted. "You know him, Snake. Griff Hutchinson."

Her world slammed to a halt. Vickey gasped and came out of the chair, her helmet bag crashing to the floor. "Ma'am?"

"You heard me, Snake. Griff Hutchinson." Lifting

her hand, she said, "And don't even start. I know the story. I don't like this any more than you do, but he's the only dude with some Indian blood in him. You can pass for South American, and so will he. Hutchinson is part Mexican, part Cheyenne and part Anglo. He speaks Spanish fluently. If you're going to try and go up against men who would just as soon kill you as look at you, you can't stand out like *norteamericano* tourists. You have to look Spanish. So that's that. I don't want to hear any arguments. Sit down."

Stunned, Vickey did so. Her head swam, and she felt dizzy. Rage began to grow deep inside her. Stomach knotting, she held her C.O.'s implacable emerald stare. Snake knew the major wasn't going to back down from the orders she'd just given her. But Griff Hutchinson was a son of a bitch, someone she'd just as soon spit on than talk to. She didn't think she could deal with him in the cockpit of her Apache much less on a mission for the crystal star. Hands clenched into fists on her thighs, she stared hard at Maya. The room was quiet, as if filled with glass ready to be shattered.

Gulping several times, Vickey finally found her voice, but it was hoarse and filled with emotion. "Ma'am...I don't think I can make this work. You're asking me to take on my worst enemy. To not only teach him in the cockpit, but work with him on this undercover assignment. I don't think I can do it...."

Giving her a piercing look, Major Stevenson said in a dark tone, "You will because it's an order, Snake."

Chapter 3

"Chief Hutchinson, you're going to have dual duties here at the Black Jaguar Squadron," Major Stevenson told him in a low voice. She sat at her desk and stared at him until he wanted to squirm in his regulation one-piece, green flight uniform.

"Not a problem, ma'am." Griff tried to smile as he sat at partial attention. Damn, she looked familiar. Where had he seen Major Maya Stevenson before? Rubbing his eyes, he just couldn't pull it out of his fogged, sleep-deprived brain.

Maya rested her chin against her hand. "Oh, it may be, Chief."

Griff frowned. He'd never served under a woman C.O. before. This was the shock of his life as far as he was concerned. When, after his thirty-day leave in the States, he'd received orders to ship out to Peru, he'd been excited, knowing it was a black ops assignment. But this black-haired woman with glittering green eyes made Griff wonder just what the hell he was getting into. "I don't understand, ma'am."

With a twist of her lips, Maya opened a file folder on her desk. "Chief, according to your personnel record here, you're part Native American. Is that correct?"

What does that have to do with anything? Griff damn near verbalized the words. But his mouth had gotten him into a helluva lot of trouble in the past, and he was aware of that weakness in himself. He should be—it had already cost him plenty. Instead of being a CWO2, he was still a CWO1, even with a year's combat experience under his belt. Normally, after successfully completing such a tour of duty, a warrant officer could expect to get a promotion. Not him.

Folding his hands in his lap, he said, "Yes, ma'am. My mother is a mix of Cheyenne and Yaqui Indian from Mexico."

"And your Dad is Anglo?"

Griff didn't like the way the word fell from her full lips. Searching the major's unreadable features, he wondered if she didn't like whites in general. That was possible, because it was obvious she wasn't white skinned herself. *Great, a C.O. who was prejudiced against white men.* Had he just jumped from the frying pan into the fire?

Griff tried to get a handle on his jittery emotions.

"What does my family heritage have to do with anything?" he asked, almost as if in a challenge. He saw her eyes flash with anger and he lamely added, "Ma'am."

Was he in front of some kind of a firing squad? The other two men he'd arrived with, both combat pilots who had served in Afghanistan, hadn't been told to see the C.O. right away. Griff felt singled out, reprimanded. Whatever the reason, it didn't bode well.

"You always counter a commanding officer's questions?" Maya demanded. She saw the anger in his gray eyes. His full mouth was thinning with obvious displeasure. Wanting to make sure this man was in full control of himself and his emotions, Maya was going to push him—hard. And she damn well wasn't going to answer his questions, either. What Hutchinson had just pulled bordered on insubordination.

Griff gulped, realizing that what he'd just pulled tiptoed on disrespect. And judging by the woman's steely voice, he'd angered her. His eyes widened momentarily as he felt the full brunt of the invisible power that seemed to swirl around her. For a second, Griff swore he saw a jaguar in place of her face. That was crazy! Blinking several times, he stammered, "N-no ma'am, my question wasn't meant as insubordination."

"What then? I wonder if you'd question a *male's* authority if he were in my shoes."

Oh, great! She *was* highly prejudiced against white males. Since landing this morning Griff had seen only one or two men among the many women in the huge cave. Maybe he should have gotten a clue from that.

"Er, absolutely not, ma'am." Scrambling, he offered her a weak smile and opened his hands. "I do have a problem putting my foot in my mouth. I'm tired from the red-eye flight and I haven't slept in twenty-four hours. It's not an excuse, and I apologize. I don't want to get off on the wrong foot down here, ma'am. I'm here for a year-long tour and I certainly didn't mean to sound argumentative."

Griff held her glittering emerald gaze and felt her carefully contained rage aimed directly at him. Seeing that his excuse didn't hold water with her, he added humbly, "Ma'am, no one told us we'd have a woman C.O. I'm used to dealing with men. We had some women mechanics work on our Apaches over in Afghanistan, but they weren't on my crew."

"And this is how you treat the females in your squadron, Chief Hutchinson? Question whatever they ask? Maybe it goes further back than that. How about to Fort Rucker four years ago?"

Griff's mouth fell open. He snapped it shut. *That* was where he'd seen Maya Stevenson! Four years ago, at Fort Rucker. She'd been in that class but he hadn't met her. The whole sordid incident came back to him in a flood of memories and he felt smothered by his shame—not to mention Maya Stevenson's lethal glare. "Er..."

Tapping her index finger on his personnel jacket, Maya added grimly, "You were in the squadron that graduated ahead of mine, Chief. You boys didn't like the first women to go through Apache flight training, just because we were female. I remember you and the gang you rode with real well. You had the approval of a number of instructors, so your little group got real ballsy. You tried to put a number of us away by humiliating us, shaming us, setting traps we'd fall into so that army officials would think we didn't have the right stuff to be combat pilots like you good ol' boys."

Hutchinson sagged in the chair. As guilt ate at him, he looked down at his hands, gripped together in his lap. "I remember, ma'am…." he whispered, his voice contrite.

"Good," Maya said savagely, sitting up. "Because I will not tolerate your questioning *any* officer—or for that matter, any warrant officer—under my command the way you just did me. If I didn't need combat-seasoned pilots as badly as I do right now, Mr. Hutchinson, I'd be throwing your sorry ass out that door and sending you back to the States so fast it would make your head swim. Do I make myself clear?"

Burning with humiliation, Griff nodded. The only way he was going to get through this was to stand up to the heat she was throwing at him. He lifted his chin and met her angry gaze. There wasn't an ounce of compassion in Major Stevenson's face. He was screwed—by himself. By the bad choices he'd made during flight school at Fort Rucker. "You're very clear, ma'am."

"Let me be even clearer, Chief Hutchinson. I will not tolerate for one moment any prejudice against any female under my command. All I need is one report of your lack of respect toward a woman and I will see you get a general court-martial. You got it?"

Oh, yeah, I got it, all right. "Yes, ma'am, I understand. I will not disrespect any female in this command."

Snorting softly, Maya sat back for a moment in her creaky chair. The door had been shut to her office since Hutchinson had come in. She didn't want anyone to be aware of his less than glorious, prejudicial past. "Well, you're going to feel like you've been singled out here, Chief. Big-time. I'm assigning you to one of the women who went through school with me. You know her well."

Sweating profusely, Griff wanted to wipe the perspiration off his upper lip, but he didn't dare. He sat at total attention. "Ma'am?"

"Every one of you Afghan-combat pilots is going to have to train in with one of my women Apache pilots. You don't know the lay of the land or the turf we fly here in Peru. For the next three months, mister, you are assigned to Chief Warrant Officer 2 Vickey Mabrey." Her lips twisted. "Also known as Snake."

Griff's mouth fell open again, this time with a gasp of surprise. Unable to recoup from his reaction, he saw the C.O.'s eyes become slits. "Yes, ma'am. Not a problem, ma'am. I'll handle it, I promise. I will respect Chief Mabrey." And if he didn't, Griff saw his dream of a twenty-year career in the U.S. Army being flushed down the cosmic toilet. Major Stevenson had her hand on the handle, but so did Vickey Mabrey.

A cold chill of dread washed through Griff. His past was coming back to haunt him big-time. Not that he didn't deserve it. He knew he did, because what he'd done four years ago had been wrong. And now he'd landed in a hornet's nest, surrounded by the very women he'd tried to get drummed out of Apache flight school. Karma had come around to bite him in the ass. He sat there drowning in his own sweat.

"Two doors down on the left is our mission ready room, Mr. Hutchinson. Get your butt over there. Snake is waiting for you. She's going to brief you on your double assignment with us."

Instantly, Griff stood up and snapped to attention. "Yes, ma'am!"

Maya gazed up at him, obviously pleased by his discomfort.

"Dismissed, Mr. Hutchinson," she stated.

"Yes, ma'am!" Griff quickly made a perfect about-face, marched to the door and opened it.

"Leave it open, Chief," she told him.

"Yes, ma'am." He moved out into the busy hall filled with U.S. Army personnel bustling in and out of their respective offices—all of them females.

Second door on the right. Griff hurried down the hall, his beret gripped in his left hand. He wiped the sweat off his upper lip and also took a swipe at his brow. Once he reached the open door marked Briefing Room, he braced himself for what he would find inside. Taking a deep gulp of air into his lungs, he tried to calm his riled emotions. *Vickey Mabrey. Snake.* Oh, God, he was truly jumping from the frying pan straight into hell.

As he entered the small room, he saw ten chairs arranged toward the front, facing a raised mahogany podium. And behind the podium stood Vickey Mabrey. As he hurried into the room, her head snapped up. The moment her forest-green eyes met his, Griff felt a cold shaft of rage aimed at him.

"Shut the door, mister."

Her voice, always husky, sounded like steel. Griff turned and shut the door. Breathing hard, he tried to force himself to slow down and stop reacting emotionally. In the cockpit, he was cool, calm and collected. Nothing ever rocked his world, and his emotions never got in the way. But they sure as hell were stirred up now.

Vickey Mabrey came out from behind the lectern. She wore a one-piece black suit that fitted her tall, lean body, and Griff recalled how she had always reminded him of a whippet dog or a greyhound. Her skin was just as gold as it had been, he noted, and her dark brown, straight hair barely touched her proud shoulders. This wasn't a woman struggling through flight school, he could tell. He saw the tilt of her dimpled chin, those glorious green eyes that had once mesmerized him. When Vickey was happy, her eyes had gold flecks in them, he recalled.

Griff frowned. He'd seen those gold flecks only once. And that was before— He didn't want to go there, and quickly shut out the memory of those ugly days at flight school.

As he came to a halt before her, he saw her put her hands on her womanly hips and give him a disdainful look that bordered on a sneer. Griff knew he had it coming and surrendered to the ordeal. He had no right to become defensive or combative. Besides, Major Stevenson had made it very clear that if he seemed disrespectful toward any woman here, his career would be fried—permanently. And there wasn't much call out in the civilian world for a combat helicopter pilot. No, he wanted his twenty. He wanted his career.

Vickey glared down at Griff Hutchinson. His cheeks were ruddy, his jaw dark because she was sure he hadn't shaved since starting his long flight from the States. His green flight suit was rumpled and looked sloppy in comparison to their sleek black body-fitting uniforms. His eyes—those gray eyes with their huge black pupils and surrounding ring of ebony—held a startled look. Was he in shock, maybe? Vickey had no idea what the major had said to him, but judging by the wild glint she saw there, her C.O. had probably nailed his sorry ass to the wall. Snake felt a rush of pleasure over that. Maybe she shouldn't, but she did.

"I see you got a proper welcome to the Black Jaguar Squadron by our C.O.," Vickey said, her lips lifting away from her teeth. Her parents often said that she had the smile of a wolf before it strikes.

Griff stood there looking at Vickey. She was a CWO2; he was a CWO1. He was below her in rank and she was his boss. "Yes, I did, Chief Mabrey. She ordered me to report to you."

Good, he was being respectful. What a pleasant, unexpected surprise. Vickey eased her hostile stance and allowed her hands to fall from her hips. She took a long look at the man who had caused her so much pain. With his short black hair, thick, straight eyebrows and large, eaglelike gray eyes, Griff Hutchinson had bad-boy, dark good looks. His nose was Native American—like a beak of a raptor. His cheeks were high, prominent and wide. Within a square face, his chin was noteworthy and rock hard. But what had gotten her into trouble was his sensual mouth, the left corner of which hitched up in a little quirk.

Power—and blatant sexuality—exuded from Griffin Hutchinson now just as it had then. Oh, he was a little older looking; crow's-feet now creased the corners of his eyes. But what aviator didn't have those? Squinting into the sun even with dark glasses on, or the protective shield of a helmet, gave everyone crow's-feet. There were lines beginning around his mouth, too. Back in flight school, he'd been a joker and played a lot of tricks on others at their expense. But the horizontal lines beginning across his broad brow hinted at seriousness—that maybe he wasn't the immature brat he'd been four years ago. Vickey would soon find out.

"Sit down," she told him, pointing to the chair behind him.

Nodding, Griff took the chair. He saw Vickey pick up a clipboard from the lectern. She had an incredible womanly grace to her; she always had. And how beautiful she was! He tried to hide his surprise over how she'd filled out, matured as a woman in four years. In flight school she'd been like a gangly whippet who had not yet grown into her body. Her lips, full and wide, had appeared too large for her oval face. She'd always had high cheekbones and golden skin that told of her

Navajo heritage and sleek, dark brown hair that shone with gold highlights in the sun.

Taking a cue from her, Griff pulled out a notebook and pen from his flight pocket. As she sat down in front of him, her legs wide, the clipboard resting on her thighs, he sensed her power, authority and confidence. Her self-assurance came from being a combat pilot, Griff knew. And from what little he'd been told, this black ops was all about air combat, which was why he'd leaped at the assignment. If he'd only known who ran the squadron he'd have avoided this one-year gig like the plague. But it was too late now.

Needled by Griff's presence, Vickey picked up her clipboard and flipped through several pages of material. Bile was building in the back of her throat and she felt a latent rage boiling in her tightly knotted gut. *To hell with it.* She dropped the papers back on the clipboard and rested it again on her left thigh. Giving him a glare, she snarled, "You need to know that I did *not* want this assignment with you. You're the last man on earth I'd ever want to work with. But Major Stevenson ordered me to be your trainer for the combat flights, and I'll do it. I haven't forgotten what you did to me back in flight school, mister. And there's nothing you can say or do to fix it or make it go away." Vickey smiled lethally down at Hutchinson, who held her gaze. His steady eye contact made her respect him, if nothing else. She wanted to ensure that he was contrite and not combative. If he challenged her, there would be real problems—fast.

"I understand, Chief Mabrey." Gulping, Griff knew

he deserved this. He'd been an idiot to think it was all in the past, over and done with. He'd never apologized to Vickey for his behavior or his part in framing her to get her thrown out of the school. He should have, but at the time he'd still believed women didn't belong in combat helicopters. *Stupid him.*

Vickey stared into his wide gray eyes, trying to read his thoughts. At one time, she had been drawn to this proud, handsome upperclassman. *Silly her.* Mouth quirking, she glared down at him. "What you did to us back in training was unconscionable. You need to know that I don't want this assignment with you. I don't trust you, but I'm stuck with you 24/7. I'll train you in the cockpit, no problem." Vickey grimaced and looked down at the clipboard. "But in this other assignment, you're going to take orders from me. It's *my* gig. And as much as I'd like to dump you off at the nearest bar in Lima and go on this mission by myself, I can't. The major says I need a partner, so I'm going to do it and so are you."

Griff nodded. "I hear you. I know it's too late to give you an apology, but I will, anyway, Chief Mabrey. I *am* sorry for my tactics toward you back in training. I'm sorry for lying to you." He opened his hands, his voice faltering. Her glare was eating him alive, and he saw the hurt reflected in her eyes. "I know you don't believe me."

"You're right about that," Vickey rattled, emotions plunging through her like sharp knives of rage.

"All I ask is for you to give me a chance. Let me prove to you I've changed."

Her laugh was brittle. "Yeah. Like you gave us a chance back in training? That kind of chance?"

Griff absorbed her heat, her distrust. "No, not that kind. Just give me a chance to prove to you that I've grown and learned. I hope I'm more mature now than I was back in flight school."

Her nostrils flared. "All pretty words. You know, Hutchinson, you're just the same, with that contrite little-boy look. That honesty mirrored in your voice. Oh, yeah, I fell for all of that once. But not now." Vickey jabbed her index finger at him. "As far as I'm concerned, you're a wolf in sheep's clothing, and I will *never* trust you. *Never.* You showed your true colors at school, damn near deep-sixed us and got us thrown out of class. You were part of that gang that set us up."

Griff's conscience burned as he held her wounded gaze. How could he have hurt her? Vickey Mabrey was a beautiful woman in so many ways. How had he allowed himself to go along with such a nasty game?

"Listen, Vickey." He purposely used her first name, which was unheard of in their line of work. They either called one another by their pilot nicknames or their last names. Never their first. Griff looked pleadingly up into her shocked face. "I am sincerely sorry for all the pain and suffering I've caused you. I deserve your anger. I deserve your not trusting me. I hope—" and he held out his hands in a gesture of peace "—that I can somehow make amends. I can never make up for all that I did to you. But I'm going to try."

She reared back, her voice breaking from years of withheld emotion. "You bastard, I will *never* trust you.

I don't care how hard you try or what you do. The only way you're going to get along with me is to follow orders. I know what I'm doing and you're here to listen and learn. That's *all.* Got it?"

Griff swallowed hard. For the first time he saw the full extent of the harm he'd helped inflict on Vickey Mabrey. Her forest-green eyes were riddled with pain. Her beautiful, kissable mouth was contorted with anguish, and her entire body seemed tense. A hard and cold bitterness serrated his gut. How was he ever going to fix this? Hanging his head, Griff stared down at the notebook clutched in his hands. *Somehow, I will make you trust me before this year is over,* Griff silently promised her. *Somehow, I will show you that I'm not the same person you knew four years ago. And that you can rely on me....*

Chapter 4

Vickey tried to control the emotions that buzzed in her gut like angry hornets. As she rubbed her stomach with one hand, she adjusted the clipboard on her thigh and studied the notes she'd taken during the briefing with Major Stevenson, Kai and Jake. She rattled off the information to Hutchinson in a biting tone of voice. To his credit, he took a ton of notes on what she had to share.

Whether she wanted to or not, she admired his attentiveness. Some combat cowboys would just sit there and pretend to remember everything, every detail. But anyone could screw up and miss something, a detail that might get them killed later. So at least Hutchinson had one saving grace: he'd learned to take notes.

"Questions?" she snapped after she was done with the mission presentation. Just looking at him turned her stomach into knots. The past was indelibly imprinted on the present. Of all the people she'd ever met in the world, Hutchinson and his gang were the last ones she'd ever want to see again.

Griff wrestled with his feelings as he studied his scrawled notes. Vickey had rattled off the information like a Gatling gun and he wasn't so sure she wanted him to grasp all the information. Failing to do so would get him into trouble, and Griff did *not* want to start off on the wrong foot. "Yes, this crystal star. I'm not clear about it." He gazed up into her scowling features, then moved on to admire her rich brown hair. Griff recalled how gold and red colors had danced through those shiny strands back at Fort Rucker. He'd been drawn to her but he'd been afraid to admit his feelings to the gang he'd associated with there. If they'd known he lusted after a woman trainee, they'd have ridiculed him and made damn sure that he was ostracized.

Looking back on that time, Griff realized that if he'd been more mature, he'd have left that clique, whose entire focus was to make the women trainees look bad and get them discharged from the army. His hands itched to slide across her hair as it softly framed her oval face and dimpled chin.

"Clear in what sense?" Vickey demanded, looking at her watch. They had exactly ten minutes until she could deliver his ass to the room where the three new pilots would get familiarity training of the BJS facility from Sergeant Joanne Prater. And then Vickey would be free of him—at least for now. She had a ride with Wild Woman scheduled shortly.

"Major Stevenson made note of my Cheyenne blood. I'm trying to understand our assignment to go after this crystal. She seemed to think my Indian background was important, but I don't understand how. Do you?" Griff cocked his head and held her narrowed green eyes, which were laced with impatience. Griff didn't care. He wasn't going to let her put him in the same position he'd placed her in back in training.

"This is an Indian affair," Vickey muttered. "I don't know whether you practice your people's traditions or not. If you did, you might understand better."

He shrugged. "Listen, I'm a real mix. My mom is Mexican Yaqui Indian and Cheyenne, my dad is white. I wasn't raised on a reservation. And to tell the truth, my father wanted me to be raised a Christian, and fought my mother on her belief system. So I grew up going to church."

"Well, I was raised on the Navajo Reservation and my 'church' was the great outdoors. The Great Spirit is found everywhere, not just inside four brick walls."

"No disagreement there," Griff said, managing a smile. "I'm a nature kind of guy. My mother is an herbalist. She treats the sick with herbs. She taught me how to grow and collect them as a kid. I always liked being outside with her, looking for them."

Vickey was almost tempted to ask him more about his upbringing, but remembered her tight schedule. "We can talk about your warm family another time. All I care about is that you grasp the importance of this star to the Eastern Cherokee nation. Do you?" She leaned forward and gazed into his warm gray eyes. When Griff had spoken about his mother, she'd seen all the tension flow out of him. His voice had become more animated, and he'd gestured with his large, square hands. Good flight hands, she could tell, but she tried to ignore that about Griff. In her book, he was the bad guy and could never be anything else. Maybe that was the Scorpio in her. Vickey had read in many astrological books that Scorpios, once burned, never forgot and never forgave those who had done them in. The books were right.

"I don't get it," Griff acknowledged. It hurt his pride to admit it, but he realized that if he wasn't completely honest at every turn, his career could be torpedoed. And if Vickey Mabrey was gunning for him, trying to set him up, he had to make sure he understood the turf they were playing on—completely.

"Every Indian nation has sacred objects," she said in a bored tone. "And those objects or totems are powerful."

"In what way? Powerful how?"

Summoning patience, she said, "Totems have the energy of the spirit within them. They gain more energy as humans work with them. The older the totem, the more power or force it has. In the hands of a trained medicine person, the object's incredible energy can be used for healing and positive change that can help a person, a clan or a nation."

"And in the wrong hands?"

Snake liked the fact that he put things together very

quickly, but Hutchinson wouldn't have survived a year in Afghanistan if he didn't have the smarts to connect the dots in a helluva hurry. She pushed away the shred of satisfaction she felt. He was her enemy, period. "A person who understands the foundation of energy can use it for selfish gain, greed or getting even."

"How could the star be used to get even?"

Shrugging, Snake said, "According to Kai these clan totems could send a beam of energy to someone and kill them. Typically, whoever holds it could order the spirit to channel a laserlike beam into the heart of the person they want dead. It can cause a heart attack, in other words."

"That's pretty cool stuff," Griff said, impressed. He saw Vickey frown. "I mean—"

"I know what you meant. I have to go. You're due for familiarity training on the first floor, room six." Getting to her feet, Vickey walked toward the closed door. "You and I will pick up where we left off tomorrow morning at 0800."

Griff stood and watched her walk away with pride and confidence. Vickey Mabrey took no prisoners. Sighing, he shook his head and stowed his notebook in the left pocket of his flight suit. Why should he expect anything else? Would he have forgiven someone for trying to get him court-martialed on AWOL charges? No.

"Helluva spot you've gotten yourself in, Hutchinson." Turning, Griff left the quiet briefing room. As he ambled down the hall, which was a beehive of activity, he realized again that everyone he saw was female.

This was a women's squadron. And in a sense, he realized, the upperclassmen in training at Fort Rucker had helped this black ops come into being. Wanting to find the positive, Griff decided that Major Maya Stevenson had turned something bad from that one-year class into something very good. She'd created the Black Jaguar Squadron as a response to the U.S. Army stonewalling her entire female flight class at Fort Rucker. Very smart. Savvy. But then, he'd heard that Major Stevenson's father was a general and had helped make her vision become reality.

As he took the aluminum grate steps down to the first floor, Griff looked around the huge lava cavern. It was an amazing feat of nature, he decided. The entire area around Machu Picchu was volcanic, as he understood it. And each of the curiously shaped mountains, which rose to eleven thousand feet in height, had been created by a volcano blowing its top. Who would ever think that one day this naturally-formed cave would be the home of an Apache squadron stopping drug runners? Shaking his head, filled with awe and respect, Griff decided he'd better get his butt to room six and continue indoctrination. The more he knew about the BJS, the sooner he would fit into the nearly all-woman squadron.

A smile cut across his face as he opened the door to the first floor. Reverse prejudice. At Fort Rucker, women going through training were the anomaly. Here, he was. Karma had definitely landed on him.

"I tell you, Wild Woman," Vickey said into the microphone against her lips as she flew the Apache through the blue sky, "I could barely be civil to that bastard." She had the controls for the bird. The cockpits were arranged one above the other. Today, Wild Woman was handling the weapons array and radar. They were speeding along a well-known and often used drug route between Cuzco and the Bolivian border. At twenty thousand feet, they played in the wispy white cirrus clouds that looked like a horse's mane flowing in the wind. From this vantage point, their radar would spot anything moving below them. Drug planes usually hugged the terrain, flying barely a hundred feet above the jungle canopy in order to evade radar detection. However, twenty-four-hour-a-day flights like theirs prevented such escape.

"Hutchinson remembered what he'd done to you?"

"Oh, yeah," Vickey growled, looking around. They were flying at a higher altitude than usual today, so had masks strapped to their faces and oxygen bottles hooked up nearby. "He knew. He took one look at me and his big gray eyes popped like a lemur's." She chuckled darkly.

"He's probably thinkin' you're going to screw him like he screwed you."

Sunlight lanced into the cockpit, and if she hadn't had her shield down over her eyes, Vickey would have been temporarily blinded. She grinned. "I've thought about it, trust me. One good deed deserves another."

"Now, now, Snake," Wild Woman tittered, "you shouldn't lower yourself to a male's level. Beside, trying to set him up—if you got caught like they did—well, you could kiss your career goodbye. Major

Stevenson expects better of us, and I know you'd like to even the score with him, but don't. Okay?"

"Wise words from a Wild Woman. Don't worry, I wouldn't think of dirtying my hands on that bastard. He's not worth my career."

"What was he like? Changed? The same?"

Shrugging, Vickey looked around the sky. "Who knows?" Her vigilance was born out of habit, because it was always possible that a Black Shark, its pilots paid by a drug lord to shoot them out of the sky, could be lurking nearby. The Apache lacked the ability to pick up the energy signature of the coaxial, double-bladed Black Shark, so they had to constantly rubberneck to make sure the copters weren't sneaking up on them.

"How did he take you being his commanding officer for this secret mission you have to do?"

Vickey could not tell anyone at BJS about the mission. It was top secret. As much as she wanted to confide in Wild Woman, she couldn't. "Okay, I guess. Right now, he's playing Mr. Contrite-and-Gee-I'm-Sorry-I-Screwed-You."

Chuckling, her colleague said, "Well, look at it this way, Snake. You know what he's capable of. If Hutchinson starts squirreling around with you, deep-six him."

"Don't worry, I will." Frowning, Vickey swept her gaze across the two HUDs—heads-up displays—which were five-by-five-inch green television screens in her cockpit array. Nothing showed on them. "And at the first sign of him trying to nail me, I'm running to the major and asking her to get rid of him." And she'd like nothing better. Vickey tried to squelch that small niggling feeling in her heart toward Griff. At one time, before his nasty incrimination effort, she had been powerfully drawn to him. Scratching her temple, she shook her head. How could she have been so wrong about him?

"You know," she said, "when we were in school going through training, I was actually attracted to him. Can you believe it?"

"I remember, Snake. We were bunkmates. You used to talk about him all the time. You liked his gray eyes. You said he reminded you of the golden eagles that flew over the mesas of the res where you were raised."

"You've got a damn good memory," Vickey told her unhappily.

"I can blackmail you with it." Wild Woman giggled.

"Yeah, right."

"He married now?"

"I don't have a clue."

"Was he wearing a wedding ring?"

"No..."

"That's good."

"Why?"

"Because I think you're still drawn to him. I hear it in your voice. I saw it in your eyes earlier when we were doing the walk around the bird back in the cave."

"Oh," Vickey snorted, "get lost! No way, dude!"

Wild Woman grinned. "Okay, I could be wrong, but I have good instincts, you know. I think there's a part of you that still likes this guy even though he tried to frame you."

Shaking her head, Vickey felt a frisson of fear move through her. "You're crazy!"

"Yeah, like a fox," Wild Woman snickered. "We'll just see where this top secret mission of yours leads the two of you. I hear you get twenty-four hours flying and then forty-eight off to do this secret mission. Is that right?"

"Yeah, right." Forty-eight hours with him in close proximity. Vickey wasn't sure how she was going to manage her rage toward Hutchinson. Or that damn, niggling feeling of attraction.

Chapter 5

Three days of unrelenting héll. Griff compressed his lips as he walked away from the Apache he'd just landed on the lip of the BJS cave complex. At his side, a good distance from him, walked Vickey. Her face was unreadable, as usual. This was his third six-hour indoctrination flight with her. He still hadn't gotten adjusted to the schedule around here, so he was sleep deprived. But he knew that would change over time.

Giving her a sidelong glance, he raised his voice and said, "I understand we have forty-eight hours off now?"

Vickey nodded. At 1500, the noise in the cave was at its peak. Another Apache had just landed, making talking nearly impossible as the whapping of the blades echoed through the complex. Anyone working close by automatically wore earmuffs to save their hearing. Vickey pointed to the H.Q., ahead on the right, and saw that Hutchinson understood her gesture. They would talk in the debriefing room up on the second floor.

Sweat trickled down her ribs. Mid-January was the dry season in this corner of the world, but the humidity was still nearly a hundred percent. It was like working in a sponge so far as Vickey was concerned.

She reached the metal stairs first and rapidly climbed. Shoving the door open with her shoulder, she walked confidently to the small room where pilots wrote their flight reports. Every mission needed a follow-up, written at one of the two computer terminals here and saved in the database where Major Stevenson and her staff could retrieve it and analyze it for future reference.

Vickey opened the door and left it ajar for Hutchinson. When he closed it behind them, quiet descended. Vickey sat down at the first console, her helmet bag at her feet, and in her peripheral vision saw him sit down two feet away from her. She didn't like having Griff that close to her, but there was nothing to be done about it. Pulling off her fireproof flight gloves, she dropped them on top of her black canvas bag. Then she opened the collar of her uniform, rolled up her sleeves to her elbows and cracked her knuckles. After flipping on the computer, she began to write her report, a process that now was second nature to her.

Because Hutchinson was in training with her for

three months, Vickey had to fill out a special section on him and his performance. He would receive a hard copy of her assessment. She knew he was sweating every flight with her because she could see the wariness in his eyes. The urge to lie, to make an allegation that he wasn't up to snuff, was very real. The Scorpio part of her would love to get even, setting him up just as she'd been set up for a fall. But she couldn't do it. Wild Woman was right—Vickey couldn't lower herself to a man's level. Not a chance. She was a woman, and therefore of better moral fiber.

As she typed in her name, rank and serial number on the form, Vickey grinned to herself. She felt proud of her decision. She'd treat Hutchinson fairly, come hell or high water. She wanted Major Stevenson to see her as a straight shooter—honest and reliable. Her better nature overcame her darker side, although there was no law in the universe that said she couldn't dream daily of all the nasty ways she might even the score with him.

Griff didn't have much to type into his report. He waited patiently for Vickey to be done before he spoke to her. In the double cockpits, she always rode in the top one. She'd put him through his paces, for sure. And he felt confident that he'd passed every test.

The two male pilots who had been transferred to BJS with him seemed real happy to be chasing druggies. Griff had gotten to know them slightly on the flight down to Peru, and he felt like the odd man out. CWO2 Brad Samson and Teddy Giddings were from the same Apache squadron and were best of friends. It seemed natural that they would team together, which left Griff in his current predicament. He felt thrown off balance by the fact that ninety percent of the BJS squadron were women. He hadn't learned to associate with women from a strictly military perspective. Women were to be wooed, danced with, kissed and made love to. Grimacing, Griff decided that he truly had descended into hell.

As he sat there waiting for Vickey to grade his flight abilities, Griff studied her profile. She had a long face, just like her body. She was, as she put it, a lean, mean killing machine in the cockpit of her Apache. He'd heard that she'd shot down a Black Shark last year.

Noting her intent study of the computer monitor, he decided he liked the way her unruly dark brown hair kept dipping forward and how she automatically pushed it back across her shoulder. Her gestures were graceful, her movements reminding him of a ballerina. Even her walk, on legs that seemed to go on forever, was lithe and flowing. Maybe it was her face that made him most aware of her as a woman. Her broad forehead, with strands of dark hair falling across it. Her aquiline, very Indian nose with fine nostrils that would often flare like a wild mustang scenting the air. Her full lips, so often compressed with intensity…

Vickey didn't try to be anything but herself, even in the cockpit. She was comfortable with her sexuality and made no bones about it. She didn't wear makeup, but so what? Griff figured overly made-up women were living behind a mask. Silently, he applauded Vickey's strength of character not to hide herself.

Relaxing in the chair, he enjoyed this twenty-minute reprieve in their silent war with one another. This was the only time he could sit and look at Vickey Mabrey and not receive a glare in return. Griff was coming to grips with the fact that she hated his guts and barely tolerated his presence. She was with him only because she was under orders to train him. The knowledge hurt in some deep compartment of his heart, but he also understood why she felt that way. He would, too, if she'd tried to sabotage his career in the army.

A slight smile tipped one corner of his mouth as Vickey once again pushed an errant lock behind her shoulder. This time she slid the shining strands behind her ear with her index finger.

Griff allowed himself the pleasure of studying her high cheekbones, broad and golden-skinned. And her eyes, the intelligence glittering in them adding to their allure. He could see a fierce, intense passion in them, as well. His gut told him that she lived by her emotions, which made her the strong woman she was. Why hadn't he realized all of this four years ago? Before he'd been part of a plan to get her discharged?

Pushing that aside, Griff simply basked in Vickey's natural beauty, absorbing her goodness in lieu of all the bad vibes that pooled between them. Her brown brows were angled over her widely spaced eyes. Thick, dark lashes framed those wolflike alert eyes of hers. She didn't miss anything, Griff decided.

Dropping his gaze to her lips, he smiled to himself. She had a sinner's mouth, in his opinion. Her lips were full and soft, the corners gently tilting upward—evidence that she laughed a lot. But she never smiled at him. When one of her women friends would approach her, he'd see a completely different side of her: spontaneous, humorous, laughing a lot and zinging back one-liners that made him laugh, too. When she didn't have to be serious, she wasn't, and Griff really liked that about her. In her off time from the black ops, he'd learned that she went to a certain bar in Cuzco, where she'd tango the night away and have a helluva lot of fun.

A tiny ache began in his heart. What would it be like to have Vickey in his arms while they danced? Just imagining holding her made him burn with a longing he'd never experienced with any woman before.

He watched her as she finished her report. Griff liked her strong, dimpled chin. He wondered if she'd inherited that feature from her mother, who he'd learned was a German biologist. There was a certain precision to all Vickey's actions, and he knew Germans were famous for this trait. It certainly showed when they were flying the Apache. On the ground, however, he saw her loosen up and flow. Maybe that was a gift from her Navajo father?

There were so many questions he was dying to ask her. Griff realized they were all personal ones and she'd never allow him that kind of access after what he'd done to her. Sadness enveloped him. How stupid and immature he'd been. If there was some way to change the past, he'd do it now. Vickey Mabrey was a fine pilot. She had great flight hands and she flew that helo smoothly, like melted butter through the sky. Griff was so admiring of her skills. The guys in his training squadron had been a hundred percent wrong in going after the women in the other class. Shaking his head, he realized there was nothing he could do now to undo the damage. Or the memory.

The chair squeaked as Vickey turned and glanced at Griff. She was caught off guard by the warmth in his gray eyes. Feeling uncomfortable, she growled, "Your flight was fine today. You'll be receiving a copy of my report in your box at the personnel office if you want to check it out."

"Great. Thanks."

Vickey scowled. "You earned it." There was something endearing about Griff Hutchinson. Maybe it was his ears that stood away from his head that made him seem less of a threat to her, and more like a little boy than a killer Apache pilot. Pinned back ears usually reminded her of a wolf. But Griff's face was open, not threatening as a result of his ear placement. People reminded her of animals all the time. In some ways, Griff reminded her of an open, happy golden retriever. She wasn't sure, and that kept her on guard around him. Part of her still liked the bastard, though she could never figure out why.

"What now? Are we to go on that mission to look for the crystal star? Do you have a plan in place?" he asked.

Nodding, Vickey leaned over and picked up her helmet bag. She unzipped it, stuffed in her flight gloves and closed it back up. "Yeah, I spent some time yesterday with Lieutenant Ana Cortina. She's from the Peruvian army, on loan to BJS for the last three years. She was born in Lima. I went over all the information that Kai Alseoun gave to me and asked Ana about antique dealers in Lima. She knows that city like the back of her hand. I don't know if you're aware of this, but all kinds of grave robbing goes on here in Peru. Many archeologists with two hearts would gladly buy items from Peru under the table for their museum—or steal them."

"I'm completely ignorant about all of this," he admitted, opening his hands. "I'm going to need your help." Not only that, but Griff *wanted* Vickey's help. Otherwise, he knew he was doomed with her. Seeing her expression lightening, he knew he'd said the right thing for once.

At least he could be humble. That was in his favor, Vickey decided. She crossed her legs and held his gaze. "Ana said there are reputable antique dealers in Lima. They're all in the Miraflores District, the high-end, rich part of the city. That's not where we need to start our search for this star. She said that in the poorest area there's a small health dispensary run by a couple of very old Catholic nuns. We should go there first."

He grinned wryly. "Nuns? Involved in shady antique dealings?"

Though she fought it, a grin tugged at Vickey's mouth. When Griff smiled, his whole face lit up. The darkness she'd seen in his eyes disappeared, replaced by the excitement of a little boy on the hunt for treasure. She didn't want to like him, but when his expression was boyish like this, she had no way of countering it. Brows knitting, she forced the smile from her face. "No, Ana said that they worked with Major Mike Houston for many years. They called him the Jaguar God down here because he had the nine lives of a cat with the drug dealers he took on."

"A Special Forces guy?"

"Yeah. For seven years Houston was down here raising hell with the drug dealers and stopping a lot of the cocaine trade. He was a wanted man, from what Ana told me. Houston kept a health clinic going so poor people would have good medical attention, and he fed it drug dollars. Now, from what Ana says, Perseus, the super-secret CIA branch that Houston works for, gives them a yearly budget to keep their doors open to the poor."

"And so these nuns probably know everyone, the good, the bad and the ugly."

Pleased at his grasp of the situation, Vickey said, "Bang on. Ana said these nuns know who among the locals are stealing from archeological sites. They would know the men who are giving them money, the ones who probably know about this crystal star."

"Sounds like a good place to start. I would never have thought of this angle."

"Houston mentioned to Kai Alseoun that this would be a good lead. He said the nuns were in their eighties now, and to be gentle with them."

"Eighty years old…" Griff shook his head and gave her a silly grin. "I'm twenty-seven. I can't imagine being that age."

"And in our business we probably won't reach it," Vickey said succinctly. "We're due to meet the commercial helo on the other side of the mountain. This is where we have our cover, the mining operation. You flew in there from Cuzco, already. You need to see Sergeant Prater down in personnel. She's got your uniform for our little mission."

Griff stood when Vickey stood. "Oh?"

"Yeah, you're new to the neighborhood, Hutchinson." She picked up her helmet bag and gave him a sour smile. "We need to look like South Americans. With our skin tone and dark hair we can pass for Argentineans. Prater has our fake IDs, passports and stuff down there. I worked with her on putting our cover together. We're a brother and sister from Buenos Aires, Argentina. We're pursuing our Ph.D.s in Inca culture, which is why we're here. It would look okay for us to be poking and prodding around the area for antique dealers and rubbing elbows with the shadier side of this equation. So our costumes are going to be those of university or college kids—jeans, hiking boots, knapsack, baseball cap. We'll look like typical students on a low budget." She pointed to the very expensive watch he wore. "That goes. You get a cheap watch instead. There's no way we can look like we have a lot of money on us. Otherwise, the gangs that rove that part of Lima will think we're buzzard bait. They'll attack and rob us. They don't think twice about slitting a rich tourist's throat in those nasty sections."

"Got you," Griff murmured, removing the watch from his wrist. He opened the Velcro tab on a pocket and dropped the timepiece into it. Before Vickey could get to the door, he reached it and opened it for her.

She gave him a quizzical look.

"Chivalry isn't dead," he teased as he bowed and gestured with his hand for her to exit first.

Snorting, Snake growled, "Oh, gimme a break, Hutchinson! You're not knightly material to begin with."

Ouch. That hurt. Griff straightened and lost his grin. "I had that coming, didn't I?"

"In spades." Vickey didn't look back. She wanted to be rid of him for just a little while. Surprised by his gesture, she could feel her heart warm at his thoughtfulness. Men just didn't open doors for women anymore. Well, he had. But he wanted something, too. Her forgiveness. As she strode quickly down the hall, weaving among her colleagues, Vickey wanted to go hide in her cubicle. She had to pack her gear. When she heard Griff's footfalls, heavy and solid, as he moved abreast of her, she forced herself to not look over at him.

"You know," he told her in a husky, conspiratorial tone, "whether you like it or not, you're going to have to start trusting me a little bit. We can't go out on this mission without some kind of communication open between us. And if we're supposed to be brother and sister, the bad guys will expect us to act like siblings."

Her nostrils flared. When Griff strode ahead and opened the exit door for her, she glared up at him. "You're right," she snapped. "I can play the game when I have to. Just like you did with me four years ago. So don't worry about my end of this mission. I'll carry it off."

Griff followed her out and down the stairs. The echoing sounds in the cave were constant. Several golf carts whizzed by with food supplies stacked on them, heading for the mess. On the flat, black basalt floor, Griff caught up with her. Vickey's profile was set and stubborn looking.

"I wasn't questioning your ability," he told her. "I've never gone undercover before, so I'm trying to think of how to carry it off. Have you ever done this?"

She couldn't fault him on his need to know. "No, I haven't."

"And you got this assignment because Kai Alseoun had this dream of you?"

"Yeah," Vickey said, slowing her pace a little. The clank of tools being used on the maintenance of the Apache helicopters echoed around them. "I had a dream, too. Actually, I'd had the same damn one for over a year." Her mouth quirked and she glanced at Griff, who was watching her intently. They walked close together—too close for her comfort. "These past three months, I was getting the dream about once a week. It was driving me nuts. I'd wake up screaming from it because it scared the hell out of me. I was being chased by some dark, unknown guy and I kept seeing this seven-pointed star crystal. I knew I had to get the star and run for my life. And then I'd wake up, sweating like a stuck pig. Trust me, it sucked."

Raising his brows, Griff murmured, "I'll bet it did. And you'd need every minute of sleep you could grab around here, given the schedule you're on." He was amazed Vickey looked as good as she did. No stranger to horrible nightmares, he understood her distaste for having the same one over and over again.

"You got it," she said. "So, when Kai showed up and shared the dream she'd had, I knew I was the person she was looking for."

"I remember my mother telling me that dreams are messages. My father always laughed at her for that, but I took her seriously."

"Your dad was obviously Anglo, as you said before."

"Yes. He didn't like my mother teaching me anything having to do with her—and my—heritage." Giving Vickey an intimate look, Griff took a huge chance and asked, "Were your mother and father Navajo?"

"Just my dad. Alfred Black Dog Mabrey. He's a medicine man."

"And your mother is Anglo, right?" The opposite of him.

"Right. She's originally from Germany and got her U.S. citizenship a long time ago. She came over to the States because she was in love with the Wild West and cowboys and Indians. I remember her telling me that a lot of German people are very drawn to the mystique of Native Americans. Maybe because they come from Druid stock, the original tree-and-nature people. Anyway," Vickey said, slowing down as they approached the back door to the barracks, "Ingrid Mueller, my mother, came on a grant from her university in Dresden to do plant study on the Navajo Reservation. She met my father, they fell in love the moment they laid eyes on one another, and my mother kissed off her Ph.D. and married him."

Vickey gave Griff a rueful look. "Unlike your dad, my mother didn't try to stop me from being taught my Indian heritage. She loved the Navajo beliefs and was very much a part of the natural world. Maybe because she was a biologist, I don't know."

Vickey had started to reach for the doorknob when Griff's larger hand grabbed it first.

"I'm going to continue to open doors for you," he told her, with a look that didn't leave room for argument. "It's ingrained in me, I guess, so I'm not apologizing for it. You're just going to have to suffer one more thing about me while we work together."

Vickey opened her mouth to shoot him down again, but thought better of it. "If you think this is going to erase the past, you're wrong."

Griff gave her a patient look. "I know that. And I'm not doing it because I want you to forgive me. I know you won't. I'm doing it because I want to. It's a sign of respect as far as I'm concerned."

She searched his face, especially his large gray eyes. Damn, he seemed honest. And sincere. But Vickey remembered that same look when Griff had tricked her. She'd believed him then. She wouldn't now. It wasn't in her makeup to deliberately hurt people, so she swallowed a nasty retort, shrugged her shoulders and went into the barracks.

"I'll meet you over on the mining side in an hour," she told him over her shoulder. All the women officers and warrants stayed up on the second floor. A small section on the first floor was reserved for the male contingent of the squadron.

"I'll be there," Griff called as she quickly mounted the wooden stairs.

Standing on the landing, Griff suddenly remembered that he had to find Sergeant Prater and get his undercover gear and identification. Grinning, he turned and headed back to H.Q. That was okay. He didn't mind walking Vickey back to the barracks. In fact, he'd enjoyed it immensely. His heart lifted a little and Griff felt a tiny trickle of hope. She'd talked to him. Actually talked to him about something personal. Rubbing his hands together, Griff felt the silly grin spreading across his face. Maybe he could convince her he'd changed. That he wasn't the bastard he'd once been. And somehow, he wanted to prove her wrong—that he *was* knightly material.

Chapter 6

Griff found Lima to be a dreary, gray place in January—or at least on this particular day. It was the beginning of summer in the southern hemisphere. He could see strands of blue sky every now and again as the low, somber ceiling of clouds parted, but at other times they drove through showers. They'd hailed a taxi at the airport and were heading toward the barrio where the Catholic clinic was located. There, they hoped to talk to the two elderly nuns who were friends of Major Houston. Vickey sat on one side of the vehicle, her dark blue canvas knapsack between them on the seat. Griff held his in his lap as the yellow cab dodged and ducked through traffic.

"Plenty of potholes in the roads, aren't there?" Griff

noted wryly, gazing out at the city through the windshield. Once again the cabbie had turned on the wiper blades. It was barely 0800.

Vickey nodded. "Yeah, Lima is the largest city in Peru, and the only section that doesn't have potholes is the rich district of Miraflores." She smiled briefly, her gaze restless as she perused the city around them.

"I see...." Griff watched as cars whizzed around one another on the six-lane highway. They'd taken a helicopter flight from the mountain base to Cuzco, where they picked up an Aero Peru commercial flight to Lima at 0600 this morning. He was excited by the chance to see more of a country about which he knew next to nothing.

"I didn't know this part of Peru was like a moonscape—barren dirt hills and mountains sweeping down to the sea," he mused. Lima lay within shouting distance of the blue Pacific Ocean.

"Copper mining is big in these parts," Vickey said, her face nearly unreadable. She wore a dark blue baseball cap, the rim pulled low over her eyes. "A lush jungle surrounds Machu Picchu, and where Peru borders Ecuador and Brazil. But down here, the cold Humboldt Current flowing along the coast drives away any chance of rain, so at least half the country is bone-dry desert just like this." She waved her hand toward the taller buildings of downtown Lima, visible now through the rain.

Vickey pulled out her new identity papers, created for their undercover work. One had an official stamp from the University of the Pampas, Buenos Aires.

Information had been sent to the university so that anyone who wanted to could verify their names and student status.

Tucking the papers back into her vest, Vickey tried to ignore Griff's considerable aura, but found it impossible. Somehow she had to put her feelings for him aside, both her likes and dislikes. It was a crazy combination, and she had no control over her emotions toward him—only a muzzle and a short leash on her mouth.

The taxi zipped down a narrow street where the buildings were one to three stories tall. Griff could see flowers hanging over balcony railings, making the street look pretty despite the grayness of the day.

"So, rain here is pretty rare, right?"

"Yep. This is special. Just for you."

Grinning, Griff murmured, "It's warm and wet. I guess rain is something desert folks would welcome with open arms any time of year."

"For sure. Ah, take a look. That's where we're heading. Down there." Vickey pointed down the hill as they began a rapid descent on the rain-slick streets.

The barrio was a much uglier section of town. Griff frowned at the ramshackle huts that covered the hillside. Construction materials included corrugated aluminum, plastic sheeting, weathered two-by-fours and even cardboard—anything the inhabitants could use to make a home. The taxi slowed as the asphalt turned to bright red clay, now slick and gooey in the rain.

Everywhere Griff looked, he observed dark-skinned Indians—Quechua, he presumed—wearing threadbare clothing. From what he could see, there were no sanitation or water facilities. The odors of cooking, fecal matter and urine combined, making him hold his breath from time to time when they passed through the worst areas of the barrio. As the taxi crept along between the hovels, people, mostly women and children, stared at them.

"This is terrible poverty," Griff murmured.

"Major Houston has been trying to help out in the neighborhood for over a decade now. You can see how bad off they are…." Vickey's heart bled for the people living here. Stacked next to each other as they were, the shacks reminded Vickey of houses made of cards. They were fragile, too, as evidenced by how the rain turned some cardboard walls into mush.

Amid the mire of human suffering in this cardboard shanty town, Griff spotted a small redbrick church surrounded by a white fence. The building stood out like a beacon of hope.

The taxi halted in front of the clinic. Even at this hour, in the rain, there was a line of people waiting to get inside. Getting out, Vickey paid the driver in soles and hefted her backpack as she exited the vehicle. Walking carefully in the wet clay, she made it to the picket fence and pushed the gate open. Just then the rain stopped, and a ray of sunlight pierced the parting clouds, shining brilliantly down upon them.

Griff followed Vickey to the side door of the clinic and stepped inside, where Indians of all ages stood patiently waiting. Babies were crying and mothers tried to comfort them, bouncing them in their arms.

He felt guilty that he had on such good clothes, compared to them.

At the front desk a young nun in a blue habit was working, her hair black and short.

"*Hermana*, we're here to see Sister Gabby and Sister Dominique," Vickey explained in Spanish. "I'm Victoria Rosalino and this is my brother, Griffin. We have an appointment to see them this morning?" Although the older nuns knew they were working undercover, the staff did not, so Vickey stuck to her new role.

"Oh, *sí, sí,*" the woman said. Holding out her hand, she smiled. "I'm Sister Bernadette. Please, follow me."

"Thanks," Vickey murmured, after shaking her hand. Sister Bernadette was just over five feet tall, thin and Peruvian. Her sable eyes sparkled with warmth as she bustled from behind the desk and hurried down the narrow hall.

"You look kind of busy," Vickey noted as she walked with the young sister.

"Oh my, yes, Senorita Rosalino. It's like this every day! I get so behind in my paperwork. I'm supposed to make a new file for each person." She threw up her hands. "But we need more file drawers! I'm putting them in boxes, and don't have time to arrange them alphabetically." She rolled her eyes. "We need at least two more sisters to help out, but the church has no one to give us. Somehow, God will provide."

Stopping at the end of the hall, Sister Bernadette opened a door, poked her head in and spoke rapidly in Spanish, while Vickey waited. Griff, she noted, was studying everything. She was glad he was so alert.

"Come in," Sister Bernadette whispered, and stepped aside.

Nodding, Vickey smiled. "Thanks."

Inside, two white-haired nuns in blue habits sat at metal desks. They wore no headdress, their hair short and silver. Vickey introduced herself and Griff to them. The tall, lean nun with a narrow, pinched face and gold-rimmed spectacles over piercing gray eyes stood up slowly.

"I'm Sister Dominique. Welcome, welcome. And this is Sister Gabriella."

Vickey instantly liked the short nun, who also who got up with great difficulty. "Hello, Sister Gabriella."

"Call me Sister Gabby."

Vickey found her grip strong and sure. She saw the warmth dancing in her large brown eyes. "Please, don't get up on our account."

Shrugging eloquently, Sister Gabby said, "I put my back out yesterday."

"Yes, and I told you not to try and lift that heavy water pail," Sister Dominique said, waving her thin, arthritic fingers toward her friend of many years. "We just can't do what we did fifteen years ago, Gabriella. You should have left that pail for Sister Bernadette, who's young and strong!"

Hiding a smile, Vickey sat down in front of their desks, which were cluttered with files and folders from one end to another.

"Make yourself comfortable," Sister Gabby invited. She waved her wooden cane at an electric hot plate that sat on a wooden table. "Dominique, instead of using your energy to yell at me, would you like to make our guests some good, hot tea?"

It took everything Vickey had to keep from chuckling. While Sister Gabby came hobbling around and stood in front of them, Dominique growled something in French, pouted and then went to the hot plate to warm the tarnished copper teakettle.

"So, you are friends of *mon petit chou?*" Gabby inquired sweetly, her hands folded on the top of the cane.

Griff sent Vickey a questioning look because he didn't speak French. He knew the nuns had come from France a long time ago to serve the poor in Peru.

"Oh," Vickey laughed. "Yes, ma'am. Mike Houston warned us that you would call him by his nickname, little cabbage."

The nun smiled warmly. "He is truly a guardian angel to us, Victoria. And that is a French endearment for someone who is greatly loved."

"And we do love him." Dominique spoke up, turning on the hot plate beneath the kettle. "Without his continued support, we could not be here, helping people. We use homeopathy, you know."

"Homeopathy?" Vickey looked up into Sister Gabby's watery brown eyes. The woman's hair was completely silver, cut short and neat. Her face was deeply wrinkled and kind, reminding Vickey of an aging elf.

"Yes, it's a wonderful, natural medicine," Gabby said in a conspiratorial tone, "an alternative method of treatment we were taught back in France. We have been serving God's people here with it for a long, long time. We aren't medical doctors. I have some nurse's training and so does Dominique, but we found that coming here to Peru on very limited funds, we could not afford standard medicines."

"So," Dominique crowed proudly, setting four mugs in a row on the table, "we said let's use what we know—homeopathy! It's cheap, it works and the Indians believe in it because it comes from nature."

"Of course," Gabby said, "every once in a while we get medical doctors who volunteer their help for a week or two, and we are grateful. We do what we can…."

"You obviously do," Griff said sincerely. He stood up. "Ma'am, you're making me feel bad." He gestured to his chair. "Why don't you sit down and I'll stand? With your back problem, I don't think standing is very good for you."

Sister Gabby gave Vickey a startled look. "What did you do? Bring Sir Lancelot with you?" She chuckled, smiling up at Griff. "Young man, I believe I will take you up on your invitation. Thank you very much."

Griff held out the chair for the old nun until she settled in it. "You're welcome." He turned and walked over to where Sister Dominique was preparing the tea. "Can I be of help, Sister?"

Tittering, Dominique said, "Well, of course! We never turn down help. Here, put the mugs on the tray, with the cream and sugar. Four spoons, too."

Griff patiently did everything Sister Dominique asked of him. In no time he'd poured hot water into the mugs and she'd plopped a teabag into each. With her blessing, she asked him to take the tray over and hand them each a mug, while she sat down behind her desk.

Griff served everyone. When he took the tray to Vickey, he saw some emotion in her eyes as she put cream and sugar into her tea. Unable to decipher it, he grinned and then set the tray on the only clear corner of Sister Gabby's desk. After fixing his own tea, he pulled out the chair from her desk and sat down.

"Thank you," Vickey told the nuns. "We know you're really busy here, but Major Houston seemed to think you were the people we needed to talk with."

"About what, dear?" Sister Gabby inquired, sipping her tea noisily. Lifting her head, she said in a wobbly voice, "Dominique! Where did our biscuits go? We can't have midmorning tea without biscuits, can we?"

"The rats ate them, Gabby!"

"Oh, dear." The nun gave them an apologetic look. "I'm so sorry...."

"Don't be," Vickey said, placing her palm over Sister Gabby's aged hand. The French nun gave her such a warm look that she felt some of her trepidation melt away.

Gripping her hand, Sister Gabby said, "Well, now, Dominique, they are here for a reason and I'm sure they don't want to spend all day with two cranky old nuns!"

"Humph!" Dominique said, hold her mug in both hands.

"What is it you'd like to know, dear?"

Vickey gently held Sister Gabby's hand, which was

callused and had slightly swollen joints. "Major Houston said you would know the names of some of the chief grave robbers of Incan artifacts. We're here to find a special item from North America—a seven-pointed crystal star that belongs to the Eastern Cherokee people. It was stolen a little over a year ago and we have information that it's in Peru somewhere. That's why we're here," Vickey told them. "Have you heard of anyone talking about such a star?"

"Hmm." Dominique rubbed her chin as she set her mug down on the desk. Pushing her glasses up on her nose, she frowned. "Felipe Balcazar is the man you're seeking. He's up to his neck in stolen archeological treasures here in Peru."

"But would he also traffic North American things?" Griff asked, glancing at Vickey. He saw her nod deferentially at his question.

"Oh," Gabby chortled, "Balcazar would sell his mother if he thought he'd get a sol for her!"

"That's true, God forgive him," Dominique murmured with a sorrowful shake of her head. "He's in his midforties, overweight, and partially balding, with black hair and brown eyes. Down at the pier, the main one, there are many warehouses where shipping containers come in and out. Balcazar has an office in one of the shabbier buildings. I don't know which one, but he has a sign there, a red-and-white one that says Balcazar Imports. That's him."

"But," Gabby said with concern, "you must be very careful. He trusts no one, and he's dangerous. We've heard many accounts of him and his thugs coming here to our barrio and forcing young men at gunpoint to go with them. He takes these young ones up to the mountain jungles and forces them to dig all over the place, looking for Inca burial sites."

"Yes," Dominique added grimly, "and he murders them. Many a mother has come through our front door here, in tears and hysterical. Balcazar is notorious for his cruelty. He uses young men and then has them disappear. We are sure that after he's done with them, he kills them. He doesn't want word of a burial site to leak out to anyone except his own thugs who bring the treasure down from the jungles to his warehouse. Balcazar then sells the artifacts to rich people overseas, who don't care where it came from or whose blood was spilled in the process."

Griff frowned. He didn't like the sound of this character. "And if we go waltzing into his import office? What will he do?"

"Who knows?" Gabby said. "It all depends upon what you want or what he thinks he can get from you."

"If we go ask about this crystal star?"

Dominique laughed. "Well, if he has it, he's certainly not going to admit it to you! You look like college students. He knows you must be poor if you're going to school. More than likely he'll just shrug you off."

"But you said he has a warehouse where he stores these things?"

"Yes, but child," Gabby said, "it's guarded around the clock by men with weapons. Balcazar isn't going to let you into that shabby place to go snooping about, let me tell you."

"And if you're caught, he'll kill you," Dominique added grimly.

Vickey nodded and looked over at Griff. The idea of him being shot didn't appeal at all to her. Or getting blown away herself, either. Still, Kai had warned her that Robert Marston played for keeps.

"Does the name Marston mean anything to either of you?" Vickey asked, looking back at the nuns.

"Oh, my, yes!" Gabby said. "He's in cahoots with Balcazar! Why, according to the whispers we hear among the people of the barrio here, Mr. Marston is a major buyer of stolen Inca treasure. It's known that he wants any and all pre-Columbian treasures, too."

"And what are the Lima police doing about Balcazar?" Griff asked.

"Poof! Nothing!" Dominique waved her fingers. "They get paid off, my friend. Oh, yes, payments slide under the table all the time. You cannot trust the Lima police. Do not go to them."

"Mike told us to avoid them," Vickey said. She rubbed her furrowed brow. "Is there anyone here in the barrio who could help us get into that warehouse? Someone who's been in there and knows the layout? The guard schedule?"

"Hmm. Why yes, I know of someone," Gabby said. "Juana's son, Pablo." She scrunched up her thin silver eyebrows as she glanced over at Vickey. "Pablo used to work for Balcazar, and he escaped. He was one of the lucky few who did. Pablo was kidnapped from here a year ago. That's why we know what this evil man does with our young men. Right now, Pablo

Lazaro is hiding out because Balcazar still has thugs looking for him. He wants to kill Pablo because he doesn't want any survivors to tell the stories."

"And where is Pablo now?" Griff asked. He finished his tea and set the mug aside.

"He lives with his best friend, Marcos Huisa, here in the barrio. I will draw you a map of how to get to that house," Dominique said as she pulled a piece of paper from a stack and started to scribble on it.

"I heard Pablo speak of a star," Gabby murmured, scratching her thin hair. "Once…oh, I wish my memory wasn't as spotty as it is. That's all I remember, Victoria."

Vickey smiled gently at Sister Gabby. No one called her Victoria except her mother. It gave her a warm feeling to hear her name from this old nun. "That's okay, Sister Gabby. You're doing great as far as we're concerned."

Griff felt a little pride when Vickey said "we." Maybe they were more of a team than he felt presently. He wanted to be, but she kept him at arm's length. On the flight to Lima she'd been coolly professional. No more warm talk about her mother or father. Maybe that had been a slip on her part? Griff hoped not. Rubbing his jaw, he figured their present mission wasn't going to give them downtime to chat, either. No, this was looking more and more dangerous by the moment.

"Here," Dominique said, leaning over and handing the map to Griff. "If you follow this, it will take you to Marcos's house. They don't have telephones here. No cell phones, either. These people are very poor."

"And when you reach Marcos's place," Gabby said, "be sure to tell him that we sent you. Otherwise, I'm sure Pablo, if he is there, will take off out the back door, running. They won't trust you. They'll think you're working for Balcazar."

"Thanks," Griff said, taking the paper and looking at the diagram. Although Dominique's shaky hand made a lot of lines wavy, he could follow the map without a problem. When he handed it to Vickey, their fingertips met. For a moment, Griff enjoyed the brief contact. Her eyes narrowed instantly as they touched, and she quickly pulled away, as if burned by the contact. Hurt, Griff tried not to allow the feelings to assail him too deeply. But they did. Sister Gabby had called him Sir Lancelot. Well, if the nuns saw his potential knightliness, maybe Vickey would. He sincerely hoped so, but Griff had no sure or clever way of proving to her that he was a decent and trustworthy guy.

Yeah, trust. There was that word again. Through half-closed eyes, he watched Vickey studying the diagram. Her dark brows were drawn downward, her lips compressed. Griff was getting used to how she looked when she was zeroing in on something, fully focused. As usual, her shiny brown hair slipped forward to bracket her face, and he waited for her to lift her hand and push the strands away. As she did, he secretly enjoyed the graceful movement. Did she know how incredibly desirable she was as a woman? That even her smallest gesture was worth waiting for? Sometimes Griff felt like a starving lobo wolf and she, a delectable delight he'd never get to fully savor.

Tucking all those desires inside him, Griff saw Vickey lift her head. Her green eyes were thoughtful as she held his gaze. "Looks like our first order of business is to try and find Pablo."

"I'm in agreement," Griff said. He rose and smiled at the two old nuns. "And thank you for all your help."

Sister Gabby smiled, revealing that most of her front teeth were missing. "Just be careful. Balcazar is dangerous. He shoots first and asks questions later."

Vickey eased off the chair and gently grasped Sister Gabby's hand. "We'll be very careful, Sisters."

"And ask Pablo about the star," Gabby repeated. She touched her head. "I'm *sure* he mentioned something about it…."

Chapter 7

As they left the clinic to go find Marcos's home, they were suddenly surrounded by muddy, barefoot children of all ages. The young ones danced around Vickey, hands outstretched begging for money, their dark eyes shining with hope.

To her surprise, Griff laughed and dug into the pocket of his jeans. Instantly, the children circled him, as well. Halting, she watched him smile warmly at them and crouch down until she could only see his head and broad shoulders. At least thirty children crowded close to him. Her lips lifted in a grin as he produced a bag of hard candy. Little hands eagerly stretched forward.

"Now, now," Griff chided them in Spanish, "everyone will get a piece of candy. Don't push and shove. One at a time..." And he began handing out the individually wrapped candies, one each to the wildly waving hand. Finally, as the last child, a little girl in a ragged red dress, waited her turn, Griff lifted her and set her on his thigh. Holding her gently, he placed the candy in her hand and then reached for his handkerchief.

"You've got a snotty nose, little kid," he said, and wiped the girl's nose gently several times until it was clean. Shyly, she looked up at Griff through her thick black lashes, the candy in her mouth, both hands holding it there as she eagerly sucked on it. "There, you're fit to run around now," he said, and set her on the muddy ground.

Straightening, he took the empty plastic bag and stuffed it back into his pocket. The children disappeared like fog on a hot morning. Looking over at Vickey, Griff felt his heart suddenly beat hard, as if to underscore the incredible expression on her face. No longer was she glaring at him, as she usually did. And no longer was there distrust in her wide green eyes. No, as he wiped his hands self-consciously on the sides of his jeans, he saw something else he never thought he'd see: tears. Stymied, Griff stood frozen for a moment, because that was the last thing he'd ever expected to see coming from her.

In awkward moments like this, he often became the joker. "Oh, come on," he chided her, walking up to where she stood. "Don't tell me you haven't fed these little ragamuffins before?"

Vickey blinked several times and forced the tears deep inside her. "I can be touched by simple human generosity, even from you," she growled as she swung into step with him once again. The clay surface of the deeply rutted road continued to be slippery. The odors of urine and feces stung her nostrils. People used the ditches on either side of the makeshift road as their outdoor toilet.

Griff chuckled darkly. "See? I can so be a knight in shining armor." He met her flitting gaze and saw her mouth pull into a semblance of a smile. Or was that a grimace?

"In my experience the word *knight* just doesn't go together in the same sentence with you." Vickey saw his humor-filled gray eyes darken. She reined in her Scorpio tendency to sting when the victim was down and helpless. Lifting her hand, she muttered, "Okay, okay, I didn't expect this of you."

"What? A little compassion for kids?" He squared his shoulders proudly. "Over in Afghanistan the kids always met us outside the barbed wire. I had my mother send me over big boxes of candy so I could always carry some in my pocket when I left the base and went into town on errands."

"My heart be still." Vickey dramatically placed her hand over her chest. She wouldn't admit it to Griff, but this showed a generous side of him she hadn't expected.

"Where's *your* candy?"

Laughing, Vickey patted the pack she carried on her shoulders. "In here. Jelly beans. I was saving them."

"For who? Yourself?" He stopped suddenly. "I know. For me, right?"

Her mouth curled upward, as they continued walking. Vickey was incredibly pretty when she smiled. That intense warrior look disappeared, revealing an inner layer as bright as a seam of gold in a mine.

"Get real, dude. Never for you."

"Ahh, come on, Vickey. You're telling me if I was starving to death you wouldn't feed me if you had food?"

She knew he was joking. And, for once, this felt better than maintaining that dark, grudging tension she felt toward Griff. As she observed the boyish look burning in his gray eyes, the careless, far-too-inviting smile on his mouth, she frowned. "I'd feed you, don't worry."

"Really? Evil ol' me?"

"Yes, evil ol' you."

"And if I was caught by the bad guys, you'd come and rescue my sorry ass?"

Snorting, Vickey gave him an assessing look. "That would depend…."

"Ah, I see." Griff nodded. "Fair enough. But I'd definitely rescue you."

"First of all, I won't get caught. And I know you want to make me think you can be a good guy. That's your bottom line."

"Ouch."

"You walked into that one, Hutchinson," Vickey said. Damn! She shouldn't use his real name. "Rosalino," she muttered, correcting her error.

"I just love the fact that we're supposedly brother and sister." Griff shook his head as they slogged slowly along the road. Women were out in front of their huts, leaning over small cooking fires, black kettles suspended from tripods over the flames. Children ran everywhere, with skinny, mangy dogs barking at their heels. Everyone gazed at the two of them with curiosity and wariness in their eyes.

"You would."

Shrugging, Griff stopped to look at the map, then pointed to the right. "I think we take this little lane. Marcos's house should be at the end of it."

Vickey agreed after she took the map and checked it out herself. Wood smoke hung over the barrio. The clouds were breaking up and fingers of sunlight stretched across the area, momentarily brightening the dreary place. She wiped the sweat off her upper lip as she turned down the unnamed lane bordered by shacks.

"Do you have brothers and sisters?" Griff asked as he walked at her shoulder. They slipped and slid on the wet red clay.

"I have two sisters, both younger than me."

"Ah, the older sister syndrome."

Vickey laughed. "Yeah, it sucks, lemme tell you."

Griff was delighted she'd opened up. Maybe the candy he'd given to the urchins had touched her heart and made her realize he wasn't such an ogre. "Me," he said, thrusting a thumb at his chest, "I have a kid sister and a younger brother. I'm the oldest, too." He peeked at her to see if his chattiness was being well received. Vickey seemed noncommittal rather than closed down so Griff leaped at this opportunity to share more about their families.

"My parents are cattle people from Wyoming. Running a strictly organic operation. My mother told my father that if he didn't let his cattle feed on the open range, with good food, clean water and no antibiotics, she'd divorce him."

Vickey raised her eyebrows. "Your mother sounds like a formidable woman." She saw that Griff's cheeks were ruddy from the heat. His face was far more open, his gestures showing his excitement over discussing something personal with her. Grudgingly, she listened. After all, he *had* been kind to the children and wiped that little girl's nose. Vickey didn't want to admit to herself that Griff had a nice side, but couldn't forget the child's adoring look after he had treated her so kindly. What a great father he'd make, she mused. And as fast as that thought hit her, she rejected it. One kind act did not erase their nasty past.

"Oh, my mom is hell on wheels," Griff chortled. "Dad was in the Marine Corps for four years, then came home to work with my grandfather, who had polio as a kid. Gramps was pretty banged up from it and the polio was returning, so my dad gave up his dream of being twenty years in the military, and came home to take over the operation of our ranch, the Bar H. My grandmother had died a year earlier, so the place was a mess. He hired my mother to cook for the ten cowboys that rode with the Bar H. She really whipped those men into shape, Dad tells me."

A grudging smile tugged at Vickey's lips. "I've never met a Native American woman who didn't have a warrior side."

"Bingo!" Griff said, laughing. "Yeah, my mom rode roughshod over all of them, apparently. The ranch was a disaster when she went there, the main house, too. Gramps not only was crippled with polio, he was still grieving over the loss of his wife." Griff held Vickey's gaze, which revealed her interest. Maybe the way to neutral ground was to open up and tell her about his background. Judging from the glimmer in her green eyes, she *was* interested. Heartened, he continued as they slogged through the mud.

"My mother cleaned the two-story log home that my grandfather had built fifty years earlier. It took her three months to turn it from a dump into a fairy-tale castle—that's what she told me. And she took photos before and after, so if you look at our family scrapbooks you can see the difference."

"A lot of men live like pigs, surrounded by beer cans and junk food. They don't have a clue how to man a vacuum cleaner. God forbid they should dust," Vickey said.

"Guilty as charged," Griff responded, holding up his hand.

"Oh, somehow I doubt that," she chuckled. "Your mother would have whipped you boys into shape from the get-go."

Griff grinned. "You're right on target. She did. Now, I can't say I'm Mr. Clean, but my hooch over in Afghanistan was clean even if it had dirt walls and corrugated metal for a roof, with a ton of sand bags on top. I didn't even have rats."

"Rats?"

"Yeah, we lived out in the wilds of the countryside, in a little village. Part of our mission was to be there for the people, so pilots lived among the villagers between flights and assignments. My hooch was really nice. You should have seen it. I swept it out every morning. I never left food in there because that's what the rats went after. Some of the other pilots would get food boxes from home and leave them around. If they left on a mission they'd come back to find the rats had eaten through the cardboard and left a real mess."

"Ugly."

"No kidding."

"So, what did you do with yours?"

"I always put my boxes in the chieftain's house. He'd lock them away so no one would walk in and take the stuff."

"It sounds like you shared your food," Vickey said, seeing the end of the lane coming up.

"I told my mom that the kids of the village really needed winter clothing. She went to Casper, which was seventy miles from our ranch, and solicited all kinds of clothing donations from the local ladies' clubs."

"I think I like your mom."

"Yeah, I kinda like her, too."

Vickey shook her head. "If you have such a strong, fine mother, how the hell did you go so wrong?" The question flew out before she could bite it back. Griff, after all, had apologized to her for his dark deeds of the past. She slowed her stride, wanting to apologize, but the words jammed in her throat.

She saw his face crumple. Why did he have to be so readable? She'd rather deal with an implacable Neanderthal than someone whose every emotion was obvious.

"I guess..." Griff blinked and took a breath. "I guess I had that coming...I don't know. My mom raised all of us to respect women. It just never occurred to me that women were capable of flying combat helicopters." Giving her an apologetic look, Griff saw the uncertainty in Vickey's narrowed eyes.

"And did your mom ever know what you'd done?"

Wincing, he said, "Yeah, I told her. We all got called up by Captain York, the head trainer at flight school, and were given a choice between a court-martial or losing a pay grade for the tricks we'd played on all of you. I broke down and told my parents."

"I'll bet your mother wasn't very happy." Vickey halted and turned to him. Marcos's hut was less than a hundred feet away, but she wanted to finish this conversation. If looks meant anything, she could see that Griff was clearly ashamed and humiliated by what he'd done. Folding her arms across her chest, she watched him stammer awkwardly, his hands reaching toward her.

"M-my mother cried. She was angry with me. She said I—I knew better. And I did. I got caught up with a bunch of guys who felt women learning how to fly the Apache were taking men's jobs. She reminded me that her great-grandmother was a Cheyenne warrior. A great one, apparently. There's a photo of her in our family album—a fierce-looking woman on a paint pony with a war shield in one hand and a spear in the other."

"So which was worse, I wonder," Vickey said, "your mother's reaction to what you did, or the slap on the wrist Captain York gave all you boys?"

Griff settled his hands on his hips and looked down at the red clay coating his leather boots. Mud was splattered halfway up the legs of his jeans. "Oh, no question. My mom."

"That gang you ran with were a nasty bunch," Vickey muttered.

Nodding, Griff said, "Looking back on it, I know you're right." Griff gave her a searching look. "I'm not making excuses for what I did to you, Vickey, but I'd hope you give me a little credit, too."

"For what?"

"I'm sure you know the whole story about what was planned?"

"We got the whole story, I thought."

"The leader was Tad Markley. He was from Arkansas."

"A good ol' boy Southerner who felt women should be barefoot and pregnant and not sit in the seat of an Apache."

"I know…."

Griff met and held her angry stare. "He got his hands on some Rohypnol, the date-rape drug. His plan was to lure several of you to an off-base bar and make you late coming back the next day. You would be considered AWOL, and he knew that Captain York would throw the four of you out."

"You've got it right so far," Vickey said grimly. "I remember Markley coming over to our group and inviting us to the bar after the day's written exam and flight test. We were all wired and wanted to do a little drinking to let down our hair for a while."

"Yeah, it was easy to convince you," Griff admitted quietly.

"I remember how, at the club, you hung back, like a shadow in the background.

"The other four guys were drinking and dancing with us. I should have listened to my gut, because the whole thing didn't feel right."

Nodding, Griff said, "To tell the truth, I didn't feel good about the idea of slipping that drug into your drinks. I was worried about the health effects on all of you."

Vickey remembered that smoky little bar outside Fort Rucker. It was a popular hangout three miles off base, and easily accessible by bus. The bar was a small place with a couple of pool tables, a hardwood dance floor and a blaring jukebox. Beer, the drink of choice, flowed freely. Everyone was having a good time. Vickey loved to dance because dancing bled off all the tension she carried as she tried to make her way through training. Yet her gut had screamed at her that night—and she'd ignored it, much to her everlasting regret. "So you *weren't* the one responsible for putting the drug in our beer?" she asked.

"No…Markley did it."

"You were the driver?" After they'd drunk the tainted beer, the four of them had grown very sleepy. Markley and his friends had escorted them out of the bar and loaded them into a van.

"No, I got cold feet, so I told Markley I wasn't going through with it. He just laughed off my concerns for your health."

Surprised, Vickey stared at him. Griff's face was serious, his gray eyes dark, his scowl pronounced. "What? This information never came out in the investigation afterward!"

Shrugging, Griff said, "Do you remember me coming over to you at the bar? When I knocked over your bottle of beer and most of it spilled on you? There wasn't much left afterward."

"I do remember. I was pissed off as hell that you'd spilled beer all over my only dancing dress."

"I was trying to get rid of the bottles, so you ladies would drink less of what was in them. That was why."

Vickey stood there assessing Griff. "We were never told this in the investigation."

"No, you weren't."

"You were implicated all the way."

"I know…."

"So, if you really were trying to help us, why the hell didn't you just tell us not to drink it?"

"I don't know. Immaturity…stupidity…being afraid of getting dropped by Markley and his group. At the time, I felt I needed their support. I didn't want to be singled out as a loner, or as not being one of the guys."

"Humph."

"What do you remember of that night?" Griff asked.

"I remember how pissed off I was at you for spilling that beer all over my dress."

"Yes, and you drank what little was left in that bottle and then went to the rest room to wipe off your dress."

"That's right. And when I returned, I was feeling really tired. So were the three girls with me."

"I wasn't able to get to their bottles," Griff said. "They drank a lot more than you did."

"I remember. Markley came over with his friends, saying they had a van and a nice motel room where we could sober up. I remember being hustled out the back door." She frowned. "But I don't remember you there."

"I wasn't." Griff shrugged. "I told Markley I couldn't do it. He saw what I'd done and knew why I'd done it. He'd cornered me when you were in the bathroom and told me that if I didn't have the balls to go through with it, to get lost."

Vickey rubbed her brow. "That's why you weren't in the van that took us to that motel ten miles away."

"Right."

"I vaguely recall Markley herding the four of us into that room. By that time, we were passing out. I remember lying down on one of the two beds and going to sleep. I don't even remember the guys leaving. They just covered us with some blankets and took off—"

"—Hoping that you'd sleep through 0600 the next morning, miss roll call and be hit with AWOL charges."

"No shit." Vickey looked around. The sky was turning bluer by the moment, the clouds dissipating rapidly. Drilling him with a dark look, she said, "And you were the one pounding on the motel door at 0430 the next morning, trying to wake us up."

"Yeah."

"So what really happened? Did you get left at the bar? Did Markley head back to the base without you?" She was interested to hear the rest of the story.

"That's right. I didn't have much money, and no car. Bus service didn't go that way, either. So I walked the ten miles to the motel where I knew they had put you."

"Oh." Vickey remembered waking up as Griff had pounded on the door. "You woke me up. I came out of it, staggered to the door and opened it."

"Yes. And I told you to get everyone up and back to base so you wouldn't be AWOL."

Grimacing, Vickey said, "I had such a roaring headache. You were nearly shouting at me and it felt like I had bombs going off in my head. I couldn't understand at first."

"I told you the truth."

Vickey murmured, "Yeah, that really cleared my head. My adrenaline punched in at that point when you told me we'd been set up."

"I didn't think it was right."

"But you took the fall right along with Markley and the others. Why?"

"Because I had been part of it, Vickey." Griff purposely used her first name and saw her eyes go soft. Then they hardened again. Her mouth thinned, obviously due to a lot of emotions Griff didn't blame her for having. "I did agree to the plan at first. I deserved the punishment."

"But none of what you just told me ever came out afterward." She searched his earnest face. "For all I know, you could be lying to me now."

"That's true. But what I did—knocking your beer over and coming to your motel room to wake you up so you wouldn't be AWOL—should count for something. Shouldn't it?" Griff wanted Vickey to stop painting him with the same brush as his one-time friends. He *was* guilty, but not entirely. Would she be able to sort all this out? Did she want to? He hoped so.

"Okay," Vickey said, "why are you telling this to me *now?* Why not earlier? You had plenty of opportunity there at the flight school after this whole sordid mess was uncovered."

"I was told by Captain York that if we didn't buckle down and finish our training without a hitch, we were out. He wasn't in any mood to hear the rest of the story. The newspapers had gotten hold of it and we were bringing disgrace on a national level to our program. He was interested in letting it die. Even if I'd tried to tell my side, Markley wouldn't have backed me up. And—" Griff smiled briefly "—if I'd gone to you and asked you to testify on my behalf, as angry as all of you were, do you think you would have?"

"No. You're right about that," Vickey said. "The mood we were in, we were ready to kill all of you. We didn't trust any of the guys in your class. If it hadn't been for Maya Stevenson's father being a U.S. Army general and stepping in to force Captain York to clean up this prejudice toward us, chances are we wouldn't have graduated. So, no, we weren't in a mood to be nice."

"Which was another reason I took the fall with Markley," Griff admitted. "I didn't think you'd corroborate my story or what I'd done to try and head off the whole thing."

"This is a lot to feel my way through," Vickey told him. "I don't know if I believe you or not."

Griff stepped closer to her in an effort to bridge the gap between them. "I guess I'm telling you this because we're going into some potentially dangerous areas here, Vickey. I need you to trust me. Just a little. We might have to rely on one another."

Right. He was right, but Vickey didn't want to admit it. Noting the searching look in his gray eyes, she couldn't just flip Griff off as she had before. "Look, I need time to think about this. I'm not calling you a liar, but I also see that you have a good reason to feed me this line and hope I swallow it, too."

"I know that," Griff admitted. Giving her a warm look, he said, "I don't think you're an unfair person at heart. My sense is that you'll consider what I just told you. I know you don't like or trust me. I'm hoping my honesty will create a little trust between us, because those nuns back there said Balcazar was dangerous."

To hell with it. "Look, I'll come a hundred percent clean here. I've always liked you and I was drawn to you in flight school, but I never acted on it. I couldn't. But getting thrown together with you now, I don't want to see you hurt, Vickey. I know you're self-sufficient and can take care of yourself, but I don't want anything to happen to you. Hang me for it if you want, but that's the truth." Griff saw the sharpness of her eyes suddenly grow softer by his admission. Hope rose in his heart.

Chapter 8

They struggled through the barrage of containers, tin cans and torn cardboard that comprised the front of Marcos's hut, which was squeezed between two others. The "door" was a blanket, a bright statement against the grim poverty, in Vickey's opinion. She felt Griff halt close to her right shoulder.

"Marcos!" she called out in Spanish. "Are you in there?"

No answer. The odor of ripe garbage wafted to her flaring nostrils and she grimaced. The stench was nearly overwhelming. How did anyone live with this day in and day out?

"Marcos?" she yelled more forcefully, and banged on the side of the hut. It shook beneath her fist.

Someone stirred inside the hovel, and Vickey heard movement on the other side of the blanket.

"What?" A man she assumed to be Marcos stuck his head outside the blanket.

Vickey scowled. He was drunk. The fumes of alcohol, probably pisco, assailed her sensitive nose. He was young, probably in his early twenties, and terribly skinny. The dark blue pants he wore were in dire need of cleaning. His short-sleeved yellow shirt was also filthy. "I'm Vickey Rosalino from Argentina and this is my brother, Griff. The nuns from the church sent us to you. Can we come in and talk?" At this point, Vickey didn't want to go inside the flimsy hovel.

Rubbing his face, Marcos blearily stared at them. "The nuns sent you? What are you? Law enforcement?" He looked them over with wary, bloodshot eyes.

"No," Griff said, stepping forward. "We're archeology students from University of the Pampas, Buenos Aires."

"Coulda fooled me." Marcos grinned, showing that his front upper teeth were missing. "What's in this for me?"

Vickey pulled twenty soles from her pocket. "Money, if you give us some information."

Marcos looked around, then gave her a warning glance. No doubt, he didn't want to exchange money out in the open. Soles were hard to come by and he obviously didn't want prying eyes seeing her wave the colorful bills about. "Come inside."

As she stepped into the one-story hut, Vickey saw

it had a second room with a blanket across the door. Someone else had to be living with Marcos. In the main area of the hut, there was an empty bottle of pisco on the hard-packed floor, next to what appeared to be Marcos's bed. Marcos's sleeping area consisted of straw and a couple of red-yellow-and-green-striped blankets that had seen better days. Vickey kept her back to the wall, so she could see both doorways, and Griff stood opposite her. She was pleased to note he understood her stance.

Marcos pushed his long, oily black hair away from his face. His skin was deeply pockmarked, and Vickey wondered if he'd had smallpox—not uncommon in such conditions. He sat down on his bed and crossed his legs. Looking up at them expectantly, he made a gesture for them to sit on the bare, dry floor.

"We'll stand," Vickey said. "Sister Gabby said that you were allowing a man who used to work for Balcazar Imports to stay with you. His name is Pablo Lazaro. That's who we want to talk to." She leaned down and handed Marcos the soles. He handled the money with great care, then broke into a grin.

"*Sí,* he's in there…." The Peruvian hooked his thumb toward the other doorway. "He's passed out." Running his fingers across the rainbow colored bills, he beamed. "You can stay as long as you want." He unwound from his sitting position and stuffed the bills into his pocket. "Me? I'm gonna go down to Jesus's Bar. *Adíos, amigos….*" And he brushed past the blanket and disappeared.

Vickey wrinkled her nose and looked at Griff. "Nice digs, eh?"

"My stomach's rolling." The stench of human waste was overpowering. In the corner near Vickey was a pot with plenty of fecal matter and urine in it.

"Makes two of us. Let's go wake up Pablo." Vickey shoved the blanket aside. Her eyes had adjusted to the dim light of the shack. On a wooden box in one corner of the smaller room she saw a kerosene lamp sputtering. The odor of the fuel was heavy in the room—enough to cause carbon monoxide poisoning, she suspected. Vickey spotted what had to be Pablo, wrapped in a red blanket with only his black hair visible. She walked over to him.

Griff stepped into the room, and he saw another empty liquor bottle near the sleeping youth. Remaining near the door, he watched as Vickey leaned down and gave Pablo a good, sharp shake.

"Hey, *compadre!*" she whispered, "wake up!" Again she shook him.

Pablo groaned. He muttered something and tried to cover his head with the blanket.

Pulling it out of his hand, Vickey coached, "Get up, Pablo! We want to talk to you. Now!" She rolled him over on his back and got a better look at him. The Indian youth was barely in his twenties. Hanging around his face and narrow shoulders, his black hair was grimy, as if it hadn't been washed in weeks. When he blearily opened his bloodshot eyes, Vickey stared down at him, still supporting his shoulder.

"W-who are you?" he muttered, frowning.

"Friends of the nuns down at the clinic," she told him. She tightened her fingers on his pathetically thin shoulder. Pablo was skin and bones. Food must be hard to come by, and drinking pisco like a fish didn't help. "We need some information. Wake up, Pablo! There's money in this for you if you talk to us *now!*" She jerked him into a sitting position and then released him, itching to wash her hands thoroughly with a lot of soap and water. There was plenty of evidence of flea bites—red bumps running like a highway up and down his neck.

Groaning, Pablo got up and staggered. If Griff hadn't reached out and grabbed his elbow, he'd have fallen against the sagging wall. More than likely, he'd have crashed through it, bringing the hovel down around them.

"I'm Griff Rosalino from Argentina. This is my sister, Victoria. Sister Gabby told us where to find you." He released Pablo's elbow and the man righted himself on his bare feet, which stuck out of his dirt-streaked tan chinos.

"Yeah, yeah. Gimme a minute. I gotta pee." Pablo brushed the blanket aside and reeled into the other room.

Wrinkling her nose, Vickey said in English, "This place reeks. Once he pees, let's get him outdoors. I'm gonna vomit if we don't."

Grimly, Griff nodded. "Yeah, makes two of us. I'll stay with him. I don't want him running off."

"Roger that." Vickey watched Griff move past the blanket. She heard Pablo peeing. Once he was done, she pushed aside the covering and saw that Griff was standing to one side of the exit like a guard dog, obviously anticipating that Pablo might run off. She turned to the Peruvian, who was having difficulty zipping up his pants, still so drunk that he fumbled.

Gripping Pablo by the arm, Vickey said, "You're comin' with us." She propelled him out the door and into the fresh air. Taking in deep breaths, she held on to the Indian, who staggered against her and then tried to get his feet under him once more. Griff took his other arm to steady him.

"There's a café down the road," Griff said. "Not much of one, but it's got to be cleaner than this shit house."

Nodding, Vickey tugged Pablo forward. "Come on, *compadre*. We're gonna sober you up with food and coffee, and then you're gonna talk to us…."

The Verde Café wasn't much more than pieces of plywood nailed together. The single-story structure was capped off with the ever present corrugated tin roof. However, much to Vickey's relief, the place was clean, with its rough-hewn picnic tables and hard-packed dirt floor. Light filtered through plastic windows that had been duct taped to the plywood. Run by an Indian couple, the café was nearly empty except for a mother with two snotty-nosed, cranky children at a corner table.

Getting Pablo a cup of hot coffee and a plate of *huevos rancheros* was the smartest thing they could have done. The young man sat across from Vickey and ate like a starved dog. Seeing him wolf down the meal aroused an intense sadness in her. No matter what food the café owner put in front of him, he ate it, then sipped hot coffee from a chipped yellow ceramic mug. Griff sat at his side, his brows drawn downward.

The squalls of the children, probably two and three years old, filled the air. Vickey could handle the noise much better than the horrible odors of the hovel. Here the smells of baked beans, rice and spicy Latin foods permeated the air. For that, she was grateful.

Pablo sipped his coffee, holding the mug with both hands. Grinning at Vickey, he said, "Thanks. This was a real good meal."

"We want something in exchange," she informed him, keeping her voice low. In the corner near the cook's area a portable radio was blaring tango music, loudly enough to cover their conversation. Vickey didn't want anyone overhearing what they were saying.

"Sister Gabby told us you worked for Felipe Balcazar," she said, leaning forward, her elbows on the table. "Is that true?"

The look Pablo gave her was one of shock. "Worked for that bastard? He kidnapped me and *made* me work for him!"

"Okay," she murmured, "you were kidnapped. Can you tell us about it?"

Pablo seemed even more wary. "Why? Has he sent you?"

"No, of course not! We're friends of the nuns. They told us how to find you, so relax, will you? We just need some information about him."

Pablo relaxed. "Information will cost more than just a meal."

Gazing darkly at the man, Vickey pulled out ten soles from her pocket and pushed them across the table toward Pablo. He quickly grabbed the bills and stuffed them into his pocket. "So talk. We want to know about Balcazar's place down on the Lima wharf."

"Why would you want to see him? He's a cutthroat killer. He kidnaps Indians all the time, takes us to the jungle and forces us at gunpoint to dig until we find a grave. If we don't dig, he shoots us in the head and leaves us in the jungle to rot."

"We know that," she said, curbing her impatience. "We need to know the layout of his warehouse down at the dock." She pulled out a notebook, opened it and placed it front of Pablo. Handing him a pen, she said, "Can you draw the warehouse? Entrance and exits points?"

"You two are loco. Crazy," Pablo said. He set aside his mug, picked up the pen and laboriously drew on the notepad.

Vickey grimaced. His hands were filthy. Pablo needed a bath in the worst way, but there was no running water in the area. She had seen many women washing clothes in front of their shacks by beating them with a stone in tin buckets. Pablo obviously didn't have anyone to do his laundry for him. He was probably too scared to show up at his mother's hut for fear that Balcazar's henchmen would grab him and haul him off to be killed.

"There," Pablo said proudly, pushing the notepad toward Vickey. "This is his office here, in the front. The warehouse is huge—two stories tall. There's a lotta windows on either side of it, but they're all pretty dirty and you can't see out of them. He puts all the stuff he takes from graves in strong wooden crates. When I was done digging in the jungle, they brought me back here, where I had to shred paper by the hour." Pablo pointed to the back corner of his drawing. "Balcazar used the shredded paper to pack artifacts in the crates. Then someone would hammer the top shut. Those crates would go out to a ship, or sometimes he had special crates sent to the Lima airport and flown somewhere. But I don't know where."

"What kind of stuff did Balcazar find?" Griff asked.

Pablo shook his head. "A lotta bones, that's for sure. He knows the jungles of Peru like the back of his hand. He pays Indians in those regions for information on where the graves are located. The people who live there know the land and the history. The Incas had many little towns, and now the jungle has claimed them all. If you didn't know where to look, you'd never find them. Balcazar has a whole bunch of guys hiking through the jungle, asking the locals for information. He pays them a few soles and they tell his men where the graves and temples are."

"And once they're located, he sends you there to dig?" Vickey asked.

"Balcazar never goes near the places. His men do. I was taken by airplane from Lima to Cuzco, then by bus down to Ollantaytambo, near Machu Picchu. From there, we walked down railroad tracks and into the jungle. They always had a gun on us. They'd hide them under their coats, but we knew they wouldn't hesitate to pull them out and shoot us."

"You couldn't escape?" Griff inquired with a frown.

Giving a muffled snort, Pablo finished off his coffee. He picked at the few crumbs of toast left on his plate and placed them in his mouth. "It was impossible. We always had four 'handlers,' as Balcazar called them. These guys herded five to ten of us diggers into the jungle, all of us carrying big packs with picks and shovels. The locals knew they were Balcazar's men, which is why they never tried to help us. If they had, they were just as likely to be shot as we were." Shrugging, Pablo held his cup up to the restaurant owner. She quickly brought over a tin pot of coffee and refilled his cup. Pablo thanked her and waited until the rotund woman left.

"How long were you forced to work for him?" Vickey asked.

"Three months." Pablo looked somberly down at his coffee. "I escaped one night from the warehouse. It wasn't easy. My friend, Pollero, was shot in the back and died. We'd both had enough. I was lonely for my mother, for my people. Homesick, I guess. I just wanted out and so did Pollero." Looking around, Pablo frowned and refocused on telling his story. "What I didn't realize was that Balcazar would keep hunting me. I can't go to my *mamacita.* If I do, they'll be waitin' to kill me."

"Did you ever put labels or addresses on those wooden crates holding artifacts? Or see them, at least?" Vickey demanded.

Pablo laughed. "*Señorita,* I cannot read or write."

"Oh."

"Did you ever hear the name Robert Marston?" Griff asked.

"Him? Oh, yeah. He's a big buyer of Balcazar's graveyard stuff."

Vickey shot Griff a telling look, before returning her gaze to Pablo, who sipped his coffee as if it were gold cupped between his hands. She felt sorry for the young man. "Pablo, we're looking for one special artifact. Did Balcazar ever mention a seven-point crystal star?" She automatically held her breath and fixed her eyes on his face.

"A star?"

"Yeah." Vickey grabbed the notepad, flipped to a blank page and quickly drew a sketch. Pushing her drawing toward Pablo, she said, "This is what it looks like. It's the size of my palm." She held up her hand.

Pablo fingered the notepad and examined the drawing. He gave Griff a long look and then settled his gaze back on Vickey. "What's it worth to you?"

Vickey pulled more bills from her pocket and pushed them into Pablo's awaiting hand. "You'd better have good info," she warned him throatily.

Those bills, too, disappeared into his pants pocket. Pablo looked around as the children continued squalling. Holding them in her ample lap, the mother tried to calm them by rocking them. The music blaring from the radio helped drown out their conversation. Pablo looked back at Vickey. "Yeah, I heard Balcazar talkin' one night about a star."

"Did you see it?" she pressed.

"Nah. Just heard him talkin' about it."

"What did Balcazar say?" Griff asked.

"I dunno. I was packing a big crate with Manuel. The boss was angry with Fernando, his head man running the graveyard gangs out in the jungle. I heard him say 'star' and 'crystal,' but that's all. Balcazar was really upset. It scared the hell outta us and we thought he was going to put a gun to his man's head and drop him on the spot. That's how angry he was."

"You never saw the star?"

"No. We packed a lot of statues and stuff, plus bracelets and necklaces, but no star."

"And that was all you heard?" Vickey said.

"Yes." Pablo put his hand over his pocket, perhaps in reaction to the threatening look she gave him.

"How long ago was this?" Griff asked.

Shrugging, Pablo said, "About a month ago."

"Was crystal something Balcazar often finds at these grave sites?" Vickey asked.

"No, I never saw any. Mostly emerald necklaces and bracelets, blue stones and gold. Gold cups, gold jewelry, but not crystal. We found a lot of pottery, too."

"You never found crystal?" Griff demanded darkly.

Shaking his head, Pablo sipped his coffee.

"So, a star or star shape isn't something you'd normally find in an Incan grave?" Vickey asked. They had to somehow make sure that this was the star they were pursuing.

"No. We'd find round coins and plates, but I never saw a star. That's why I perked up when I heard him say 'crystal star.' It was different." He gave Vickey a searching look. "What is this star to you?"

"I can't talk about it," she told him. There was no way she was letting out any info about it. Especially not to the likes of Pablo, who would easily pass on anything he heard for a few bills.

Tapping the notepad, Griff looked at the drawing Pablo had done. "What are Balcazar's hours of operation?"

"He goes home around ten every night."

"What about guards?"

"Oh, sure. All over the place. Arnaldo is in charge of security. He has men stationed around the warehouse day and night. They carry machine guns on their shoulders at all times."

"While you're inside packing?" Vickey demanded.

"We always stopped around midnight. We were herded back into a house nearby, where we slept. At 5:00 a.m. the next day, we were awakened, given something to eat and then were brought back to the warehouse to do more packing."

"So," Griff said, "no one is in the warehouse from midnight to five o'clock?"

"*Sí.* But the guards walk around the outside all the time."

"How many guards?" Vickey asked.

"Two, usually. They circle around it, you know?" Pablo made a clockwise motion with his finger.

Studying the warehouse drawing, Griff said, "And there are two doors to it? One in front and one at the rear?"

"*Sí.* But they are chained shut. You cannot get into them from the outside unless you had a pair of bolt cutters or a key for the locks. Besides," Pablo said, "those guards walk pretty fast. You might have two minutes at the most before they'd see you if you tried to get in one of those doors."

Too risky. Griff almost said it out loud, but decided to keep quiet with Pablo around.

"Does Balcazar have any other warehouses where he stores artifacts?"

"No. This is it." Pablo brightened. "I did hear a name mentioned along with the crystal star. Fernando was telling Balcazar about Roka Fierros."

"Who's he?" Vickey demanded.

"Roka worked under Fernando." Grimacing, Pablo touched his hairline. "Fierros is part Quero and a mean bastard. He hit me with the butt of his gun one time when he didn't think I was digging fast enough. Look, there's still a lump here where he struck me."

Vickey saw the raised flesh beneath the greasy black hair as Pablo pushed back a strand for her to see.

"Looks like a nasty cut," she murmured sympathetically.

"What's Roka Fierros to all of this?" Griff asked.

Shrugging, Pablo smoothed his hair back over the lump and said, "I don't know. That's all I heard. I thought you might want to know."

A bunch of loose threads... Griff nodded and thanked him. "I think we need to get going," he told Vickey. He could see that she was ready to move on, drumming her fingers restlessly on the rough surface of the table.

"Yeah, let's saddle up." She gave Pablo a tight look. "Thanks for your help."

"*Sí, señorita.* And thanks for the meal and your generosity."

With a nod, Vickey extricated herself from the table and bench. She threw a twenty-sole bill in front of Pablo and whispered, "Go get a bath, a haircut and some clean clothes."

His eyes widened and he took the bill. "Thank you, *señorita!* I will do so."

Following Griff out into the warm, humid afternoon air, Vickey eased the backpack onto her shoulders. After they'd walked out of earshot of anyone in the café, they halted. Griff had put his pack on and settled the baseball cap over his eyes.

"That proved to be a good interview," he said.

"Better than I'd hoped for," she said. She put her own cap on her head and adjusted the bill to keep the sunlight out of her eyes. "We've got a couple of leads, but let's hike out of this joint. All I want to do right now is get to a clean hotel room and take a long, hot shower." Vickey studied her hands. "God, I feel filthy. As if fleas are crawling all over inside my clothes."

Griff chuckled as they walked shoulder to shoulder down the road, which was quickly drying up after the rain. "Fleas didn't have time to hop on you, but I understand."

A group of children raced by them, laughing. They were barefoot, their clothes threadbare. Two dogs followed, barking loudly.

Compressing her lips, Vickey slid her fingers beneath the straps of her knapsack. "What do you think? Was he telling the truth? What was your gut hunch?"

Griff was pleased she would even ask. "Yeah, I think he was being straight with us, even if he was coming out of a drunken stupor."

Shaking her head, she muttered, "Drinking a whole bottle of pisco would ruin anyone for days afterward. Whew."

"The drink of choice down here, eh?"

"Yeah. It'll put a fire in your gut in a helluva hurry." Vickey managed a smile. "I ought to know. I've had a few pisco hangovers myself. More than I care to admit." She saw Griff's answering grin. Since their talk, she felt better. Somehow, looking into his warm gray eyes, she wanted to believe what he'd said about his part in the fiasco at Fort Rucker. But did she dare?

Chapter 9

After calling in their information via the Iridium satellite phone Vickey was carrying, she and Griff decided to take a taxi to the wharf area. It was late afternoon by now, and the sky was clear. As they drew near their destination, Vickey wrinkled her nose again because the sea breeze reeked of oil.

When they came down the hill toward the wharf, she frowned. Tanker ships anchored out in the deeper water were arranged in a semicircle, awaiting their turn to come to the terminal to off-load the fuel they carried. The resulting pollution was severe.

The taxi dropped Vickey and Griff off at the Del Oro Laguna Restaurant, one frequented mostly by dockworkers who manned the huge cranes and unloaded cargo containers from ships. Vickey knew she and Griff stood out sharply. They got some curious looks, some hostile ones. The wharf area wasn't a tourist destination in Lima, hence their being out of place.

The restaurant reminded Vickey of a truck stop. Late afternoon was lunchtime for Peruvians, who ate on an entirely different schedule than North Americans. *Desayuno*—or breakfast—was served around 11:00 a.m., and lunch between 3:00 and 5:00 p.m. Most people didn't sit down to supper until 8:00 to 10:00 p.m., very late at night for Vickey's digestive system. She'd never adjusted to the local mealtimes.

The restaurant, filled with workers who ate ravenously after all their hard, physical work, had few tables available. Griff spotted an empty one in a corner. The place was filled with cigarette smoke, but luckily, there was an open window next to the table, offering some relief from the noxious air. As soon as they sat down, a young girl, who looked to be the owner's teenage daughter, served them menus and glasses of water. She smiled shyly and left them to peruse the menu.

Vickey sat next to the window and placed her knapsack on the chair beside her. Taking off her baseball cap, she set it on top, then quickly ran her fingers through her flattened hair, arranging it into some semblance of order around her face. Griff was covertly watching her, she noticed, with an admiring look in his eyes. That made her feel disgruntled. Quickly lowering her hands, she took the menu and opened it.

"Quite a choice here," Griff stated, noting her scowl. "Asian, Italian, Latino."

"There's a huge Japanese population in Lima," she told him. "And a number of Italian people, as well. It's a cosmopolitan city with a lot of cultures and nationalities."

"Give me pasta and I'm happy," Griff said, grinning. His back was to the noisy group of laborers. Vickey had the best location in the restaurant. From her position she could see the door and everyone who came in and out. He felt a little uncomfortable, but he trusted Vickey's alertness.

"Pasta goes straight to my hips," she said. "I like it, but my dad has diabetes, and I have hypoglycemia as a result of his genes. My body makes fat cells out of pasta immediately." She patted one hip. "It all settles right here, so I avoid it like the plague."

"I'll eat it for both of us." Griff grinned again and the waiter, a young man dressed in a white shirt and black trousers, came to take their order. Griff asked for a big bowl of spaghetti with garlic bread, while Vickey ordered fish. After the waiter left, Griff placed his elbows on the table.

"You're as lean as a greyhound," he confided. "I don't see an ounce of fat on you."

With a slight grin, Vickey said, "Trust me, I have fat. Diabetes is endemic to Native Americans, and it runs in my dad's family. The doctors warned him that if he had kids, the disease would skip a generation, but we'd have low blood sugar—just the opposite of diabetes, which is high blood sugar. That's why I always carry protein bars with me. I can't afford to have my sugar drop in the middle of a flight." She pulled one of the bars from a pocket of her pack and showed it to Griff. He took the foil-wrapped bar and studied it. "My mother sends a box to me every month. She worries about me fainting dead away in the cockpit and crashing." Vickey chuckled darkly.

"It's that severe?" he asked, handing back the bar. As she took it, their fingers touched. He absorbed the brief contact and gave her a slight smile. This time she didn't recoil as if he were the plague personified. That was progress.

"It can be. Low blood sugar means the body isn't able to pull stored sugar into the bloodstream. I know when I'm getting that way—I get really cranky and irritable."

"And you faint?" Griff found her having such a critical medical condition at odds with her being one of the fiercest combat pilots in the squadron.

Vickey held up her hand and ticked off each symptom by touching her splayed fingers. "Cranky and irritable. Then I get light-headed and dizzy. And if I'm stupid enough not to eat a protein bar at that point, yeah, I could faint. But I don't let it get that far. I control it, just as my dad controls his diabetes with his diet. After he was diagnosed with it, my mom put him on a strict regime and he's been fine ever since. He doesn't have to take an insulin shot, so that's good news."

"Can you take anything for your low blood sugar?"

"I eat a lot of small meals daily, plenty of protein,

and stay away from most carbs, especially pasta. My body, unfortunately, converts starchy carbohydrates to fat instead of to energy I can use. Not a good thing."

Griff appraised her. "From where I sit, you're in incredible shape." He saw her face became darker, and realized Vickey was blushing.

"My father's people all have my build—lean and tall. I inherited that from him."

"And the blood sugar problems."

"That, too." Vickey saw the waiter heading toward them with coffee, cream and sugar. Once he'd served them and left, she said, "What about your parents? They got any serious medical problems?"

Griff leaped at the chance to have a normal conversation with her. He poured cream into his coffee and stirred it. "My dad broke his back riding a bull about twenty years ago. He recovered, but he's had back pain off and on ever since. He had three kids and when we got to our teens we did a lot of the ranching chores he couldn't do."

"So, you were a cowboy?" Vickey saw him flush and avoid her stare.

"Well, I wouldn't say that. I rode a horse, roped, branded and stuff like that, but I'm not a true cowboy. Those dudes are married to the saddle and would rather have four legs under them than their own," Griff said with a chuckle.

"You were drawn to the air," Vickey stated before sipping her coffee. She looked at him over the rim of the cup. "An eagle, not a ground pounder."

Nodding, Griff said, "Yeah, the sky always called

to me. My father never understood it. My brother is still at the ranch, helping him keep things going. He loves that life. My sister is a newspaper reporter in Denver, Colorado."

"Did your desire to fly cause problems with your father?"

"No," Griff said, setting the cup down, his hands resting around it. In the background, someone put money in the jukebox and a rumba came booming out of it. He leaned forward so that Vickey could hear him. "My father was in the Marine Corps for four years before he came home to help run the ranch—I told you that. He loves the land, but he also understood my need to find a career that involved flying. I think he hopes I'll come home someday and sink roots."

She saw the sad, wry smile that flitted across his well-shaped mouth. The more she got to know Griff, the more their own past seemed—well, in the past. Still, Vickey refused to forget what he'd done to her and the other women, even if at the last moment he had changed his mind and helped them.

"What's your sister's name?" Maybe his problem with women stemmed from childhood. Vickey saw Griff's brow wrinkle momentarily. He turned the cup around in his hands before he answered. She felt tension in him. The rumba ended and the normal restaurant din returned, much to her relief. She didn't like loud, noisy places.

"Candy. Candace, actually. She's the youngest."

"Spoiled rotten?"

He laughed. "Yeah, I guess. My mother shielded

her from my father because he's a rough kind of cuss. Candy didn't want to be a tomboy even though my father tried to turn her into one. I guess he had problems with women or relating to them."

"What about your mother?" Vickey knew patterns existed in families, and his was no different.

"My mom is a strong woman. And proud. She told me that when she married my father shortly after he came out of the Marine Corps, they fought like cats and dogs." Griff picked up his mug and took another sip of coffee. As he lowered it, he murmured wryly, "They still do. She doesn't take anything he tries to lay on her. My father, as you can probably guess, is real old-fashioned."

"We call them Neanderthals."

Chuckling, Griff said, "Yeah, that fits."

"So, you picked up his Neanderthal attitude and that's why you didn't think women should be flying combat helicopters?" She held his widening eyes as she zapped him with the bold question. His mouth opened and then shut. Vickey flashed him her lethal smile. "I'm trying to figure out where your belief that women can't be as good as any man originated."

Nodding, Griff said, "Gotcha."

"I'm not keeping score. I just want to understand what drove you to do it."

"Fair enough," Griff murmured. "My little sister, Candy, was very feminine. She disliked ranch work and didn't like to get her hands dirty. She hated riding a horse. That's not her fault, I know. That's just the way she is. My mother sided with her and I grew up in a family that fought daily. My father was stiff-necked about a woman's place being in the home and, of course, my mother died laughing about that. She could do anything he did, just as well."

"If you saw your mom being empowered, why didn't you see other women the same way, then? I don't understand."

"I've asked myself the same thing many times, especially after we got hauled in front of the C.O. and reamed for what we did to all of you." Griff gave her a quick glance. Her green eyes were narrowed and thoughtful. This time he didn't feel as if she was going to attack him. She really wanted to understand. That signaled to him that Vickey was willing to try to forget the past—or at least put it into perspective and, hopefully, move on. That was the best Griff could hope for under the circumstances. He had the rest of the month with her as his air commander, and there was no way he wanted the war to continue between them. Peace was better, and no one wanted it more than he did. And if he was brutally honest with himself, he'd have to admit he was attracted to her quiet, intense nature.

Griff liked Vickey's ability to ask the right questions, to probe, dig and try to understand the larger picture. That was an indication of good people-managing skills, and he felt safe enough to be frank with her as a result.

"I'm not going to sit here and blame my father for the way I behaved. My mother was so damn angry at me she just about disowned me after she found out what happened at Fort Rucker. Believe me, I got my ears burned off by her in a series of phone calls."

Vickey laughed and said, "You had it coming. She's Cheyenne and I've yet to meet an Indian woman who wasn't strong and resourceful, the backbone of her family. Women are the quiet warriors on reservations. I saw that time and again on the Navajo res where I was raised. The men did all the strutting, crowing and bragging, but it was the women behind the scenes who held everything together."

"Right. It wasn't any different in my family. My mother rules." Griff grinned. "But if you ask my father, he'd say he did."

"So, you took on your father's belief that women were second best?"

"I did. I wanted to show him that he could trust me. Early in school I got knocked around by a bully and his friends. I kept coming home with black eyes and a bloody nose. My mother told my father to give me some boxing training so I could learn to defend myself. So he did. I think he was ashamed that I couldn't fight my own battles."

"Were you little for your age?" Vickey asked. Griff had grown up into a tall, strapping male, and few men would round on him without thinking twice about it. He was well muscled and obviously worked out with weights on a regular basis.

"I was a runt," Griff admitted, and caught her fleeting smile. "All this bullying happened in the first four grades. When I was in sixth grade, I grew tall and left those days behind, much to my father's relief."

"So, you were a skinny little kid and your mother got you boxing lessons?"

"That's about it. My father had been a boxing champion in the Marine Corps. I really liked the time he spent with me, showing me how to fight. I don't think he enjoyed it because it took him away from ranching, which is demanding, never-ending work."

Nodding, Vickey began to understand a little more about Griff. "Was he an absentee father, then? You wanted more time with him than he had to spare?"

"Yeah, I guess so. Although, if I went along to check on the herd or help in the corral or barn, I could spend time with him."

"But he didn't talk with you much?"

"We had ten wranglers who worked with us. I was more a shadow, the kid who trailed along in the rear."

Hearing the pain in his voice brought out her compassion. Vickey set down her coffee cup and was tempted to say something comforting, or even touch his hand. The waiter brought their meal, which jolted her back to reality. She had ordered fresh broiled trout with lime juice and rice. The bowl of steaming, spicy pasta in front of Griff was large enough for two men to eat. Picking up her cutlery, Vickey murmured, "You sound like you never really had the father you needed. Your dad was too busy, too preoccupied with ranching demands."

Griff took a spoon and fork and cut into a meatball with relish. "That about sums it up." He gave her a searching look. "You're pretty good at sizing things up. Sure you aren't a shrink in disguise?"

Smiling, Vickey said, "Wild Woman says it's because I'm a Scorpio. We're always digging under the carpet to see what lies beneath it." She popped a piece of trout into her mouth.

"I like that about you. You pull the truth out of a person. You don't take things at face value, but instead search for reasons behind their actions or reactions."

"In your case, yes," Vickey said, cutting the fish with her knife and fork. "I see two sides to you, Hutchinson. One is the good guy, the other the untrustworthy bad guy. I'm pretty confused by you, if you want the truth." She leaned forward and dropped her voice to a near whisper. "And after we're done here and night falls, we're going to try and break into that warehouse. I want to know who I'm working with, that's all."

Buoyed by her admission, Griff kept his spiraling feelings of hope to himself. Upbeat, he focused on his spaghetti, which was covered with a fragrant garlic marinara sauce. "You got a special guy in your life?" He hoped not, but didn't want to look too closely at why he felt that way.

"Me? No. I've been down here four years and the only men I've been around are at the dance joints in Cuzco. Until very recently, the BJS was all-female."

"If it had been a mix of male and female, do you think you'd have a relationship?"

Vickey sighed. "Listen, after what happened at Fort Rucker, I gave up on men except for dancing and drinking purposes. There's still a lot of underground prejudice against women, in the military and out, and

I can feel it a mile away. Besides, I like the women I work with. It's been a helluva four-year ride down here."

"But don't you get lonely for a man?"

"Sure I do, but we get R & R once a month. I go to Cuzco with Wild Woman and we party hardy, believe me. I like men, contrary to what you may think. I love to dance. There's something primal about dancing that lets me release all the tension that's built up over the month." Her lips twisted. "That and a few shots of pisco."

"Blowing off steam from this nonstop combat," Griff murmured. He stirred his pasta, then forked up more of the strands.

"That's about it." Vickey realized that his face had lost a lot of strain. Was it because they were talking like normal human beings and not always on guard or at one another's throats? More than likely. Vickey understood that the way she handled their situation would dictate its outcome. In her heart of hearts, she really didn't want to be at war with Griff. He was, after all, a fellow pilot. Not everyone could fly combat or the Apache. Squeezing more lime juice over the last of her trout, she asked, "What about you? Is there a woman at home waiting for you to come back from this one-year gig?"

Why did she even care? Vickey sighed internally but kept her expression neutral as she put the lime wedge back on her plate and looked up at him.

"Not anymore." Griff mumbled. Some of his appetite fled. "I had a woman in the States, but six months into my duty over in Afghanistan, she wrote me a Dear John letter. Seems she didn't want to deal with the anxiety that I might be shot down and killed."

"I see…." Vickey dug her fork into the fluffy white rice. "That's a lot to ask of a civilian. I've seen more than one relationship crumble over that particular issue. We don't have safe jobs, that's for sure."

Nodding, Griff said, "Yeah, I'm getting that. I'm not into one-night stands. I don't believe in them. I was hoping to meet a woman who honored what I do, knowing that I wanted to spend twenty years in the army before getting out."

"So, you're a little burned on civilians, eh?" Why did she feel glad about that? Vickey wondered. It wasn't that she was happy Griff had been wounded by this woman and her decision. Then what was this glee? Vickey felt lighter, happier all of a sudden. Griff was a free agent, with no ties.

"There's not much else to look at," Griff complained. "As a warrant officer, I can't engage in a personal relationship with any enlisted woman. And I'm not an officer, so those women are off-limits, too."

"And you can't fraternize with warrants above you in rank, either." He was a CWO1. That meant he could only show interest of a personal nature with another CWO1, not a 2 or a 3, which were higher in rank. Now why did she feel so bummed out that she was a CWO2?

"That's right. It severely limits the playing field." Griff finished his spaghetti and pushed the bowl aside. He took his paper napkin and wiped his mouth one last time. "Besides, I'll be spending the next year of my life down here, and if it's anything like combat in Afghanistan, there won't be much time to have a personal life."

Depressed by his realistic admission, Vickey held the fish spine and pulled off the last flakes of meat with her fork. "That's true."

"Besides," Griff said, mustering a smile, "I'm sure my rap sheet has followed me down here and word of what I did back at Fort Rucker has already spread around BJS. So I don't think any CWO1 woman in this squadron is going to look at me with anything but a glare."

"Word does get around," Vickey admitted dryly. She felt a twinge of hurt for Griff. "Look at it this way—penance for your sins."

He gave her a sour smile. "That's how I'm taking it."

"Dark night of the soul time."

Nodding, Griff dropped his wadded up napkin into the bowl near his elbow. "I'm trying to be graceful about it."

"It becomes you."

"Yeah?"

"Yeah."

"So, you're not as pissed off at me as before?"

Shrugging, Vickey said, "No."

Weight slid off Griff's shoulders. More than anything, he wanted Vickey's forgiveness. He wanted someone to understand that at the last moment, he'd done the right thing. He'd walked ten miles to reach the motel, wake the women up and get them back to the base in time. Sitting there, Griff realized he wanted Vickey to acknowledge that. In some ways, this situation reminded him of the one with his father when he was young and being bullied at school. How desperately he'd wanted his father's attention, his care and concern. His protection.

Looking at Vickey, noting her guarded gaze, Griff knew he didn't need those things from her, but he did want her understanding. Maybe lunch had provided a small bridge of hope between them. She no longer glared at him. No, the look in her eyes was softer. Muted. Did he dare hope?

"Let's mosey on out of this cancer joint. I need some fresh air," Vickey muttered. "We can do a little reconnoitering around the dock area, size up Balcazar's place and pretend to be gawking tourists."

"Good idea." Griff rose, scraping his chair on the wooden floor. Leaving enough money to cover the bill and give the waiter a sizable tip, he watched as Vickey picked up her cap and settled it on her head. She shrugged into her knapsack and nodded at him. Griff took the lead, threading among the tables of noisy dockworkers. The stench of sour sweat and unwashed bodies permeated the air. Didn't men in South America use deodorant? he wondered. If they did, it wasn't working. Mixed with the scents of flavorful Latin spices and thick clouds of cigarette smoke, it was enough to gag a maggot, in Griff's opinion.

When he opened the door for Vickey, she raised an eyebrow. "Forgive me for being a Neanderthal," he murmured with a grin as she shouldered past him. Seeing the hint of a smile on her full lips, he felt his spirits rise even more.

The strong scents of ocean brine mixed with petroleum assailed them once again as they walked along the wide metal dock. For the next half mile, warehouses stretched in a soldierly row, facing the Pacific Ocean. Behind the warehouses rose a high hill scattered with boulders and long, green sea grass.

"You're a Neanderthal, all right," Vickey said, strolling slowly at his shoulder.

"But I do have some saving attributes?"

Grinning, Vickey murmured, "Maybe a few."

"Like?"

"Don't push your luck, Hutchinson. You're lucky I sat down and had a meal with you. That's as good as it gets. Now, let's go find Balcazar's warehouse."

Preening inwardly, Griff murmured, "I'd like to repeat that meal with you sometime in the future when we're not doing stealth missions."

"Oh," Vickey laughed, "dream on!" And yet her heart thrilled at his huskily spoken suggestion. Griff was, indeed, an enjoyable dinner companion, but she was damned if she was going to tell him that. Like a good Scorpio, she kept lots of secrets, and this was simply another one she stored deep in her heart.

Chapter 10

"Are you ready?" Vickey whispered the words near Griff's ear. It was 0200, and sparkling stars studded the ebony sky. Lucky for them, it was the new moon, so darkness hid them as they lay between huge sandstone boulders on the side of the steep hill. The warehouses were poorly lit, the shadows deep and pervasive. From their vantage point, they could watch the sentries who guarded Balcazar Imports.

Griff nodded. They had changed into black spandex one-piece uniforms at a local motel and watched television until it was time to go. It was easy to leave the tawdry motel at the tip of the hill that looked down on the wharf area and sneak down in the darkness. Looking at the green dials on his watch, he whispered,

"As soon as this guard passes, you should run like hell for that rear door."

Nodding, Vickey pressed against the boulder. From where they knelt, they could see without being seen. The two guards, both big men with smoothly shaved bald heads and AK-47s on their shoulders, were very good about timing their rounds of the warehouse. As the night wore on, however, they smoked more cigarettes and grew lax.

Vickey and Griff had checked out the rear door at dusk. Surprisingly, it had no chain or padlock. Vickey had been taught by Wild Woman how to use lock picks, and she had a set in her damp hand right now. Shoving them in the thigh pocket of her black suit, she quickly pulled on a set of thin gloves of the same color. They didn't want to leave fingerprints.

Wiping a bead of perspiration from her brow, she watched the thick-set guard in jungle fatigues move languidly toward the front of the two-story warehouse. The building was at least three hundred feet long and had a peaked corrugated roof. It was built of aluminum and set on a wooden and steel I-beam frame. None too steady if a bad storm blew in off the Pacific, Vickey thought as she prepared to sprint to the door.

They had three minutes before the guards made a complete round and met one another at the rear door once again. She wasn't sure she could jimmy the lock in that time since it might take several tries. However many times it took, she would succeed. Wild Woman had taught her well. Her friend had a very interesting past, knowing about such things, though she'd never explained why she had developed such talents.

"Get ready...." Griff whispered roughly. He crouched behind her as she pushed herself to her feet, then reached out and quickly squeezed her shoulder. "Be careful, okay?"

Glancing at him over her shoulder, Vickey saw his shadowed eyes burn with concern—for her. Something had happened during their late lunch at that wharf restaurant. Vickey couldn't name it—could only sense it.

Griff's fingers brushed her shoulder in a caressing gesture. She felt his worry for her. Shaken by the intimacy he'd automatically established with her, she gave him a tight grin. "Don't worry, Lone Ranger. Tonto, here, will do her work."

An unwilling grin split his serious features. Griff forced himself to release her shoulder. God knew, he wanted to keep touching her. She felt firm and well muscled beneath that black spandex. "Tonto?"

"Yeah. Remember back in flight school? Your handle was the Lone Ranger?"

Griff had nearly forgotten. "You don't forget anything, do you, Ms. Mabrey?" He said it in jest, hoping to lighten the tension around them. Glancing up, he saw the guard disappear.

"Go!"

Nodding, Vickey dug the toes of her black boots into the loose, sandy soil. It was beach sand, basically, and they'd built the entire wharf upon it. What a waste of a good beach, Vickey thought as she raced down the slight incline, the salt grass slapping against her legs as she moved like a silent shadow toward the rear door.

A light at the point of the roof weakly illuminated the door. Climbing the three concrete steps, Vickey quickly pulled the set of tools from her pocket. She breathed hard and kept her mouth open to lessen the harsh sounds. Her hands shook as she placed the first pick into the lock. Opening a door like this was an art, Vickey had discovered. But she was shaking badly, worried about being discovered. Griff was to flash the red laser light from his pistol when it was time to leave. What time was it?

Sweat dribbled down her face. Scrunching her brow, she worked the picks and soon heard something click. Pulling them out, she tried the door. It didn't budge.

Damn!

Again, she stuck the thin metal picks into the lock.

A red light blinked on the door in front of her—Griff's signal to hightail it out of there. *Now!* Quickly, Vickey pulled the tools free, turned and leaped to the sidewalk. In seconds, she was sprinting back up the hill, among the huge sandstone boulders scattered about. As she ran, she tripped on a clump of salt grass, the strands wrapping like tentacles around her ankle. With an *oomph* she landed hard on her belly, her arms thrown out in front of her. Her chin took the brunt of the blow.

Vickey gasped as the wind was knocked out of her. She rolled over on her back and tried to get up, but the way she'd landed, she couldn't move. *Hurry!* She knew she had exactly one minute before the guard would discover her! Rolling back on her belly, she heard a soft whisper of sand. It was Griff! Looking up, she saw him reach down, wrap his fingers about her right arm and haul her upward. In seconds, he was dragging her back to safety.

"Thanks...." Vickey managed to gasp before collapsing in a heap behind the boulder. Panting, her hands against her chest, she tried to pull in a deep breath, but it was impossible. She bowed her head and tried to muffle the harsh sounds escaping from her. The guards might hear her.

"Vickey?" Griff demanded hoarsely. He knelt down on one knee, his body against her back as she leaned forward, trying to breathe. Automatically, his hand went to her shoulder to steady her. "Are you all right?" Fear rose in him. Had Vickey hurt herself when she tripped? Was she seriously injured? Griff hovered worriedly over her, one ear keyed for the guard's raspy boot sounds coming their direction along the concrete sidewalk.

Vickey felt Griff's powerful presence surrounding her. "I'm...okay. Just got the air knocked...out of me. Gimme a second...."

Relief hurtled through Griff. He kept his hand on her upper arm, shielding her with his body. The guard was nearing the corner, and Griff peeked around the boulder. Sure enough, the guards met, talked a little in low voices, turned around and headed back toward the front of the building once more.

"It's okay. They don't know we're here," he whispered near her ear. He could smell the sweet fragrance of Vickey, her hair momentarily brushing against his mouth as he spoke. Her breathing was becoming steadier. Both hands were pressed to her chest, her head bowed.

"I fell and had the wind knocked out of me," Vickey finally croaked. Griff's hand felt good. Somehow, he made her feel safe in a highly unsafe situation. Maybe it was his nearness, or his firm, steady grip on her arm.

"Take your time," Griff counseled. She lifted her head and pushed her hair off from her sweaty forehead. Releasing her, he sat down and faced her. "Your right ankle got tangled in that salt grass on the slope below us. Nasty stuff."

"No kidding," Vickey muttered. Griff had brought up one leg and wrapped his hands around his knee. She could barely see the dangerous look on his angular face. "I'm okay now. Thanks. You saved my bacon out there. I couldn't move. I couldn't breathe...."

"My pleasure," he told her quietly.

She watched him warily. "If you hadn't been there and been thinking fast, they'd have discovered me."

Griff searched her wide, vulnerable eyes. She wasn't looking at him like he was some two-headed monster now. "Maybe," he whispered, leaning toward her, his thigh brushing hers, "this is where we can start building a mutual trust with one another?"

Griff was right. Perspiring heavily, Vickey wiped her brow with the back of her gloved hand. "You earned points with me on that one, dude."

His grin widened. "Good." He looked down at the picks in her left hand. "Any luck with the door?"

"Some. I heard the tumblers click. I thought I had it, but it wouldn't open. I have to go back."

"Give yourself ten minutes."

Good advice. Vickey's chest ached because the air had been knocked so violently out of her when she'd crashed into the slope. What a stupid thing to do. She should have been more careful. More alert. She knew that grass was long, thin and strong. Next time, she would be more cautious.

A few minutes later, a convertible filled with four shrieking, singing young women barreled down the wharf road. Vickey used her infrared scope and saw that the women were definitely drunk and having a helluva good time. The driver of the red convertible slammed on its brakes and honked loudly in front of Balcazar's warehouse. Vickey moved to the edge of the boulder, where she could see the closest guard walking out to the car. He was calling to one of the women and waving his hand, which held a lit cigarette. The women squealed greetings in return. Vickey saw the second guard saunter up to the convertible, as well, shouting out a welcome.

"This may be our lucky night," she muttered, turning to Griff. "Keep watch! I'm going down there now!" She grabbed the picks and quickly slipped from behind the boulder, skirting through the shadows to the rear door.

This time, she heard three more tumblers move as she shakily worked the picks. And when she tried the door, it opened. Turning, she stood and gestured for

Griff to quickly join her. Within seconds, she saw him striding down the slope. The noisy chatter from the front of the building continued nonstop, and Vickey silently thanked the young women for their impromptu visit. They knew one of the guards. What luck! It was obvious both men were bored out of their skulls, so any diversion was more than welcome to them.

Vickey pushed the door wide and moved inside the dark and cavernous warehouse. Griff ran lightly up the stairs, breathing hard as he slipped inside. Vickey quietly shut the door and locked it once more.

"Good going," he rasped. Setting down the knapsack, he dug out two small Maglite flashlights and handed one to Vickey.

She knelt at his shoulder and chuckled. "Women raising hell at two in the morning around here. Who woulda thought?"

Grinning, Griff said, "Bless 'em all. They'll keep those guards engaged for a while, but we have to be quiet." He saw Vickey rise to her full height and begin to scope out the area. Each flashlight had a red plastic cover so it wouldn't glare or catch undue attention. She peered around.

"You thought the office would be a good place to start?" Griff walked to her side. All around them, stacked nearly to the ceiling, were huge wooden crates on steel supports. Plenty of them had open lids. Vickey went over and dug her hand into one.

"Yeah, the office," she whispered. Picking up shreds of paper, she added, "Packing material. These boxes are big enough to carry a human inside of them."

"Probably for the big pots they find," Griff guessed as he looked into the deep, well-built wooden crate.

"Yeah…." Vickey turned and quickly hurried down a narrow concrete aisle between canyon walls of crates. Through the thin aluminum walls of the warehouse she could hear the women talking and giggling. Stopping in front of the office, she tried the door and found it locked, so she drew out the picks and went to work again. In no time, she had it open. Inside the office, the venetian blind on the only window was closed.

Vickey and Griff moved quietly into the small office and observed a small wooden desk piled high with teetering stacks of paper. Behind the desk were three green metal filing cabinets comprised of four drawers each. Vickey pulled the top drawer of the first one open. Griff followed her and opened the drawer of the third, leaving the second file between them so they had room to work.

"We need to find something with 'star' or 'crystal' on it," she whispered to him. Every label on the top of each file was sloppily handwritten in Spanish.

Groaning, Griff rasped, "This bastard doesn't do alphabetical order. This file drawer is a mess. How about yours?"

"Purchase orders." She quickly flipped through the dusty files. Shining the red light down into the drawer, Vickey worried about getting caught. Her heart was racing like a freight train. Having Griff nearby was a help. There was something secure and protective about him that made her feel better. It wasn't logical, maybe, but she couldn't deny it. Grimacing, Vickey forced herself to look at each tab.

"All purchase orders here! By number." She pulled one file out and tried to figure out how the hell Balcazar was keeping his system. Kneeling on the floor, she set the thin folder before her and quickly perused its contents, page after page.

"Anything?"

"Hell no! Wait..." Vickey's breath hitched. "I think I got it!"

Griff waited as she scooped up the file and set it on his opened drawer.

"Look. He's doing this by month and year, not by name of the buyer. Or name of whatever it is, like any reasonable person would do..." She pointed to the tab.

"You're right." Griff looked at the folder in the drawer he'd opened. The noise outside was growing louder, creating a real party atmosphere. He could hear both guards laughing and talking with the drunken, giggling girls.

"The crystal star was stolen fourteen months ago." Vickey quickly counted back on her fingers. "We should be looking in April of last year."

"Okay," Griff said, returning to his drawer.

Jamming the file back into place, Vickey scanned through the thousands of tabs. Sure enough, the files were organized by month and year, and this drawer held the current year. Quickly shutting it and making sure it locked quietly, she moved to the middle set of file drawers. She dropped to the second one. Griff shut his drawer and moved aside as she pulled it open.

"Pay dirt!" Vickey rasped. She jerked out a thin file and placed it on the desk. Hands shaking as she opened it, she saw it held several dozen sheets of paper. Griff held up his Maglite so she could quickly skim through the pile. One page involved a gold statuette, the next a piece of pottery. An emerald necklace was described on a third.

"This guy deals in high-end theft. All these papers document certain graves, their location and the contents he's stolen from them."

Griff leaned over, his eyes narrowed as she pulled up each sheet to rapidly scan it. "Gold? Emeralds? This guy is doing some serious grave robbing."

"Yeah, and wouldn't some government officials here in Lima love to know about it?"

"Others wouldn't." Griff pointed to names at the top of a few pages. "Look. Some of these dudes are government officials here in Lima."

"Two-faced bastards," Vickey breathed softly. "They'd give away their own country's history to turn a sale." Her heart dropped. "Griff..."

"What?" He saw her pull one paper from the file and hold it up for him to read.

"It's the star! Look!" She traced the text, typed in Spanish. "It says one Eastern Cherokee crystal star." Excitedly, she read the document more closely.

"Look at the name at the top," Griff told her.

Breath hitching, Vickey whispered, "I'll be damned. Robert Marston! Kai was right! This implicates the bastard directly!"

"Was it shipped to him?" Griff tried to read in the poor light.

Rapidly scanning the text and a few hand-scribbled notes, Vickey said, “No, I don’t think so.” She quickly laid the paper aside and went back to the other documents. Her hands trembled. What if they were caught? Those guards would shoot first and ask questions later. Gulping, she tried to read several other sheets on the stolen artifacts. After scanning five, she whispered, “The others were shipped. All to different buyers. None to Marston except this one.” She held up the sheet she’d read. “It says nothing about being shipped. Only that it was delivered here to Balcazar. The name has been blacked out, so we don’t know who delivered it to him.”

“And the notes?”

“Gibberish,” Vickey muttered, studying them through narrowed eyes. “I can’t make it out. Maybe a name? Roka? I dunno, his scribble is like hen scratching and I can’t read it.”

Griff stiffened. He turned. “You hear that?”

Instantly, Vickey went for the pistol at her side. “What?” Her pulse bounded, and fear chilled her. All of a sudden, she realized there was no more noise outside the office. Had they been so intent on what they were seeking for that the women had driven off and they hadn’t realized it? Were the guards back on duty? Swallowing hard, Vickey listened. Griff pulled out his own pistol.

She didn’t know *what* he’d heard. She’d heard nothing out of the ordinary herself. Griff slid around her and moved to the door of the office. They’d shut it, and the blinds were drawn. Turning, she took the paper implicating Robert Marston and quickly stuffed it into her right thigh pocket.

Vickey moved with pistol upraised to where Griff stood. Her heart was thundering, and she couldn't hear anything above its loud beat. "What did you hear?" she whispered in his ear.

Opening the door a slight crack, Griff looked out. The cavern of the warehouse was completely dark except for the light outside the rear door, shining dimly through the dirty windows. He felt Vickey move to his side, her body pressed against his.

"Something…like a door opening," he told her very quietly. "I don't know. I can't place it."

Nodding, Vickey gestured for him to exit. "We need to leave." Turning back, she quickly put the file back in its drawer and shut it.

Griff carefully opened the door and stepped out into the darkness. Flashlight in his left hand, pistol in his right, he waited for Vickey to join him. Once she was out, she quietly turned and shut the door. There was no time to lock it. Trying to do so might make too much noise.

The hair on the back of his neck stood up. Something was wrong. He could feel it. What? How Griff wished he were sitting in the cockpit of an Apache right now. He would have infrared, radar and a real-time television video screen in front of him. If anyone had entered the warehouse, Griff would switch to infrared and their body heat would instantly give them away. Damn, he'd rather be in the air than on the ground like this.

He signaled for Vickey to go first, and she chose to

walk down the center aisle. His heartbeat soared. Tasting fear, Griff sensed that their enemy was very near. Had the guards seen the flash of their Maglites in the office? It didn't matter. What did matter was getting the hell out of here in one piece.

He saw Vickey moving quickly, both hands on the grip of her pistol as she stepped silently along one side of the aisle. At every cross juncture, she stopped, looked both ways and quickly continued onward. The door was only a hundred feet away now.

Griff chose a secondary aisle parallel to the main one. He halted at the first juncture. Sweat was leaking down his temples and following the line of his clenched jaw. He could taste the salt on his lips as he nervously licked them.

Another sound!

Griff froze. The sound was so close he could swear he felt it. Lifting his chin, he saw Vickey disappear down the end of the row and head for the door.

"Don't move, hombre...."

The cold steel of a gun barrel was thrust into Griff's back. Fear stabbed through him. Where was Vickey? At the door? Escaped? He wasn't sure. Griff smelled cigarette smoke from the guard who had his weapon trained on him. How had they known he and Vickey were in here? His mind raced for answers.

"Drop it or you're a dead man...."

Raising the pistol, Griff braced himself. Where was the other guard? Just as he wondered, he heard a yelp deep in the cavern of the warehouse near the exit—a man's startled voice.

"Don't move!" the guard behind him growled. "Drop your weapon or I drop you."

Griff leaned down and placed his AK-47 on the floor at his feet. As he slowly straightened, he heard the other guard scream. A gun went off. Two more shots. The blasts echoed and reechoed around the warehouse. Griff flinched, and the guard behind him cursed. Somehow, Griff knew, Vickey had engaged the second guard, who'd been skulking around trying to find her. Who had fired first? Was Vickey wounded? Dead? A thousand questions cartwheeled through Griff. The guard behind him cursed again and moved to his side, shoving the muzzle of the weapon into his face. The man looked anxiously toward where the scuffle and gunfire had erupted seconds earlier.

"Ernesto!" he bellowed. "Ernesto! Are you all right?"

Griff had to take a chance. He swung his arm up and caught the guard's weapon, tipping the muzzle toward the ceiling. The guard yelled and pulled the trigger, releasing an explosion of sound. Griff had to escape! Making a twisting turn, he balled his fist to hit the guard.

And then he heard someone run up behind him. Too late! White-hot light shot through Griff's head. He grunted and pitched forward to the floor, unconscious.

Chapter 11

Damn the bad luck! Griff was a prisoner! Vickey stayed low behind the boulders. Less than thirty minutes had elapsed since she'd seen Felipe Balcazar roll up in his black Mercedes Benz. The Peruvian, in his midforties, was grossly overweight, with a potbelly hanging over his belt. The man obviously gorged daily on very rich food paid for by all the graveyard stealing he'd done over the years.

Balcazar was accompanied by four bald muscle men in army fatigues. They had an arsenal of weapons on them, which meant there was no way Vickey could fight her way into the warehouse and rescue Griff. Frustration ate at her. Fear for his life sat like acid in her gut. She didn't want him to die!

In her fight with Ernesto, the guard who'd come at her in the warehouse, Vickey had lost her pistol. The guard was dead and she'd gotten away with only a bullet nick to her right arm. It was little more than a crease in her skin, burning more than bleeding. Her pistol had been struck by his second bullet and ripped out of her hand. Her fingers were deeply bruised and swollen, but that was all. Flexing them now, Vickey felt pain from the movement, but at least she had all five of them. She was grateful for that, for worse things could have happened.

She wiped the sweat from her brow and remained hunkered down behind the boulders where they'd hidden earlier. Was Griff all right? Were they interrogating him? Could he lie his way out of this? Vickey didn't think so, because she'd killed the guard. Balcazar must know this was a serious breach of security, and she was sure he wasn't going to let Griff go on a whim.

Somehow, she had to rescue his butt. But how? Right now, there were six somber, heavily armed guards prowling around outside the warehouse, guns locked and loaded. Vickey scanned her surroundings to find an opening to get back inside the warehouse. Balcazar's black Mercedes Benz was parked out in front.

A truck came chugging down the road and slowed. Vickey watched as the driver backed it around to the rear, where a loading door was unlocked by the guard. Someone inside the warehouse pushed a button and the corrugated panel began to slowly rise upward.

Very shortly, she saw a number of large wooden crates, one at a time, brought out by a forklift and set upon the lowered tailgate of the truck. When the driver pushed a button, the crate rose even with the truck bed. It was then pushed inside by two or three burly guards. The wooden top of each crate box was handed up, but Vickey noticed they weren't nailed down. It didn't make sense to her.

Anxious over Griff's safety, she glanced down at her watch. It was 0300, and the sparkling stars still winked silently overhead. Should she call the police for help? No, she'd been cautioned not to, because Balcazar had paid enough of them off. Major Stevenson had warned her there would be no help or intervention if she and Griff found themselves in trouble. Grimacing, Vickey wiped her smarting eyes.

Very soon, the truck was completely loaded with crates. One guard threw a couple of crowbars, a large box of nails and several hammers in the back, near the open tailgate. Vicki's heart leaped as she saw Griff being brought out, his hands tied behind him. He was stumbling badly, as if semiconscious. The guards escorting him snarled at him and hustled him to the front of the truck. After opening the passenger side, they thrust him roughly into the front seat. One guard shoved him again, climbed in beside him and slammed the door. It was too dark to see how badly Griff was hurt. Her gut told her he was in rough shape.

Balcazar ambled leisurely out of the warehouse, puffing on a big Cuban cigar. He shouted, "Manuel, take the truck to the airport, to our plane. This shipment goes to Cuzco tonight! Hurry!" He waved his hand in an irritated gesture. "Take that bastard with you," he added. "Into the plane. I'll deal with him when we get to Cuzco."

Balcazar went back inside. The loading dock door whined to life and began to descend. Once it was closed, the guard locked it, then hurried back into the warehouse with the driver. Suddenly, no one was about except for Griff and the guard in the front seat. From their vantage point, neither could see her if she moved toward the vehicle.

Vickey's head spun with plans and options. Making a split-second decision, she sprang to her feet and sprinted toward the rear of the truck. Hurtling down the sandy slope, careful to avoid the clumps of salt grass, she made it to the vehicle. The tailgate was still lowered. With a soft grunt, she hoisted herself up into the bed of the truck in one smooth motion. Grabbing one of the crowbars, she slipped along one side of the truck walls toward the cab area, barely able to fit her body between the tightly packed crates.

There were six of them, she noted. Were they filled with pottery? Vickey knew better than to situate herself between the front of the truck and the crates. If the driver slammed on the brakes, the whole heavy load could slide forward, pinning and crushing her. These were not lightweight crates, but solidly made, heavy wood.

Breathing heavily, she quickly ran her trembling fingers around the top of the crate next to her. As she'd already noted, the heavy wooden lid was loose. Why?

Were they going to put in more items once they reached the hangar? Gripping the crowbar, Vickey slid forward as far as she could in the cramped space available. The crowbar was a weapon as well as a tool she'd use shortly.

As she squeezed downward, trying to making herself small and unseen, she heard men's voices again. It was Balcazar and the driver. Would they put a guard in here? Or just raise the tailgate and close up the truck? Vickey wasn't sure. From her position kneeling on the floor facing a crate, her back jammed against the outside wall of the truck, she knew she couldn't be seen. Her black clothing made her nearly invisible.

Holding her breath, her heart slamming into her ribs, she waited. She strained to catch sounds from the cab, but heard nothing. Was Griff all right? She slid her hands upward and placed her palms against the crate. She hoped like hell Balcazar's henchman didn't drive like a wild man. Even a minor shift of the crates during a turn could crush her where she knelt.

Gulping, she heard Balcazar giving the guard orders as they neared the tailgate.

"You get this load into the plane, pronto. I'll join you at the airport. I have a quick run to make in Miraflores. I want these crates cared for, Manuel. No hard driving. Pretend you are carrying eggs. These pots are very old. They're well packed, but we can't afford to have them break. Understand?"

"*Sí, patrón,* I do. I will drive this truck as if my mother were in back."

Snorting loudly, Balcazar said, "You'd kill your mother if I asked you to."

"*Sí, patrón,* that is true. But I will care for these pots. You can depend on it."

"If any arrive broken, you're dead, Manuel. Understand?"

"*Sí, sí, comprendo.* What about the gringo? What do we do with him?"

"Keep him tied up. Hustle him onto the plane and keep him out of sight. I don't want any Customs agents to spot him. You know how to do that. We always put the plane in the shadows behind Hangar 2. Do that tonight. Juan will guard him. This hombre is up to something. He's not talking now, but he will talk to me in Cuzco, one way or another. Get going! We must do this under cover of night."

"*Sí, patrón.*"

Vickey tensed. She saw the guard named Manuel come to the rear. He was a heavily muscled man with a bald head and a black handlebar mustache bracketing his thin mouth. Like all the guards, he wore military fatigues. An AK-47 hung over his shoulder. He reached up and pressed a switch, and with a grinding noise, the platform began rising once more.

Sweat dripped into her eyes, stinging them. She blinked rapidly and remained frozen in the dark shadows as the tailgate was pushed up and locked into place. Manuel then hitched himself up on the bumper, pulled down the heavy tarp over the upper half of the truck and tied it. Darkness was complete.

Good! Vickey released a shaky breath, her heart

pounding so loudly she thought for sure he'd hear it. But he didn't. Closing her eyes, she sagged a little. Manuel leaped off the tailgate, walked to the driver's side and got into the cab. She couldn't make out what he said to Juan, the guard. It didn't matter.

Once the engine fired up, Manuel eased the truck quietly out onto the roadway. Good as his word, he made the turns carefully—as if eggs were indeed in the rear where Vickey rode. Her luck was holding, and she waited for five minutes. The truck was going roughly thirty miles an hour down the straight stretch through the warehouse district. In another few minutes, he'd reach the main highway leading back to Lima. There was only one airport, the international one. Vickey was very familiar with its layout. She knew Hangar 2 was on the north side of the tower. A lot of cargo planes were kept there. Lifting her hand once again, she shakily wiped her perspiring brow.

Once the truck gears ground, beginning the climb out of the dock area, Vickey stood up and retrieved the crowbar. The space was tight, so all her movements required effort and caution. The truck groaned as it crept slowly up the long, steep incline. She pulled out her Maglite from her vest and flipped it on. There was no window at the front, so no one would see the light.

Turning to the crate next to her, Vickey pushed the heavy wooden top aside. Leaning over, she peered in and saw a thickly wrapped pot about one-quarter the size of the box, nestled among a lot of shredded newspaper and other packing material. Hoisting herself up, she carefully climbed inside the crate. There was plenty of room for her.

She eased the pot to one corner, set the crowbar on the floor and scooped packing material over it, then pulled the crate lid back in place. Somehow, she had to lie down, curl around the pot and arrange the packing material around her. If they were loading these crates and Griff on the plane, she was going, too.

But why did they leave the tops open? she wondered yet again. That was one of the things that scared her. If they unpacked the crates at the hangar, she was dead meat. Vickey was betting they'd put the hammer and nails in the truck so they could close the crates at the airport before loading them on board the plane. At least, that's what she hoped.

Curling herself in the fetal position around the pot, which she'd moved back in the center where it belonged, she spent the next fifteen minutes pulling packing material over her. Was it enough so that she couldn't be spotted? From her cramped position, her head resting on her outstretched, curved arm, Vickey did the best she could. Unless some fool dug into it, she was invisible.

Her mind whirled. Would there be Customs people around Hangar 2? Did they leave the crates open for inspection? Were the Customs agents in cahoots with Balcazar, too? Bribes, Vickey knew, were common in South America. Money talked. She lay in the dark, breathing in the distinct odor of newspaper ink. It was hot inside the crate and she was sweating heavily. To keep her blood sugar level, she pulled a protein bar from her pocket and ate it.

She tried to think of all the possible ways this scenario could play out—and how she could rescue Griff and live to tell about it. Whether she wanted to admit it or not, she cared for the guy. Little by little, she was finding out he wasn't the ogre of the past. He'd changed. Grown. And Great Spirit help her, she was drawn to him whether she liked it or not. As Vickey lay on her side, feeling like a pretzel wound around the large clay vessel, she realized that even if she hated Griff, she would risk her life to save him. He was an American. A soldier. One of her kind. Though he'd once deserved punishment, he didn't deserve to die. Vickey was going to try to prevent that from happening.

"Sit down!" Juan snarled at Griff. The guard shoved him down on a nylon-net seat of the DC-3 cargo airplane. Light filtered weakly throughout the interior. The gun barrel of the AK-47 swung away from him, and Juan barked orders to the men who were loading the heavy, bulky crates, one at a time, into the hold of the aged aircraft.

Griff's wrists were bloody from trying to ease the ropes so he could get out of them. His head throbbed as he looked around. Balcazar had had his henchman, Manuel, strike him repeatedly, and his skull was aching. Griff hadn't known that DC-3s were still flying. They had started air service in 1935, and he knew the aging dinosaur had flown during the Vietnam era. The DC-3 had been the workhorse of the global fleet fifty years ago, but now? For all he knew, the last of the planes had long ago gone to a boneyard to be dismantled, the aluminum sold to smelters. Considering the age of the plane, he realized this was going to be a helluva heavy cargo load to get into the air. Would the aircraft even get off the ground?

Griff glanced back toward the crew working and sweating to get the crates on board. Once the truck had reached the airport, the driver had pulled it between two hangars, deep in the shadows. Griff had been hauled out of the cab and made to stand near the tailgate as each crate was lowered and taken by forklift to the DC-3 sitting nearby.

Two men stood by as each crate was taken out. The top was removed, and they'd cut open a hundred-pound sack of beans and poured the contents inside. *Beans!* Griff had wondered why. And then he'd overheard one guard telling another the legumes would act as shock absorbers, settling around each rare pot to stabilize it and the packing material. Plus, if any Customs people started sniffing around, and opened one, all they'd see were dried beans. A smart move, Griff had thought.

And then he'd heard Balcazar snickering that the crates would be moved to the Customs warehouse in Cuzco after they landed. There, they'd be opened, inspected and given a label verifying the contents: dried beans. The top would then be nailed shut and the crate would be shuttled in a few days on another Peruvian airline back to Lima. From what Griff could gather, not all Customs agents in Lima could be bought off. By sending the crates to Cuzco, where the Customs people could be persuaded to turn a blind eye, the shipments "passed" and "inspected" so that officials elsewhere wouldn't bother to look inside. And then each crate went to its own special destination, to a client who, Griff was sure, paid a lot of bucks for each. Balcazar was clever, he'd give him that.

The crates were all loaded. The guards had put enough nails in each to keep the top on, but hadn't permanently hammered down each lid. No, Customs in Cuzco would have to peer inside and confirm a shipment of beans. Then the crate would be sealed shut.

What would they do with him? Surreptitiously, Griff continued to try to loosen the heavy hemp cords that bound his wrists. Not only did his shoulders ache, but his elbows screamed in pain from being yanked back in an unnatural position. Feeling warmth trickling down his aching fingers, Griff realized it was blood. Given the circumstances, he knew he had to escape or he was dead. As he sat there struggling to loosen his bonds, his thoughts turned to Vickey. At least she'd gotten away. She'd killed the other guard, but they'd found her smashed pistol. A bullet had struck it. Griff wondered if she was wounded. Bleeding to death? Dead? Had she gotten away? Was she hiding or hurt? He couldn't stand the anguish building in his heart over those tortured thoughts.

Dammit, what a mess! Griff hadn't realized a silent alarm had been triggered when they'd jimmied the lock on the office door. According to Balcazar, the shrieking alarm had gone off in his bedroom, where he was sleeping. He had called the guards and told them someone had broken into his office.

And there Griff and Vickey were—caught red-handed. They weren't very good thieves, after all. His thoughts turned back to her, charged with emotion. He cared deeply for her, he admitted. Well, that realization came too late, didn't it? He watched as the last crate was loaded and the doors of the aircraft were shut and locked. Why hadn't he told her how he really felt before this all happened? The way things were going, she would never know he liked her. Despite their sordid past, Griff was drawn to her—and he always had been. Which was why he'd gone to rescue her and her friends and get them back on the base so they wouldn't be discharged.

Shaking his head, Griff saw Balcazar heft his considerable weight up the steps and into the plane. He was smoking a cigarette this time, the butt glowing red. He wore several gold chains, some quite heavy, hanging halfway down his sunken chest. His silk shirt, short-sleeved, was open down to his protruding gut. Griff grimaced. The bastard probably thought he was a turn-on to every woman around.

Juan came back over and sat down next to Griff, the AK-47 resting in his lap. He took out a handkerchief from his back pocket and mopped his perspiring brow.

"Everything ready, Juan?"

"*Sí, patrón.* It's all loaded. We're ready to go."

Balcazar turned and looked into the open doorway to the cockpit, where the pilot was already seated. "Get us to Cuzco, Chapis."

Griff watched the other three men clamber on board and sit across the aisle in the short row of nylon seats. The door was shut, and the cargo space became very dim. Balcazar headed to the copilot's seat, and Griff wondered how he'd fit his porcine body into that small space, but somehow he did.

Manuel lit up a cigarette and inhaled deeply. The other men did the same.

The plane's Pratt & Whitney reciprocating engines sputtered to life. Griff wondered if the old dog was going to shake apart, the airframe was trembling so badly. He wanted to ask when the last maintenance check had been done on this DC-3, but decided not to. The guards didn't look that sharp. And under the circumstances, Griff didn't want to invite their interest. He'd already been beaten once. And he was sure that once they got to Cuzco, roughly an hour and a half flight, Balcazar would deal with him again. If only he could escape! But how?

"Hey, Juan, those crates are getting heavier every time!" Manuel called teasingly from across the aisle.

The DC-3 eased forward.

"Tell me about it!" Juan growled. He sucked on his cigarette and blew out a thick stream of smoke. "I swear, that one crate weighed twice as much as the others. What the hell was in it? The world's largest grave pot?" All the men snickered.

Shrugging, Manuel wiped his brow and grinned. "Twice as heavy? Amigo, you're getting old is all!"

"Humph, that one crate was heavier than hell itself! You wouldn't know, though. You weren't the one pushing it into this plane."

"Maybe two hundred pounds of beans were poured into it instead of a hundred?" Manuel teased.

All the men laughed some more. Juan didn't. He scowled and continued to smoke.

Griff listened to the sounds of the Pratt & Whitney engines. This old plane was a rattletrap, or more than likely, a death trap. And what about oxygen? They'd be flying at fourteen thousand feet to get over the Andes to Cuzco, which lay at twelve thousand feet. Looking around, Griff guessed the plane didn't have that capacity. There were no oxygen bottles or masks, either.

He turned and looked at Juan. "Is this plane pressurized?"

Shrugging, the guard said, "You mean, does it have oxygen?"

"Yeah."

Manuel snickered. "Hey, gringo! You have to be tough like us! The only oxygen on board this bucket of bolts is up in the cockpit. They put the masks on when we go above ten thousand feet. Us?" He beamed and shoved his thumb into his chest. "We just sit here and take it. We're tough! Why, we don't even wear seat belts, either." He laughed.

Griff shook his head. They'd be flying at fourteen thousand feet for nearly an hour. At ten thousand feet, oxygen was sparse. The lungs had a hard time taking and breaking it down for distribution to the red blood cells and the brain. The resulting hypoxia, or oxygen starvation, could cause many different symptoms, among them hallucinations, forgetfulness and bizarre behavior, not to mention lack of coordination and lousy judgment.

As he sat there, sweating heavily, Griff knew that an hour's exposure wouldn't kill them, but it sure as hell would play havoc on their systems. What would happen to these goons? Griff had gone through high-altitude training with the Apache, which could fly to twenty thousand feet with the pilots on oxygen. Was this his chance? Would the hypoxia hit them in such a way that they'd start giggling? Become less observant? Lose their focus on him? All that was possible.

But what about him? The hypoxia was going to hit him, too. Luckily, Griff knew his symptoms. Every pilot had to go through high-altitude training courses in pressurized chambers, so that they knew exactly what their particular hypoxia symptoms would be. That way, they'd know to get on oxygen immediately and stave off the worst deadly symptoms that might sneak up on them. Hypoxia killed, but it took time.

This flight could be his chance. He'd have to wait and find out.

He turned his mind to his cabin mates. It was obvious these thugs of Balcazar had taken this flight many times. Juan pulled out a small bottle of pisco. They began to pass it around.

Griff recalled Vickey saying that pisco was a potent, kick-in-the-ass liquor. If these idiots were drinking alcohol while hypoxia was setting in, they were going to be useless when they landed at Cuzco. More than likely they'd become happy drunks, acting like giddy children barely able to walk and talk, much less shoot straight.

That could very well be his chance to escape. Alcohol and hypoxia made a potent mix. Silently, Griff urged the men to drink up as they continued to pass the bottle from hand to hand. Smiling to himself, he carefully worked away at the biting ropes that bound him. Even though hypoxia would grip him, too, he would be the most clearheaded of this group. And he prayed that would help him find some way to escape. Because if he couldn't, he was dead.

Chapter 12

By the time the plane landed, Griff was freezing and trembling. There was no heat in the back of this bucket of bolts, and while the guards had on protective clothing and jackets, all he wore was a borrowed set of clothing, thin spring polo shirt and jeans, which they'd forced him to wear instead of his black spandex suit. Teeth chattering, Griff listened to the hilarity, the giggles and guffaws of the guards, who were drunker than hell on pisco combined with hypoxia symptoms. Their weapons had dropped to the deck of the DC-3 long ago. They were like six-year-old boys. *Unbelievable.*

As the airplane parked next to a huge hangar, the engines were cut. It was still dark outside, from what

Griff could see. A series of weak red lights flickered on along the top of the fuselage. Griff no longer felt his arms, though his shoulders burned like fire. In a way, this worked to his advantage because he could tug at the biting ropes and feel no pain since they were behind his back. He couldn't feel blood running down his fingers, either. The only thing besides his shoulders that ached was the side of his jaw where Manuel had slugged him during the brief interrogation with Balcazar in his office.

Griff wondered how the boss would react to his being drunk and high. He didn't have long to wait. The pilot exited first, then Balcazar slowly squeezed his bulk out of the cockpit seat and through the narrow door. When he saw his men giggling and laughing, his round face filled with rage. He lumbered toward them, and when he reached the first guard, he slapped him hard.

The man yelped and tumbled to the deck.

"You stupid fools! What are you doing back here?" Balcazar raked the group with a black look. He saw the empty liquor bottle lying on the deck near Griff's feet. "Drinking?" he roared.

The second guard saw Balcazar's hand coming. He dodged it and leaped to his feet.

"I do not allow drinking on this flight! Damn you all!" Felipe Balcazar glared at the men as they scrambled to pick up their weapons and stand at wavering attention in the cramped confines of the DC-3. "This is stupid! You're so damn drunk you can't off-load these crates now. All of you except Manuel, go into the hangar office and pour coffee down your gut until you're clearheaded. Then, come back out and unload this precious cargo! But not before!" He lifted his leg, his boot connecting with the shin of another guard.

"Oww!" the man cried, leaping back and crashing into Griff.

Griff was knocked to the floor, landing hard on his side. His head slammed onto the metal deck, and he saw stars for a moment from the impact. No one cared if he wore a seat belt, either.

"Get him up!" Balcazar snarled. "Manuel, you stay here and guard him while the rest of you sober up enough to unload this cargo. Now get going!"

Manuel grabbed Griff by the arm. He was a big man, obviously taking plenty of steroids to pump up his five-foot-ten-inch frame to look more like the Hulk.

Griff gritted his teeth as he felt his shoulders scream with pain. Hissing out his breath as Manuel thrust him back into the nylon seat, he saw everyone exit the plane. Manuel wove drunkenly toward the front door and stairs, and peered. Looking back, a frown of warning at Griff, the guard snarled, "You stay put, gringo." And he exited the aircraft.

Griff saw the flash of a lighter outside the plane near the door. Smoke from Manuel's cigarette drifted back inside. Shivering, Griff looked around in the gray light leaking from the open door of the hangar. It was cold as hell at this elevation, even in summer. Cuzco didn't have high temperatures any time of year, especially at night.

Griff tried to listen for Manuel. The guard's boots could be heard on the tarmac as he slowly walked around the tail of the plane, smoking his cigarette. This was Griff's chance!

Thunk.

What the hell was that noise? Griff scowled and looked behind him. It came from the crates stowed in the rear of the DC-3.

Thunk.

Or was it his imagination? He wasn't sure. Shaking his head, he struggled to recover from the hypoxic symptoms. Was he hallucinating?

Thunk.

There it was again! What the hell was going on back there? Squinting, Griff peered through the gloom, but saw nothing. It was simply too dark to make out more than the outline of the crates.

He could still hear the grate of Manuel's boots on the tarmac. The man was near the tail of the plane, from what he could tell.

The strange thunk came again. No, Griff wasn't imagining it! And it wasn't coming from the guard. Griff staggered to his feet and stared into the darkness, toward the massive crates. Did Balcazar have something alive packed in one of them?

Thunk.

His heart skittered with anxiety. Blinking, Griff could swear he saw one of the lids slowly rise. He gulped and his heart began to pound as the lid was pushed back.

What the hell?

There were more sounds—the rustling of paper and…something else. Griff couldn't make it out. Eyes slitted, he swore he saw movement. What was it? *Who* was it? His heart galloped with anxiety as a dark shadow emerged.

Weaving on his feet, standing near the exit door, Griff felt his mouth drop open as the shadowy figure tiptoed out of the darkness.

"Vickey!"

"Shh! Dammit!" She spat out shredded paper that had gotten in her mouth. As she ran her hands through her hair, beans flew in all directions. She saw Griff's eyes widen at her sudden appearance. In fact, his mouth had dropped open. She could barely walk on her cramping legs and feet that had gone numb a long time ago. She also had hypoxia, she knew. Gripping the crate next to her, she steadied herself as she made her way toward Griff.

Pulling a knife from the ankle sheath strapped to her right leg, she reeled forward. Her balance was off, thanks to the flight. "Turn around!" Her voice was hoarse and raspy. She spat again and more bits of paper flew out of her mouth. Hands trembling, Vickey grabbed his bonds. The ropes were thick, but slippery. With blood. Griff's blood. Taking the blade, she sawed at his bonds for several moments. There! He was free! The cords fell away.

Groaning softly, Griff leaned forward. His shoulders ached and he couldn't lift his hands at all.

"You okay?" Vickey demanded, sliding her hand across his shoulders.

"I can't feel my arms at all. Blood circulation is gone."

"Yeah, okay." She looked around. "Where's your buddy?"

"Outside having a smoke. He'll be coming back at any moment."

Vickey nodded. She kept the knife ready. Since she had no pistol, it was her only weapon. "We gotta get outta here! Pronto."

"No kidding." Griff straightened. Already, he was feeling his arms come back to life, the pain sharp and stabbing. He tried flexing his hands. "He's got an AK-47 on him," he warned.

"Call him in," Vickey whispered tautly. She hurried to one side of the door, her mind whirling. She wasn't completely solid on her feet yet, either. More beans fell out of her uniform onto the deck, making little pinging sounds as they bounced. Grimacing, Vickey gestured to Griff, who sat down in his seat and pretended his hands were still tied behind him.

"Manuel! Get back in here! I need to take a leak, dammit!" Griff called.

Heart hammering, Vickey heard the guard laugh. He was obviously still high. She heard him step under the nose of the plane and head for the door, where she stood off to one side. Knife in hand, she waited tensely.

"Hey! Come on! I need to take a leak!" Griff yelled. His gaze was glued to the door. Licking his dry lips, he saw Manuel emerge out of the darkness. His steps were heavy as he climbed the aluminum stairs, a cigarette hanging from his mouth.

"Quiet down, gringo," he growled as he entered the aircraft.

From behind, Vickey launched herself forward. She was nearly six feet tall and the shorter Peruvian was an easy target. She leaped upon him, pressing the knife solidly against his throat as she wrapped her other arm around his thick, short neck.

"You move, you son of a bitch, and I'll slit your throat. *Comprende?*" she whispered harshly.

Manuel croaked and froze. A fine, thin cut opened on the skin of his neck. Instantly, he dropped the AK-47. His eyes went wide as her arm held him in place.

Griff tottered to his feet. He leaned down, and dizziness assailed him. Nearly pitching over, he dropped to his knees instead, reaching out and gripping the rifle.

"Damn," he said. "The hypoxia. I can't even walk straight yet."

Vickey smiled savagely. "I know the feeling, dude. Okay, get down on your knees." She hissed the order into the guard's ear. To make sure he understood, she pressed the blade harder against his throat. His Adam's apple bobbed. With a cry, Manuel quickly dropped to his knees. As he did, Vickey released him. Griff had the AK-47 trained on him. Straightening up, she switched the knife to her other hand, then relieved him of the pistol he carried.

"Now what?" Griff asked her in English. "We got four more of these goons in a hangar drying out right now. Plus Balcazar."

Nodding, Vickey said, "Yeah, I heard it all." Breathing hard, she said, "They say anything about the star?"

"No."

Leaning over, Vickey put the blade to Manuel's throat. "Okay, *compadre,* tell us about that crystal star," she said in Spanish. "What do you know about it?" She pressed on the blade. Manuel hissed out a breath, his eyes wide with terror. "Tell me or I'll slit your throat!"

"No, no! Don't! I'll tell you everything I know!" He cried softly. Lifting his hands, he looked up at Griff. "Tell her to remove the blade. I'll tell you."

"I'll remove it *after* you tell me," Vickey snarled into his ear.

"Okay, okay. One of the guards, Roka Fierros, he stole the star! He stole it a month ago. Patrón Balcazar is furious. The star is worth a million U.S. dollars. Senor Robert Marston was to buy it, but now it's gone."

Frowning, Griff shoved the barrel of the AK-47 into Manuel's chest. "Where's this Fierros?"

"Aiyy-yee! I don't know. I swear I don't!" Beads of sweat peaked on the man's wrinkled brow as he gazed pleadingly up at Griff.

"The lady doesn't play fair, my friend, so you'd better tell her everything. She *likes* to kill men...." Griff grinned.

Croaking, Manuel squeezed his eyes shut, gasping. "No...no! Have mercy."

"You know *something,* hombre," Vickey rasped. She pushed on the knife and felt it cut the skin of his throat. Blood ran in tiny rivulets down his sweaty flesh.

"Don't kill me! Don't!" Manuel shuddered and cried out.

"Then tell us where Fierros is!" she demanded angrily.

"The last thing we knew he was in Agua Caliente, down by Machu Picchu. Patrón Balcazar had someone, a snitch, tell him that he saw Fierros walking out of town down the railroad tracks, which is the only way to get through that jungle. It's along the Urubamba River." Choking, Manuel tried to wriggle back, but Vickey's legs and body kept him right where she wanted him. "Roka was overheard at a local bar saying he was going to the Valley of the Ghosts, to the Villecamba temple complex, one of our graveyard sites where we were digging in the jungle. It's about fifty miles south of Agua Caliente."

"What's there?" Griff demanded.

"I don't know, I swear! Maybe he was going to meet a buyer. Who knows? Patrón Balcazar was going to send us to find him as soon as we unloaded these crates. That was to be our next assignment, the day after tomorrow—to go to Villecamba and find him."

Snorting, Vickey released him and shoved him violently down on the deck. Straightening, she growled at Griff, "We'll tie him up and gag him. We need to leave."

Griff's hands finally had some feeling back in them. He passed Vickey the hemp ropes that had bound him, so she could secure Manuel's hands tightly behind his back. *Instant karma, dude.* The guard wore a neckerchief. Griff took it off and tied it around the guard's mouth so he couldn't call out for help. Then, planting his boot on Manuel's chest, he slammed him back to the deck. "Move a fraction of a millimeter," he rasped at the guard, "and she'll come back and finish slitting your throat."

Manuel lay silent, his eyes huge with fear.

Straightening up, Griff said, "Okay, let's vamoose!"

Nodding, Vickey lurched for the door. Nearly falling down the stairs, still unsteady from hypoxia, she heard Griff following closely behind her.

"Neither of us can walk straight," he whispered, wrapping his arm around her shoulders. "Lean on me. We'll get out of here together."

It was a wise move. Vickey slid her arm around his waist. As they crept around the tail of the DC-3, they saw the huge hangar directly behind it. There was no movement, no sound. The lights were on, glaring through the smudged windows at the rear of the building. Looking around, she saw the main tower about a quarter of a mile away.

"This way!" she hissed, tugging Griff along with her.

They had to make a run across the tarmac. If Balcazar or any of the guards came out of the warehouse, they were as good as dead. Griff seemed to understand that, and they broke into an awkward run, bobbing from side to side, helping one another along. Hypoxia was a bitch as far as Vickey was concerned.

In the distance, she heard the familiar noises of baggage carts and other diesel engines getting in place to accept incoming traffic at 0600. There were no planes landing or taking off yet. Cuzco had flight curfews, restricting domestic and international flights to land and take off at certain specified times. It was nearly 0500 and the sky was lightening in the east. Soon, the international flights would be coming in. They always landed at daybreak.

Running hard, Vickey and Griff made it to the airport's cyclone fence, which had razor wire stretched across the top. Once there, Griff released her. There was a gate! He pointed to it.

"Come on," Vickey whispered. Reaching it first, she opened the gate and stepped out to the other side. Griff quickly followed, breathing hard. He obviously wasn't used to the high altitude.

Scanning the airport grounds, she saw a green taxi, the driver asleep inside. Going over, she pounded on the window. "Hey! Wake up!" she called.

The man, in his twenties, yelled and jumped. His eyes widened enormously as he looked out the window at them.

"Get in," Vickey told Griff, opening the rear door.

Griff stumbled in, feeling highly uncoordinated thanks to the hypoxia. It would take a couple of hours to get rid of the symptoms completely, but he'd be no worse for wear, fortunately.

Vickey had left the AK-47 hidden in the weeds near the gate. Leaping into the front seat with the driver, she told him where to go: the Liberator Hotel near Plaza de Armas.

The driver careened along cobblestone streets that had been built by the Incas centuries earlier. The buildings were tall, all made of gray and black granite blocks fitted together so perfectly it seemed that a machine must have cut them. But Griff knew it hadn't. The Inca buildings exemplified some of the finest stonework in the world.

Few people, except one or two vendors and the homeless, were on the streets of Cuzco at this time of morning. Vickey ordered the taxi to drive up to the front door of the hotel. Once they arrived, she gave the driver a wad of soles and got out. Griff followed on wobbly legs. He was glad to be here. The hotel was obviously first class. The doorman, dressed in a green-and-gold uniform, opened the door for them and greeted them in English.

Vickey headed straight for the registration desk. With shreds of paper still clinging to her black one-piece uniform, she knew she looked like hell. Lucky for them, no one was in the massive lobby at this hour. Vickey didn't want to be ogled by a group of tourists, wondering who she was, with her strange outfit.

The only clerk at the marble desk, a woman with dark hair and brown eyes, looked a little shocked as Vickey hurriedly approached. The BJS kept a number of rooms at this five-star hotel for personnel on R & R or TDY—temporary duty—assignments. Vickey had long ago memorized the code, and gave it to the clerk. Of course, the reservation wasn't listed under BJS, but the mining company that was their cover. The woman nodded and quickly gave her a key card to a suite.

Griff had sat down in the lobby to wait for her. His

beard stubble was dark and he had blood on the side of his mouth. Haggard and unkempt, he looked more like a beggar than someone who could afford such a expensive hotel.

Vickey walked over to him, weaving as she did so. "Come on, Griff. We've got a room." She slipped her hand beneath his upper arm and helped him stand. In the light, she could see that his mouth was cut and his jaw was swollen. "You look like something the cat dragged in, fella. Let's get a hot bath and clean up. We're safe here."

Safe... Damn, that word sounded good. "I'm glad you know what you're doing," Griff muttered, following her. His feet wouldn't obey, so they wove like a drunken couple down the carpeted hall toward the bank of elevators at the rear of the lobby.

Chuckling dryly, Vickey punched the button and the shining brass doors opened promptly. "Yeah, this is my turf now. Let's go."

There was no need to cajole him. Griff stepped into the sumptuous elevator, which had a painting of an Inca emperor on the rear wall. The doors whooshed shut. Groaning, he leaned back.

"Helluva night..."

"Yeah." Vickey felt sorry for him. "You got the worst of it from the looks of things."

The elevator opened on the penthouse floor. Stepping out, Vickey led him to the suite, opened the door and pulled Griff inside.

He stopped and looked around. "This is quite a place," he said in surprise. The drapes, purple brocade with gold edging, surrounded a massive rectangular picture window with a panoramic view of Cuzco. Gazing around the suite, he noticed the furniture was dark and heavy, of a Spanish style. A round marble table held a green-and-gold vase filled with fresh, tropical flowers.

Moving past him, Vickey said, "Let's get to our bathrooms. We have two, Griff—one for you and one for me. Come on."

Stumbling with exhaustion, Griff followed Vickey through the huge, spacious penthouse suite. His wrists throbbed with pain and he looked down to see the blood clotting on his hands and fingers.

"Here's yours," Vickey said, pushing open a white door edged with gold. "A bathtub and shower. Mine's next door." She pointed through an open door that led to another bedroom. "I'll be in there cleaning up."

"Okay."

"You all right, Griff? You look like death warmed over." Vickey walked up to him and grasped his arm. Her heart twinged with anguish as she saw how much of a beating he'd taken from Balcazar.

Just the tentative touch of her fingers on his arm steadied him. "Combination of stress, hypoxia and no sleep for over twenty-four hours." Griff managed a weak grin. Vickey looked strong and capable in comparison. Oh, her dark hair was mussed, but her green eyes were focused, and she seemed strong and unwavering.

"Okay, we can call a house doctor to patch you up if you want after your bath."

Shaking his head, he murmured, "No. I just need to get something to eat after I get cleaned up. I'm starving to death."

Grinning, she said, "What do you want? I'll call room service before I jump into the shower."

"The biggest damn beefsteak they can rustle up, medium, and a baked potato."

"Man after my own heart." Vickey smiled up into his face. "I'll make that two. But I like my steak real rare."

"Why am I not surprised?" Griff smiled warmly at her and then staggered into the white-tiled bathroom.

Her fingers tingled as she turned and headed into her room. That one smile, filled with what? Something Vickey didn't want to define. At least not now. Griff's eyes held an emotion that startled her. And it affected her deeply, her heart pitter-pattering a little more than it should.

Shrugging it off, Vickey picked up the phone to order their meals. They'd managed to find out a lot about the crystal star. As soon as she bathed, she'd call BJS and report. Then they'd hang out here and eat, get some sleep, and plan for the next step of their mission—to find Roka Fierros in the Valley of the Spirits.

Chapter 13

"Hold still…." Vickey breathed softly as she dabbed the cloth against the injured corner of Griff's lip. There was something deliciously sinful about holding his recently shaved rock-hard jaw in one hand and carefully blotting his sensual mouth. She knelt on his huge king-size bed, one foot on the floor, her other leg braced against his hip.

"I'm not moving…." Griff murmured. Vickey had just showered, her dark hair damp and hanging in fragrant strands about her shoulders. With only a towel draped around his hips, he had been surprised when she'd walked into his bedroom. She wore civilian clothes, beautiful ones. Beneath her sheer white silk blouse with purple orchids painted across it, he saw a pale pink silk camisole that worshipped her upper body and made him hotly aware of her breasts. The black silk pants flowed around her hips and legs and emphasized the fact that she was a woman—one who made his entire body come alive with desire. When Vickey had offered to clean his cuts and bruises, Griff couldn't say no. She'd directed him to sit on the edge of his bed while she dropped the medical items next to him.

Hope threaded through his chest as she cupped his face with her long, spare fingers. Her touch was gentle and nurturing. Griff was glad he'd shaved. His hair was still beaded with droplets of water because he hadn't towel dried it yet. Under the circumstances, he didn't care. He was too involved in absorbing Vickey's nearness—her knee against his thigh, her torso pressed lightly against him.

"This is gonna hurt," she whispered, her eyes narrowing, brows drawing downward as she gently cleaned away the dried, caked blood. He had a wonderful mouth. Why hadn't she been aware of that before? Vickey smiled to herself as she worked.

"Won't hurt as much as getting hit there—"

"Stop talking, Hutchinson!"

"Okay." Griff slid her an amused glance. She was grinning. He did, too, in response.

"Oww!"

"I told you—don't move."

The pain was slight compared to the pleasure Griff was receiving, flooding his body with sweet yearning.

"You smell good."

Vickey chuckled. "You smell better than you did." Actually, seeing Griff like this—with a white towel around his hips, stretching halfway to his knees—made her appreciate him in a new way. He obviously worked out lifting weights, his torso was so solid and firm, with well-defined muscles running across his chest and down his arms. Dark hair covered his forearms as well as his chest. Male. Yes, Griff was *very* male. Vickey fought her attraction to him. But he was not the monster she'd thought before. The last few days, their harrowing escapes, had changed her perspective.

"There..." she said, satisfied as the cut came clean. Leaning down, she looked at it closely, her eyes only inches from his lips. What would it be like to kiss this guy? Probably pretty awesome, Vickey thought, smiling to herself as she examined the nasty, deep cut.

"Bad?"

"Probably stings like hell."

"Oh, it does," Griff said. He felt her brush his cheek with her fingertips. Skin tingling wildly, he closed his eyes and relished the fleeting contact. What would it be like to make love to this wild, independent woman? The thought electrified him. Heated him. Made him sizzle. Opening his eyes, Griff slanted her a glance. "Do I need stitches?"

"No, I don't think so. It's less than half an inch in length, but it's deep." She lifted her head and touched his jaw. She liked having an excuse to touch Griff like this. "How about your teeth in that area? Loose?"

Lifting his hand, Griff gingerly tested his jawline.

"Yeah, a couple of them seem to be. No big deal. I can still eat." He smiled up at her.

"Speaking of eating," Vickey said, picking up a tube of antibiotic ointment, "they'd better hurry with our food. I'm ready to eat a whole cow, dead or alive." She squeezed some of the ointment onto her index finger, knowing Griff was watching her. She glanced down and saw the warmth and invitation in his gray eyes. Yeah, she felt it, too—that heated connection between them. But did she want to go there? And why would she? The past was still too alive for her, the memories too strong to overcome. Still, that little-boy smile lurking at the corners of his well-shaped lips got to her. Held her heart. It was a euphoric feeling.

"Okay, hold still. I'm putting antibiotic on that cut because where we're going tomorrow, into the jungle, little things like this can blow up and become seriously infected within hours. Bacteria goes wild in that kind of environment."

"Sounds bad," Griff said as her fingers slid across his chin to hold his jaw steady once more. Closing his eyes, he felt her gently smooth the ointment into the smarting, burning cut. Vickey's touch made the pain go away. Literally, the realization blew Griff's mind. If Vickey touched him, his pain miraculously disappeared! "You should have had a different career," he mumbled. "Been a nurse or something. When you touch me, the pain goes away."

Feeling heat moving up her neck into her face, Vickey realized his compliment was making her blush. She was glad Griff was looking away so he couldn't see her reaction. Giving a mirthful laugh, she said, "Must be healing hands from my father, the medicine man."

"Hey, I'm serious, Vickey. You have a warm, soothing touch." Griff tried to look at her but she held his jaw firmly so he couldn't move.

"Stay still."

"Okay."

"Were you like this as a kid, I wonder? Did you drive your mother bats by constantly moving? Were you a hyperactive six-year-old?" she teased huskily as she finished the job. Vickey rose and gathered the medical items. Then she walked to the coffee table, which had a plush upholstered couch on either side.

Griff eyed her tall, lean body as she sauntered away from him. Good God, she was all legs and muscle. Griff wondered what those legs looked like bare, then remembered her question. "Yeah, I was a handful at home," he admitted with a chuckle. "Ants-in-the-pants kind of kid, you know?" He tentatively touched the doctored corner of his mouth. The flesh was swollen the entire length of his face. He'd taken several punches in the warehouse. Sliding his fingers up his recently shaved skin, Griff felt the swelling continue to his temple. So far, his jaw was bruised purple, but he'd somehow escaped a bona fide black eye.

Vickey set the items on the coffee table and looked over at Griff, who still sat on the bed. His muscular thighs were half covered by the thick terry-cloth towel. His legs were powerful and sprinkled with black hair, and she itched to touch them. "I'll bet you were trouble," she said.

The look in his eyes made her excruciatingly aware that she was a woman. Nervously, Vickey touched the damp strands of her hair. Griff Hutchinson was too big of a magnet to her, sexually speaking. It had been a long time since she'd encountered a man she wanted to sleep with. And the truth be known, a one-night stand wasn't her gig, either. If she made love with a man, it had to be for much deeper reasons than simple sex. Scorpios played for keeps. And they weren't bed-hoppers.

Frowning to herself, she turned away as a knock sounded on the door. Good, their food had arrived.

"I'll get it. How about you dress and meet me in my suite?"

"Roger that," Griff said, sad that their intimate moment had been shattered by the sharp knock on the foyer door. His skin still tingled where she'd grazed his flesh. Lifting his hand, Griff touched his jaw again as he shoved himself to his feet.

The woman sure as hell knew how to turn him on, there was no doubt. And he'd seen the longing in her glorious forest-green eyes. Desire for him? Was that possible? Griff hoped so, because he really wanted their ugly past to be buried once and for all. Vickey was a challenge to him in every way. But a good one. Smiling cockily, he headed to the clothes closet.

Vickey had told him that the penthouse had two suites, one for women and one for men. In his closet he found all sorts of men's clothing, in a full range of sizes. He flipped through the rack, hunting for something to wear.

Griff's stomach growled as he heard Vickey greeting the bellhop who had brought their meal. Damn, he was starving—and not just for food.

"Where do we go from here?" Griff asked Vickey as they sat at the linen-draped table. Their massive porterhouse steaks and baked potatoes slathered with butter, sour cream and chives had been eaten by two hungry wolves. There hadn't been much talking while they'd devoured their meals. Reaching for his coffee, he met Vickey's gaze. She sat across from him, their toes touching occasionally beneath the table.

"While you were having your bath, I called BJS," she told him. "On the Iridium phone we keep here in this hotel room for just such need. I contacted Lieutenant Klein, who's coordinating this operation for Major Mike Houston of Medusa. I filled her in on what we'd found out so far. She was thrilled that we have the actual papers that showed the crystal star was to go to Robert Marston."

Vickey smiled. "As she told me, this is *real* evidence—something that can be taken to court as proof of his criminal activities. I know Kai Alseoun is going to be *very* happy about this, because she and Jake suspected Marston all along, even though they had only circumstantial proof of his involvement. So this nails Marston's coffin shut with the law."

"We're kinda new to this espionage game," Griff said before sipping his coffee, "but we did okay for a first outing, I think. At least we're still alive."

Vickey sat back in the chair, looking sated. Her

green eyes were half-closed, and he could swear he saw those glints of gold in them. Was it his imagination? Probably. They were both reeling from exhaustion, not having slept in the last twenty-four hours.

"We need to focus on Fierros now," Vickey said, picking up a morsel of potato skin smeared with sour cream and popping it into her mouth. Griff looked damn inviting in the navy short-sleeved shirt and jeans that fit his body as if made for him. The man had a helluva shape to lust after. Why hadn't she been aware of that before? Pushing the dicey question aside, Vickey knew now was not the time to ponder that dangerous topic.

"I'm familiar with the area where Roka Fierros is," she admitted with a sly smile.

"You are?"

"When I'm not flying combat missions, which gets me hyper as hell, I take the edge off by doing lots of hiking in the hills and mountains around there. Often when I get forty-eight hours off, I'll hike twenty to fifty miles, stay out under the stars one night and hike back to BJS the next day. Or I'll have them drop me by commercial chopper somewhere with the agreement they'll pick me up at a certain time the next day. I take these hikes, use my digital camera to hunt down orchids and then send the pictures to my mother, who is a biologist. She keeps hoping I'll stumble onto a new orchid that can be named after her." Vickey chuckled. "It gives me something to do, gets me out of the cave and back into nature, where I feel alive." Shrugging, she said, "Maybe that's my Indian blood expressing itself."

Impressed, Griff said, "You're a nature lover, for sure. I wondered what you gals did when you got some time off, besides dancing. Not that you get much, judging by the flight roster."

"No joke. That's why you three guys being sent down here is a huge relief to all of us. We'll get more downtime, more sleep and rest between combat missions. Major Stevenson knows that if we're exhausted, we won't be alert in the sky."

"So, you were happy to see me, after all."

Vickey gave him a dark look as he teased her. "Don't pat yourself too much on the back, Hutchinson."

"Yeah, I know. I'm an ugly reminder from your past come to haunt you in the present." Griff saw her wince slightly as she set her coffee cup down on the table. And if he wasn't crazy, he could swear her cheeks became pink beneath her golden skin. Why would she be blushing? Had he screwed up again? Foot in mouth disease? It was his worst trait.

"You were a surprise, there's no question," Vickey said, moving the plates to the center of the table.

"I was the last person on earth you'd ever hoped to see. That was the message in the look you gave me."

Nodding, Vickey said, "Guilty as charged." She warmed to the soft glint in his gray eyes. "It was a jolt."

"And now?" Griff challenged lightly. Although he tried to make his tone teasing, his gut clenched, because he really wanted Vickey to start realizing he wasn't that person from her past any longer. Seeing her brows knit, he held his breath.

"All things considered," she admitted slowly, moving her fingertip on the linen tablecloth, "I'd say you've changed from when I knew you earlier."

Griff released the breath. His stomach unclenched a little—but not completely. "And?"

She tossed her head, sending her tresses bouncing. Usually, she kept her straight, sable hair tamed in a chignon at the nape of her neck, but she wasn't flying right now. And she liked the feminine feel of her shoulder-length hair swirling freely about her face. Seeing the hopeful look burning in Griff's eyes, Vickey pursed her lips. Despite her past pain, she had to be truthful. "Okay. Yeah, you've changed. I like what I see. You've been honest and we've worked well as a team."

Nodding, Griff saw the contention in her narrowed green eyes. The gold flecks were gone now. He felt as if he were pushing up against that invisible shield Vickey held solidly as protection from him. Why wouldn't she defend herself? He'd tried to harm her in the past. Though he wished the shield would dissolve, Griff was mature enough to realize that wouldn't happen. At least, not yet.

"You're incredible to work with," he replied. Seeing her eyes widen slightly, he smiled. "You're bold, courageous and you've got a set of titanium balls when push comes to shove. If you hadn't thought outside the box and gotten into that crate, well, I don't think I'd be sitting here talking to you right now."

Warmth flooded Vickey because Griff's praise was genuine. She saw it in his eyes, heard it in the sincerity of his voice and the way he opened his hands. Flight hands. Strong, sensitive hands. She found herself staring at his square palms and long fingers. What would it be like to have him touch her gently? Explore her slowly with delicious, heated strokes? Arouse her to pleasure? Groaning internally, Vickey shut that door once more. She was having a helluva time keeping Griff in partner mode versus potential lover.

"It wasn't exactly pleasant sitting under all that shredded newspaper and then having a hundred pounds of dried beans poured over the top of you, trust me." She grinned wryly.

"You had to be cold. There was no heat in that bucket of bolts."

"I had no coat or jacket, true. I was probably a little warmer than you, though."

"How'd you handle the hypoxia?" Griff wondered.

"My symptoms are that I get giddy, hysterically funny and drunk. My brain farts, and my legs go wobbly. I lay in that crate snickering to myself a lot, with my hand over my mouth so no one could hear me."

Snorting, Griff said, "Trust me, it was so noisy in that plane no one would have heard anything. I'm surprised the damn thing didn't fall apart on us in the air."

"Yeah, it was a really old plane," she agreed with a laugh.

"And when I heard those thunking sounds, I was wondering if the plane's tail was finally falling off."

"Really?" she asked with a deep laugh. "I heard the guard go outside and I knew it was the only chance I'd have to get out of that box. I used the crowbar I had put inside the crate with me, banging it against the lid to loosen the nails they'd tacked it on with."

"Well," Griff said, admiration in his tone as he held her smiling gaze, "it scared the hell out of me. I wasn't sure *what* was going on. And when I finally saw you, I didn't know it was you. It was real dark and all I could see was the vague outline of a person. I wondered if you were a Japanese ninja come to sneak up on Balcazar and his guards to kill them. And then I thought I was in trouble because if you were his enemy, I was dead meat, too."

"My, my, all these wild imaginings," Vickey chortled.

"You have to admit," Griff said, "that with all that paper falling around you, and beans clattering to the deck, you weren't easy to recognize."

Nodding, Vickey said, "The bean monster."

Laughing heartily with her, Griff felt heat blaze through him in response. "You need to smile more," he told Vickey when their laughter had subsided.

Giving him a sardonic look, Vickey stood up and dropped the linen napkin on the table. "Our work isn't exactly humorous, going after druggies and knowing Black Shark copters are just waiting to blow you out of the sky, Hutchinson. Not a funny place, you know?"

"I understand, but you look so beautiful when you smile. All that seriousness just melted away."

His quietly spoken words touched her heart. "I'll keep that in mind," she told him softly. Vickey looked around, exhaustion invading her. "We have the whole day to rest and catch up on lost sleep. Dallas is sending the commercial helo to pick us up tomorrow at 0800. There will be new weapons on board for us, new knapsacks with food and water supplies. She said Major Stevenson decided to allow us to continue the search instead of going back to base to fly our regular missions. We'll get dropped twenty miles from Villecamba, where Roka may be hiding out. We'll hike in on foot and try to find the bastard. We can't land on top of him or he's liable to take off."

"Good thinking," Griff exclaimed, standing up. He could see dark shadows gathering beneath her eyes. They were both beyond tired. In fact, his feet felt like weights, and it was tough to keep his eyes open. "Listen, with this hot food in my stomach and no sleep for twenty-four hours, I'm gonna hit the sack. How about you?"

Vickey moved the rollaway dining table out to the foyer and opened the door, leaving it in the hall for the bellhop to pick up. Making sure the door was locked, she walked back to where Griff stood. The look in his eyes, tired or not, sizzled through her.

What would it be like to sleep with him? Oh, the thought was there, but it wasn't a serious one. Vickey didn't sleep around, not without a deep, continuing commitment. Still, she saw the invitation burning in those gray eyes that held her captive.

"Me? I'm going to my bed, to sleep until I wake up."

Disappointment seeped through him, but Griff nodded. "Same here," he murmured. Lifting his hand, he said, "I'll see you in about eight hours."

"Roger that." Vickey turned and went to her bedroom, quietly shutting the door behind her. Now, why was she feeling so crappy about this? She'd clearly seen in Griff's bloodshot eyes the yearning, the silent request that she come to his bed. Shaking her head, she began to unbutton her blouse as she sauntered toward the king-size bed with its purple silk duvet.

Fatigued, she didn't plumb the depths of that dilemma. Clearly there was a connection between them—a good one that was coming to life over time. Man to woman. *Why?* After draping the clothing over the back of a chair, she walked naked to the bed and pulled back the covers. The soft white cotton sheets felt remarkable and welcoming as she slid between them. Earlier, she'd closed the heavy, sumptuous purple-and-gold drapes. The room was dark and quiet.

As her head hit the goose-down pillow and she burrowed into it, her last thoughts were of Griff. He'd turned out to be a good partner in this chase to find the crystal star. He was just as bold, daring and courageous as she was. And not once had he wimped out, been stupid or not listened to her counsel. With a sigh, Vickey felt every bone in her body releasing and sinking down into the thick, welcoming mattress beneath. Yes, a lot had changed with Griff Hutchinson. She was seeing him differently. Maybe time did heal all wounds. Vickey still wasn't sure, but so far, he was showing promise.

Promise for what?

Her mind turned to mush. The last picture in her mind was of Griff smiling at her with his smoky eyes, clearly inviting her to share his bed….

Chapter 14

It was 6:00 p.m. and the evening sunlight lanced through the gauzy white sheer curtains to where Vickey and Griff sat eating their second meal of the day. After sleeping a good eight hours, Vickey felt refreshed and ready to tackle the next step in finding the crystal star.

Griff hungrily attacked his second porterhouse of the day. Vickey smiled to herself as she finished off her own grilled tilapia.

"Wild Woman dropped by about 1500," she told Griff. "She's my Apache partner. We fly a lot together, sharing air command on missions." Patting the Iridium phone on the table, she added, "The one I was carrying down in Lima got crushed when I had that fight with the guard in the warehouse, so I threw it away after I escaped. I'm glad Dallas said to use the one from the hotel and loaned us another one for when we go into Villecamba. Next flight crew that comes into Cuzco will replace the one we're taking in the penthouse. One always has to be there so we can contact the squadron."

Griff pushed his empty plate aside. Vickey had gone ahead and ordered dinner for them. He'd gotten up less than an hour ago and been surprised to see the meal rolled in by a waiter just as Griff emerged from his shower. He wondered if she had a sixth sense about his hunger. "The satellite phone is important," he agreed. Wiping his mouth with a linen napkin, he set it aside and pulled the dessert, chocolate cake, toward him. Might as well bulk up on carbs, because she had warned him that the hike they were going on wasn't a pleasant stroll over flat land. Just the opposite: jungle covered mountains and valleys.

"It's our *only* link. Cell phones might work in Lima and Cuzco, but outside the cities they're useless. Peru is still wild and untamed." Vickey added her plate to Griff's. She had ordered cheesecake with strawberries, smothered with whipped cream.

"I didn't hear Wild Woman come in," Griff murmured between bites. Vickey had dressed in the same clothes as before, and she looked even more enticing to him. She never wore makeup, but in his mind, she was perfect without it.

"Lieutenant Dallas Klein came with her," Vickey said, slicing off a bit of cheesecake with her fork. "We talked tact and strat while you snored away in your suite." She grinned at Griff, enjoying his discomfort. Seeing his face turn a little red, Vickey added, "Hey, we all snore, okay? Get over it. It's a natural human thing to do."

"Beautiful women don't snore."

He was teasing her, that warmth from his gray gaze blanketing her. "That leaves me out. I snore. Just ask anyone in our barracks. I'm always getting bitching from the other women about it." Vickey chortled.

"You're still beautiful to me," Griff said, meeting her wry smile.

"Compliments are going to get you nowhere, Hutchinson."

"Couldn't you call me Griff? I call you Vickey and you answer me."

Shrugging, she said, "It's habit, using last names or pilot handles. No one calls anyone by their real name in the military. You know that."

"So? Does that mean you won't call me Griff?" He made a point of holding her guarded gaze.

"I use people's first names when I like them."

Ouch. Well, Griff deserved that, he supposed. "Okay, that's fair enough." She didn't like him? He didn't believe that for a heartbeat.

Damn, why did she feel badly? It was the truth. Or at least it had been. Vickey touched her chest momentarily, then scowled. "Dallas, the X.O., filled me in on a lot of stuff regarding Balcazar and his theft of those pots we flew with. She called Mike Houston at Medusa. Mike worked down here for seven years with the Peruvian army. He said the military were the people that should know about Balcazar. The police department wasn't to be trusted. He said some people on the force were good, solid citizens, but a lot of the others took bribes and looked the other way."

"Which is why we were ordered not to call the Lima police for anything," Griff said, enjoying his chocolate cake.

"Right on. He gave Dallas a few names of top military officials who she could contact, to tell them about Balcazar, what we saw in his warehouse and how he was getting the stolen artifacts out of Peru to buyers around the world."

"When Balcazar was interrogating me, he wanted to know everything."

"And you told him?" Vickey asked. She couldn't help but notice the swelling along Griff's face was going down, and the cut on his mouth also looked better. She was glad.

"I told him nothing. I gave him the spiel we'd decided on. I told him we were Ph.D. archeological students from Argentina. I told him we were on a crusade to rescue stolen archeological items. That explained the black suit I was wearing. Lucky for us, our knapsacks and other equipment were behind those boulders. Balcazar had to believe me because there was no other proof."

"And the crystal star?"

Shrugging, Griff said, "He didn't know what we were looking for. You'd placed that file back into the cabinet after I heard that noise. It was the guards entering the rear door, although at the time we didn't know that." He sipped his coffee. "When you jimmied Balcazar's office door open, it tripped off an alarm at his home. He called the guards and that's how we were nailed."

"I should have guessed," Vickey muttered darkly.

"Well, we weren't exactly trained for stealth like this," Griff stated, consoling her with a smile.

"Agreed. While I was stuck in that crate feeling like I was suffocating to death, I was really wishing for the air-conditioned comfort of my Apache cockpit."

"That makes two of us," Griff chuckled. "So what are the military officials going to do? If they jump on Balcazar now, it might tip off Roka Fierros that we're going after him."

"Dallas knows that. She relayed to the generals that we're still on the mission. They aren't going to do anything until we're done. Although they said they would contact Interpol, and no matter where Balcazar sends the particular crates we flew up here with, they will be spotted and followed by police in those countries. Right now, according to Dallas, they're all going to lay back, wait and watch. What they want to do is understand the extent of Balcazar's thievery and try to nail everyone on both ends of it."

"Good," Griff exclaimed. "That makes me feel like our suffering was worth it." He smiled darkly.

"You suffered a helluva lot more than I did. I was just curled up in a cramped, dark box. Probably a little warmer than you because I was surrounded by paper and beans."

Chuckling, Griff nodded. "No argument there. I was freezing. A cotton polo shirt, jeans and the hiking boots they loaned me don't keep one toasty at fourteen thousand feet."

"That's over now," Vickey murmured. She got up from the table and walked toward the two sofas flanking the mahogany-and-glass coffee table. "Bring your coffee over here. Wild Woman brought a topo map of the Villecamba district where Roka Fierros is supposed to be hiding out. Let's take a look at the area and familiarize ourselves with it."

Picking up his cup and saucer, Griff ambled over to the cream-colored sofas splotched with orchids of many colors. Vickey patted the seat next to her, then spread the map across the coffee table. Sitting down beside her, Griff placed his cup and saucer to one side so it wouldn't accidentally spill on the relief map.

Vickey tried to ignore Griff's quiet maleness. He had an aura of steadiness and confidence around him. And he looked damn good after getting all that sleep under his belt. His beard needed to be shaved once more, but the stubble accentuated his maleness—a dangerous quality—to her.

Putting her finger on the map, Vickey said, "Here's Machu Picchu, the archeological temple complex. This place pulls in at least three hundred thousand tourists a year from around the world. The palace was built about 1500 by Patchacuti, the Inca or king. The stonework was done by the Coya, who were defeated by the Incas and then placed into slavery to build Machu Picchu and other important sacred sites. The

Coya originally came from around the Lake Titicaca area, and are considered master builders by archeologists today.

"Patchacuti used Machu Picchu as his winter palace. The temple complex sits at eight thousand feet, rising up out of the steamy jungle below. The Inca's summer palace was in Cuzco, which sits at nearly twelve thousand feet and is a helluva lot colder in winter. That was why the Inca went down to the jungle—to avoid the nasty winters up here in this city."

Vickey tapped the map. "Here's what you need to understand, and believe me, archeology thieves know it well—Machu Picchu was more than just a winter palace for the Inca and his entourage. It was also a major sacred site. When a British sailor brought smallpox to South America after he was shipwrecked in Brazil, the disease spread like wildfire throughout the entire continent. It wiped out over eighty percent of the people under the Inca's rule. Millions died. There was chaos by 1500, and by the time the Spanish landed on Peruvian shores, the Incan empire was already in terrible disarray. Their whole way of life was torn apart because the loss of life had been so severe."

Vickey moved her finger to another point on the map. "Here's our base—the BJS. It's roughly fifty miles from Machu Picchu, hidden in one of the lava peaks that rise up out of the jungle. Over here is where we're going—roughly fifty miles from Machu Picchu in a different direction. This is the mystical and mysterious Villecamba. Apparently when Bingham—an explorer from Yale University—rediscovered Machu

Picchu he heard legends from the locals about a place known as *Espiritu Valle,* or the Valley of the Spirits. Villecamba was whispered to be the most mystical and sacred of all the Incan temple complexes ever built. Yet no one could find it. Finally, in the 1960s, it was rediscovered—a complex created with the same quality of stonework as that produced by the Coya people right here." Vickey tapped the map again.

Griff leaned forward, studying the curved lines that indicated elevation changes. "It looks as if there are mountains here, and then the landscape descends to sea level jungle."

"Right on," Vickey declared. She brushed her hair away from her face. "Villecamba is still mostly hidden by the jungle. The only way into it is by following peccary and jaguar paths. The jungle is so thick that you might travel half a mile a day, using a machete to chop your way through. So we're going to get dropped relatively close to Villecamba—here, on the side of this mountain." She leaned over the map again. "We'll land on the slope at eight thousand feet and hike down a good ten miles to the jungle below. We'll have to cross the Urubamba River, which is no small feat, but there's a footbridge. We can use that to get to the other side. From there, we need to pick up peccary trails leading toward Villecamba. Dallas gave me a schematic of the trails. A long time ago we started mapping the surrounding jungle, because cocaine was moved by porters—captured Queros who were threatened at gunpoint by drug dealers. We have good intel on this area insofar as trails are concerned."

"What about Villecamba itself?" Griff murmured, looking at the topo map. "Is it entirely covered over with jungle now?"

"Parts of it have been cleared of vines and trees because from time to time different archeological groups have been down there, working with the Peruvian government. But it's slow work and doesn't get a lot of funding. There are only a few areas where you can see sections of gray, black and white stonework."

"And why would Fierros be there?"

Shrugging, Vickey said, "I don't know. But if you look at the map, you can see there are peccary paths all around Villecamba, spreading out like spokes on a wheel. Roka could be waiting for someone who could be hiking in to meet him in secret. Remember this, Griff—communication is primitive in much of Peru. He might have had to pay a messenger to run the trails from Villecamba to Bolivia to get to a buyer. That buyer might take a week just to get his buyers lined up. And even then, the potential buyer would have to hike a good hundred miles to reach Villecamba. So a month seems like a reasonable amount of time for Roka to try and off-load his stolen property. He might be selling the crystal star to a buyer who's sending an emissary to give him the money and retrieve the object. Those are my best guesses."

"Couldn't Fierros stay in the city and do the same thing?"

"Chances are Balcazar would find him. Roka deals with the same clients he does. And I'm *sure* Balcazar has put out an all-points bulletin on this guy to nab him for stealing the star. The file I read showed Robert Marston had placed a deposit of half a million U.S. dollars on that star already."

"Then Balcazar is sweating bullets on this," Griff said. "He *has* to get that star back if it's already been partly paid for."

"No kidding. And that means we have to get to Fierros first. Since Balcazar suspects he's hiding out in Villecamba, we're liable to run into his guards there, too. We have to get in there now."

"I overheard Balcazar and his guards talking about that," Griff said, sitting back. "They said they were going to get the crates packed and labeled, then he was going to send those same men to find Fierros. Manuel told us virtually the same thing."

"Then we need to beat him to it."

"Do you think Balcazar will fly them directly to Villecamba by chopper?"

"There are only two ways to Villecamba—on foot or by helo. I don't know what Balcazar will do. If he had any brains, he'd drop his men far enough away that Fierros wouldn't hear them coming. Otherwise, he could take off on any of those footpaths, just as he could with us. So they've got to surprise him."

"Like we do."

"Yeah." Vickey gave him a slight smile. "So, you up to this next leg of our mission? How's your jaw? Your mouth? Your teeth?"

Touching his jaw, Griff said, "Feeling better all the time. My teeth aren't as loose." He met her concerned gaze. "My mouth hurts like hell, but the cut is deep and it's going to take a while before it mends."

Vickey spontaneously turned and captured his jaw in her hand. "Let me look? We can't afford to let infection set in. Once we get into that humid jungle, all bets are off." Her fingertips tingled as she touched his sandpapery jaw. The look in his eyes changed; she saw desire flare like glowing coals in their depths. Tilting his head gently, she studied the corner of his mouth. "Looks good. Maybe a little more antibacterial ointment before you go to sleep tonight."

"Will you put it on me?" His mouth curved. It hurt to smile, but he enjoyed her closeness. This time he saw those flecks of gold in her eyes. Vickey's mouth seemed so soft, begging to be kissed. Yet Griff knew she wasn't interested in him as he was in her. Laughter came to her eyes, as she released his jaw. "Not this time." She sat back, hands on her thighs.

"Too bad."

"I felt sorry for you before."

"I was hoping you did it because you cared a little for me."

"Oh, Hutchinson! Get a grip, will you?" She rose from the sofa and gathered up the topo map. Her heart sped up, both in panic and excitement. Could he tell that she was drawn to him? She hoped not. After folding the map, she straightened and looked down at Griff. With a boyish smile lingering on his features, he looked so damn good to her. Vickey focused on his male mouth and once more wondered what it would be like to kiss him.

"Hey, I've got a what-if question for you," Griff said, not satisfied with her brush-off. He saw yearning in her eyes—for him. He was positive of it now. And he wanted to pursue it.

"Uh-oh..." Vickey sauntered over to the other couch and sat down with one leg tucked beneath her, the map resting on her thigh. "What's your question?"

"Back in flight school—"

Groaning, Vickey tipped her head back and closed her eyes. "Oh, don't go there, Hutchinson."

"I want to."

She opened her eyes and scowled at him. "What about flight school? I thought we'd covered everything about it before."

"Not *all* of it," Griff asserted as he sat up. "At one time, you were drawn to me."

Vickey snorted, "Dude, you are smoking something."

"No," he insisted, watching her shift uncomfortably. "Before all hell broke loose, you and I liked one another."

"In your dreams."

"Every time we met at mess, for breakfast, lunch or dinner, you would give me that look."

"What look?"

"The one you've given me a couple of times here. In Peru."

Her mouth quirked and thinned. She wanted to avoid this conversation altogether, but she saw stubbornness in Griff's face. He wasn't going to let her off the hook.

For now she wanted to keep quiet and let him continue.

"That look, as I define it, says you like me. You're interested in me. Woman to man." Griff noticed her golden skin turn dark with a flush. *Good!* He felt a sense of victory. "And I'll admit very readily I was drawn to you back then. As a matter of fact, before all this stuff blew up, I wanted to date you." There, it was out! He sat back and watched for her reaction.

"Date me?"

"Yes."

"I don't believe you."

"You can't hide from me. I see it in your eyes sometimes. A certain yearning…"

"You still have hypoxia symptoms, Hutchinson. There's no way I'm drawn to you."

He watched as Vickey suddenly stood up and smoothed the front of her pants. She *was* blushing. And he saw fear in her eyes. Why fear? Because she might like him despite what had happened? Griff sensed it. But, by the look on her face and the set of her jaw, he knew she wasn't going to admit anything.

"Just remember. I was the one who woke all you ladies up after you'd been given that drug. I came to your rescue." Griff kept his tone teasing and light.

Standing near her bedroom door, her hand on the gold doorknob, Vickey stared at him. "That's true. I think your conscience got the better of you, Hutchinson, that's all."

Griff walked over to Vickey, his own hands tucked in the pockets of his jeans. Seeing the wariness in her eyes, he halted a good six feet away from her. "I came back because I cared about you. I couldn't stand the thought of you being washed out of school, because then I would never have any hope of getting to know you better. Maybe, if things had gone differently, I would have had a relationship with you." Griff pulled his hands from his pockets, as if to reach out to her. "I admit it was a selfish act on my part. I didn't really care about the other women, but I cared about you. So if you're going to hang me on this, never forget or forgive, at least know the real truth of the situation." He gazed into her widening eyes. Just as quickly, her face became closed and unreadable.

"You did it because of *me?*" Vickey's heart wouldn't stop pounding. Griff was tall, dark and handsome. The ladies going through flight school had secretly drooled over this flyboy. And so had she, but she'd never admitted it to anyone. Gazing up into his sincere looking features, Vickey shook her head. "Hutchinson, you are so full of bullshit...."

"You'd like me to be, but I'm not, Vickey."

"And so what do you want out of this little admittance? Me to believe you? Forgive you? Change my mind and think you're knight material, after all?"

His mouth curved ruefully. "All of the above?"

"Oh, dude, you are so far out of the water on this." She jerked opened the door. "I'll see you at 0600 tomorrow morning. I'm ordering us breakfast at 0630, and at 0800 we'll go to the Cuzco airport, where we'll be picked up by Wild Woman. We'll be taken by commercial helo to that mountain just above Villecamba. Good night."

The door slammed, and Griff felt her rebuff. Sighing, he looked around the quiet suite. Well, what had he expected? She was a tough woman warrior who took no prisoners. And in all fairness to her, he *had* taken part in that horrible plan—until the last moment. But she refused to see that or admit it. Griff ran his hand distractedly through his hair, and walked back to the table. With so many emotions churning inside of him, he wasn't ready to sleep just yet. He picked up the white china pot and poured more hot coffee into his cup.

As he stood there sipping it, he smiled to himself. Vickey Mabrey might be spouting all kinds of protests, but if he was any judge of women, he could still see that she kind of liked him, despite everything. Even the fact they were separated by one rank would make him work even harder to attain it so he could have a relationship with her.

It was a place to start. If they survived this mission, Griff was assigned to BJS for a full year, and he was going to pursue her whether she liked it or not. And as long as he saw that yearning in her eyes for him, as far as he was concerned, it was a green light to go after her and try to win her over. Somehow, he had to make Vickey realize he wasn't a complete bastard. That there was a little bit of the white knight in him, after all.

Chapter 15

"Nice place to sit out the night," Griff observed, standing near the edge of the only meadow he'd seen since they'd been dropped into the Villecamba area. At dawn they'd flown from Cuzco back to BJS for a change of clothes and orders. Major Stevenson confirmed that they should continue the hunt for the crystal star, since they had such a strong lead. They would miss two days' worth of mission-flying, which didn't make Griff happy. He'd rather be in the air than a ground pounder like this.

Vickey finished digging a hole where they'd build a small fire to heat water. The hole would hide the flame from any prying eyes. The smoke would rise, but the jungle would hide it, the leaves breaking it up so that no telltale stream of smoke would give away their position. "Yeah, it's the *only* meadow around here. And it's natural. Made by the Great Spirit a long time ago."

The meadow, full of green grass and colorful wildflowers, had a small stream running through it. The sky was a dull blue with low clouds that seemed to be settling over the jungle for the night. The sun was in the west, the rays long and slanted.

Griff was glad to be there. The peccary path they'd found after getting down off the slope of the mountain earlier had been a tangled affair. All day long, he had tripped on exposed roots on the slick clay surface. Woody vines would grab at him from the sides of the narrow trail.

Hunkering down, he helped Vickey scoop away dirt from the fire hole. "Five miles from the ruins, eh?"

"Yeah." Vickey wiped the sweat off her brow with the back of her hand and glanced westward. "That trail opens up quite a bit after the meadow. At a fast walk with our gear, we can easily make Villecamba in about two hours tomorrow. I think getting a good night's sleep is in order. No sense in trying to hike the last five miles while we're tired and hungry. I want to surprise that bastard, not walk in at dusk, chase and then lose him. We need to formulate a plan of attack after we eat."

Griff nodded in agreement. Monkeys were howling in the distance. Birds made their final calls of the evening to one another. To Griff it sounded as if everyone was settling in for the night as dusk fell.

In no time, they had a small fire going. Vickey pulled out some MRE—meals ready to eat—from her large knapsack and placed an aluminum pot over a small tripod above the fire. The flames would heat the water she poured into it from her canteen.

Griff, in the meantime, was hanging their nylon hammocks in trees nearby. No one slept on the damp ground in the jungle unless they couldn't help it. The mosquitoes were bad enough. All the other inhabitants, some poisonous, others just annoying as they crawled upon a person, bit or stung them, were something else again. Griff hung their knapsacks on limbs of nearby rubber trees. Their bark was smooth and made it easy to tie valuables up off the ground.

In the distance, Vickey heard the rumble of thunder. It wasn't unusual to have storms pop up several times a day or night. Jungle conditions always made the weather unstable due to the high humidity. Vickey was glad that her hiking gear was waterproof. However, her black cotton tank top wasn't. Long ago she had bundled her hair in a ponytail behind her protective baseball cap, the visor keeping the constant drip of water from the canopy from striking her eyes and face.

Listening for Griff, she smiled to herself. He'd been an intrepid partner, hauling most of the heavy load on his shoulders. They each had an AK-47 rifle and a pistol issued to them at BJS. She felt better having weapons. It was tough to carry them in Cuzco, since it was against the law for anyone but police and military to have firearms. Even with a permit, which they had, they still could land in hot water with local authorities.

"Finished." Griff came and hunkered opposite where Vickey crouched near the fire. After spreading a plastic sheet beneath him, he settled down against the smooth gray bark of a rubber tree and opened his MRE.

"Ah, spaghetti. My favorite. What do you have?"

"Chicken, I guess. I hate these things," she muttered, tearing hers open.

"I'm spoiled after the food at the Liberator Hotel."

"Aren't we all? What I wouldn't give for another porterhouse steak right about now…."

Seeing the water begin to bubble, Vickey took a tin cup and scooped some out, pouring it into Griff's packet when he held it forward. The hot water would moisten the spaghetti and make it edible.

They ate their supper as the last rays of sun disappeared below the horizon. Darkness would come rapidly now. Monkeys continued to howl to one another. Vickey found a nice rubber tree near Griff's and spread her plastic tarp before she sat down. No sense in getting any more damp than she was already.

Griff glanced over at her. She had her back to the trunk, legs up against her body and the MRE packet balanced on her knee as she ate her dessert of peaches. "So tell me, what kind of kid were you growing up on the res?" he asked, with the hope that she'd continue to be open with him. Ever since his declaration to win her heart, she had seemed slightly less prickly and more reachable. It wasn't much to go by, but Griff wasn't going to let any opportunity slip through his hands.

"My siblings and I were half-Anglo, so the kids at the school always made fun of us." Vickey held out her golden-hued arm. "There's a hierarchy on any res. The more Indian you are, the more you're one of them, versus being white or part white."

"You grew up having your hair pulled a lot, didn't you?" He smiled at her.

She saw his teasing expression. "Listen, the res is a rough place. Hair pulling? Try real fights. The only way you prove to the full-bloods that you deserve their respect is by beating the tar out of them, instead of them using you as a punching bag."

"They'd beat up on a girl?" Griff asked, raising his brows.

Snorting, Vickey said, "Gender didn't matter! What mattered was that I learned to stand my ground and fight back." She curled her left hand into a fist. "Just like you, it was my dad who taught me how to fight. He was a boxer in his younger days and was pretty good at it. I was in the third grade and came home with a bloody nose one day from school. I wouldn't cry, but it hurt like hell. My mother was upset and he told her to calm down. He was the one who took me to the bathroom and cleaned me up."

"I thought medicine people were peaceful."

"Ever hear of Sitting Bull?"

Griff grinned. "Yeah, the Sioux chief who raised hell with the U.S. Army?"

"Same one. He was a medicine man. So was Crazy Horse. Some of the finest medicine people were our greatest warriors. They knew how to use their powers, *all* of them. My dad was no different. After he cleaned me up, we went for a walk, hand in hand, back to the corral. He told me that there were times in life when we had to fight."

"Meaning women had to fight, too?"

"Oh, gimme a break, Hutchinson!"

Laughing softly, Griff finished his MRE, munching on the soda crackers. "I was teasing you. Remember, my father drilled it into me that women were soft and incapable of defending themselves."

"Proved you wrong, didn't we?"

"In spades. I'm a convinced man." He saw a smile lurking at the corners of her mouth. "So your dad began giving you boxing lessons?"

"Yeah. Every day when I came home from school he'd put a pair of kid's gloves on my hands after wrapping them, and we'd go to the horse corral, which we made our 'ring.'"

"You liked it?"

"Yeah, I loved it. It gave me a sense of power and self-confidence."

"Did you ever have to use it in school?"

Chortling, she said, "Count on it. After about four months the same group of bullies picked on me again. And I picked back. This time," she said, satisfaction in her tone, "I wasn't the one walking away with the bloody nose."

"Do you think every woman can be a fighter like that? Or does it require special genes?"

"I don't know." Vickey put the MRE package aside, having consumed every morsel. After wiping her mouth with the paper napkin, she said, "Is every man a fighter? Is there a special gene that makes him a warrior?"

"Got me," Griff murmured. He got up and poured hot water into the cup she held out to him. "I think there is a type of male who likes combat."

"I don't think anyone likes combat," Vickey said, thanking him and stirring her freeze-dried coffee with a stick. "I think some people thrive on competition. Doesn't matter their gender, they just like to win." She grinned. "I'm one of them."

"That's me. I like the challenge," Griff said, sitting back down after pouring hot water into his own cup. He tore open sugar and cream packets, emptying the contents into the steaming cup of instant coffee. "Competition. Yeah, that rings true."

"Were you assertive as a kid?" Vickey asked him, sitting with her knees drawn up, her elbows resting on them. In the growing dusk Griff's face was darkly shadowed. He'd shaved this morning, but already his beard was coming back. Her heart yearned to reach out and touch that very male face. She quelled the desire.

"My father was a supercompetitive type," Griff said. "I played football growing up."

"I'll bet you were the star player, too."

Giving her a glance, he said, "I played pretty well."

"Humble, too. My heart be still."

"You thought I'd brag?"

"Yeah. Most guys do."

"I'm not most guys, Vickey."

Sipping the coffee, she nodded. "You proved that by

what you did in coming to wake us up and get us back to Fort Rucker before we were AWOL," she admitted. She found herself looking at Griff differently now. Maybe she was feeling a little kinder and far less hostile.

"I have a conscience. I know right from wrong."

"What you guys pulled on us back at Fort Rucker is something a woman would never do. Not individually, and sure as hell not as a group. I turned that fiasco over in my mind for a lot of years and I've come to the conclusion that males, when threatened by females, will do whatever it takes, right or wrong, to bring them down and put them in their place."

"You ladies had the best flight percentages of all the classes going through Fort Rucker at that time," Griff said. Then he added, "It created a lot of jealousy, but probably more to the point, it scared the hell out of the men."

"Scared them?" There was derision in her tone.

"Yeah. They figured if your all-woman class continued with such high percentages, in the nineties, that you would take most if not all the slots available for new combat helo pilots."

"That's not competition. That's sheer stupidity on the men's part."

Griff nodded. "No question."

"What were your flight stats?"

"In the nineties."

"So you weren't sweating getting an Apache helo slot after graduation?"

"No."

"But the guys who dreamed up this little drug fest didn't have high flight scores?"

"Right."

Giving a shake of her head, Vickey muttered, "I don't understand it. There was a lot of competition within our all-woman class, but we didn't decide to hamstring someone if they flew better than we did. We just buckled down and resolved to fly better the next time around."

"I know…." Griff knit his brows as he looked down at his coffee cup. "It was wrong."

"Men who don't have the right stuff are pissed off when women are better at flying than they are. They can't handle losing to a woman, so they lash out. What's wrong with *this* picture?"

Griff gave her a tender look and said, "That's it in a nutshell." Risking everything, he changed the subject. "Vickey? What do you see yourself doing in the next couple of years?"

She searched his face for signs of insincerity, but saw none. So she shrugged and looked up at the darkening canopy. The screams of the monkeys were finally dying down. "I hope to get rotated out of here in another year. I'll have spent four of my six mandatory years here at BJS. I love what I do, but I'd like a change."

"So, you're going to continue on with a twenty-year career in the army?"

"Yeah, aren't you?"

"I want to." Griff scratched his head. "What about personally? What do you see yourself wanting or doing?"

Finishing her coffee, Vickey eased to her feet and went to place the empty cup back in a special zippered pouch. "I love to ride horses, but that's impossible unless you go to Lima. I miss the res, the desert. I get to visit my family for thirty days every year, but I'd like to be able to drop in and see them more often than that."

Griff got to his feet, threw out the last of his coffee and walked over to his pack, which hung next to hers. "By personally, I meant, you know, like get married? That kind of thing?"

He was inches away from her. She could feel his warmth and strength as he held her gaze.

"Marriage? Dude, I don't think so! I'm only in my midtwenties. I don't even want to think about such a thing until I'm around thirty. My mother was right—later marriage is the only way to go for a woman. I saw too many girls on the res get pregnant when they were eighteen or nineteen and have three or four kids by the time they got to my age. They were tied down and didn't have a life of their own." She gave her dark green pack a pat, then went back to the fire and hunkered over it.

"Career before a family?" Griff asked, joining her. He grabbed the plastic and sat cross-legged as she lifted the pot of water off the tripod.

"Living life as I want to is more like it. Marriage is a huge step. I'm not ready for it yet. I've still got adventure in my soul that I have to experience first."

"How do you see relationships?"

Vickey gave him a dark look and set the boiling pot to one side. "Fun. How about you?"

"I like having a woman in my life for a lot of reasons. One of them being fun."

"Yeah, and the others all start with *B*—for bed."

"Ouch, no fair. That's not true. Well, not entirely true."

Chuckling, Vickey unzipped a pocket of her vest and pulled out a candy bar. She unwrapped it and chewed on the chocolate with pleasure. "Thanks for being honest. I don't like guys who hide their true motives."

"I know."

"So what does a woman in your life get from you?" she asked, watching him intently from beneath her lashes. With night falling, their surroundings were swathed in different shades of gray. The monkeys were settling down and the buzz of insects began to take over, a different orchestra coming on stage for the nighttime.

"I like talking with her," Griff said. "Trading ideas, thoughts and experiences."

"So, she's more than just a bed warmer for you?"

Brutal. Griff grinned. "I like women who speak their minds."

"Ah, the honesty card?"

Nodding, Griff watched the coals glimmer in the fire pit. "But I haven't found her—yet." Lifting his head, he held Vickey's curious gaze.

"So you're not in love?" Now why would she ask such a ridiculous question? Irritated with herself, Vickey saw his mouth draw into a boyish smile. Griff picked up a nearby stick and slowly began to peel the bark off it.

"No, I'm not in love."

"Tell me more about your last relationship."

To the point. Her mouth was feral looking, and so were her eyes. She was definitely a hunter, and Griff found himself getting excited all over again. He liked Vickey's multifaceted personality, the many layers to discover. "She was a United Nations volunteer in Afghanistan. Hell on wheels. A redhead."

"Ah..."

"Her name was Cindy and I met her six months ago. She was your age. Raised in California, where her family had avocado orchards. She was very rich. Very...pampered." He frowned looking down at the twig in his hands.

"But...?" Vickey wanted him to say more, but damned her burning curiosity. What kind of women did Griff like? Whether she wanted to admit it or not, she was comparing herself to his ex-girlfriend. It was silly, but she couldn't help herself. Why should she care *what* kind of woman Griff liked?

"Cindy was hot-tempered and spoiled."

"Nothing wrong with a temper. Better to get it out than bottle it up," Vickey said. "I'm well known for blowing up around BJS when things go wrong."

"Showing your emotions doesn't bother me," Griff said, feeling her undivided interest. He was glad, because it meant she cared. Maybe by revealing his checkered past he could get her to see him differently. Griff hoped so. Taking a deep breath, he said, "Cindy was spoiled rotten because she was rich. I think she took this job to show her family that she was capable of humanitarian deeds."

"So, it was a whim for her? An adventure?"

"Yes."

"And she met you? Mr. Flyboy Hero?"

Hearing the derision in her tone, he chuckled. "Yeah, she had stars in her eyes for any guy in uniform."

"You must have stood out. There were a lot of Apache pilot studs over there. Not to mention Special Forces A team types. All hero material."

Hesitating, Griff said, "Yeah, I guess…"

Feeling as if he was holding out on her, Vickey leaned forward. "Why did she single you out then? There had to be a reason."

Griff looked away unhappily. This was not where he wanted the conversation to go. "Oh, she was at a function in Khandahar."

This was getting good. He looked so damn uncomfortable now that he refused to look her in the eye. "What kind of function?"

Grimacing, Griff muttered, "Medals were being handed out."

"Oh?" Perking up, Vickey saw his demeanor had gone from cocky to humble. *How come?* Now, she was really interested. Her Scorpio curiosity was burning to know. Sitting up, Vickey asked, "The general was handing out medals to people? To you?" She saw him wipe his mouth and look away.

"Yeah, I guess."

"What kind of medal?" she pressed.

"Just a medal…"

"Dude, you are acting like I'm a dentist pulling a tooth out of your mouth. What's to get into knots over?" Vickey asked.

"I just didn't think the conversation would go in this direction."

"So what kind of medal?" she persisted.

"Silver star."

Vickey sat back, stunned, while he stared down at the twig as if it were his life. *A silver star?* Those medals were not handed out like candy. On the contrary, receiving such an honor meant that Griff had done something very heroic. And it made sense that this red-haired woman would zero in on him. A silver star made a person an instant, genuine hero. Giving him a sharpened look, Vickey prodded, "Tell me about it. How'd you get it?"

"Ah, hell, Vickey, I didn't want to let you know about it. It's not important." He threw the twig into the fire and began searching for another.

Griff Hutchinson was humble? Blinking, she sat there digesting his discomfort. This startling new facet of his character appealed to her more strongly than any other. Okay, he was drop-dead handsome, but that wouldn't get her to budge from her previous opinion of him. But seeing his face flush and humility broadcast in his features, she was fascinated. Maybe she'd been a little too harsh toward him.

"Mind sharing with me why you got awarded a silver star?" she pressed.

Griff found another twig, longer this time, and began to snap off small pieces and drop them into the smoldering fire. "My Apache took an RPG, rocket propelled grenade, hit. My tail rotor got dusted. We landed on a hill at a Special Forces position that was getting overrun by Taliban. My partner was wounded. I dragged him out of the chopper to safety behind their line. I picked up a weapon and joined the guys. We finally repulsed the Taliban. That's all."

Vickey gave him a long, searching look. "You must have done a helluva lot more than that to earn a silver star. The devil's in the details. Mind sharing the *rest* of this story with me?"

With a sigh, Griff muttered, "I outflanked the Taliban. I had a rifle and plenty of ammo, and under cover of darkness, I slipped from our hilltop position and found theirs." Griff gave her a flat look. "I didn't take any prisoners. When it was all over, they were dead and we were alive."

"And the Special Forces team? Why couldn't they have done this?"

"Because they were all wounded and they hadn't seen the lay of the land from the air like I had." Griff shrugged. "I've got good night vision, and come from a ranching family. My Dad showed me how to hunt, track and sneak up on an animal. This wasn't any different."

"And you did it all single-handedly?" She was impressed.

"I had to," Griff told her quietly. "My partner was dying. Slowly bleeding to death. I knew we had to get back to Khandahar fast or he was going to die. I didn't want to wait for daylight, when the troops could finally come and try to extract us."

"I see." She saw pain etched in his face, his mouth turned downward and thinned. "And your friend?"

"He died anyway. The Special Forces medic tried to help, but he was so badly wounded that he was unconscious most of the time."

Quiet settled around them. Vickey listened to the soft orchestra of crickets singing and frogs croaking. Giving Griff a probing look, she said, "That says something about your character. You deserved that medal."

"I didn't want you to know."

"Why?"

He lifted his head and held her shadowed gaze. "Because I wanted you to see me, not my past. Not my medals, either. I wanted you to understand that I'm not the same guy as before."

It was on her lips to ask why, but she was afraid to. Vickey saw frustration in his narrowed eyes. The line of suffering across his mouth made her ache. She wanted to go over to him, crouch down and put her arms around him. That's what he needed. Clearly, Griff was still hurting from that firefight. She would be, too.

"I guess, putting myself in your position, if I lost a friend I flew with, I'd be devastated."

"I was. Still am."

"How long ago did this happen?"

"Six months ago."

Her heart opened to him and she didn't struggle to suppress it. "And this U.N. volunteer? Stars in her eyes for the guy who had the silver star, right?"

"Right." With a sigh, Griff threw the last piece of his twig into the fire. "Only I was too stupid to see it coming."

"Stupid? I don't think so. Hurting? Needing comfort? Grieving? Any human being wants to be able to turn and crawl into the safety of someone's arms when they feel like that, don't you think?"

Her words, so softly spoken, soothed the ragged edges of his grief and anguish. Griff held her tender gaze. Right now, Vickey looked completely accessible to him. Open. Vulnerable. "You know," he said hesitantly, "this is the side of you I've always wanted to know."

She smiled briefly. "What? My softer side?"

He managed a thin smile. "The compassionate woman that lurks beneath the warrior disguise she wears so well."

"Well," Vickey whispered, getting up and going to her hammock, "maybe we made some progress in that direction tonight. Together." She looked over her shoulder. Griff was still sitting by the fire, which had finally gone out. She could barely see him. "What you did was heroic, Griff."

He felt her words rifle across his heart. She'd whispered them huskily, with emotion. And she'd finally called him by his first name. Turning, he lifted his head and stared at her as she stood by her hammock. "I don't want you to see me that way."

"No?"

"No. I want you to see me as a regular kind of guy."

"You're hardly that."

"I want you to judge me on daily things. Not this. Not one event in my life."

"Well," Vickey said dryly, "I was sure as hell judging you by one event in your life since Fort Rucker. This new event makes me see you differently. Better, maybe." There, it was out. She felt some relief telling Griff how she really felt. Sitting down in the hammock, she lifted her booted feet into it and swung gently. After pulling the lightweight mosquito netting over her and tying it at both ends so it was like a tent around her, Vickey lay back. Her pistol was at her side. She'd wear it tonight no matter how uncomfortable it was.

Going to his hammock, Griff felt many loads begin to dissolve from his shoulders, and joy start to flood his entire being. Fixing the mosquito netting to each end of his hammock, he murmured, "You know Cindy? The redhead?"

"Yeah?"

"I finally figured out why she wanted me. It was the hero thing. When I realized that she was going around bragging to the people she worked with, I cut it off."

"Good for you." Vickey put her hands behind her head and closed her eyes. "Maybe bad guys can turn into good guys. Do you think it's possible?" she whispered.

Smiling to himself, Griff climbed into the hammock. "I think everyone is part good and bad. We're a mix of both." He tried to get a glimpse of her in her hammock, which was about ten feet away. The darkness was thick by now, so he settled for listening to her voice.

"And you like me anyway."

"I like you, Vickey Mabrey. For better or worse." Griff lay down and got comfortable. It felt good to stretch out and relax even with his boots on.

He heard her chuckle. "You're incorrigible, Hutchinson."

"But *you* like *me* a little, anyway?"

"Yeah, I hate to admit it, but I am interested." Then she added, "And it's not because of that silver star you earned."

"Yeah, right."

"Gotta trust me on that one."

"Just call me Griff, will you? That will make my day, week and month."

"Okay. I can do that, Griff."

Satisfaction thrummed through him. "Good. Thanks." That meant she was taking their relationship, what there was of it, to a new level. Heart singing, Griff closed his eyes. His happiness was short-lived as he realized that tomorrow, at dawn, they would sneak quietly into Villecamba and begin their search for Roka Fierros. Either of them could die because Fierros was armed and dangerous, no question. If the guy had the balls to steal that crystal star from right under Balcazar's nose, then he had guts to kill anyone who threatened him. If they found him, he wouldn't go down without a fight. And that meant either of them could be wounded or killed.

That last thought kept Griff in a light, restless sleep. He'd just made a serious breakthrough with Vickey, and it could all be destroyed in a heartbeat. There was no justice in the universe, he decided. None at all.

Chapter 16

At 0600 long wispy fingers of clouds descended over Villecamba. This part of the world was known as Spirit Valley, although Vickey knew that locals talked it up as "Ghost Valley" to heighten the mystical quality of these ruins. The site lay mostly hidden within the arms of the jungle.

Vickey crept through the dewy grass. The tangling greenery grew against the gray-black square stones of the outer wall where she walked, rifle in hand. Behind her, Griff silently followed. With luck, they'd find Roka Fierros just getting up and having breakfast.

Because of the foggy conditions, Vickey could barely see twenty feet ahead of her. With each step, she placed her soaked boots, not wanting to trip. She was thankful that she was familiar with the layout, since she'd come here many times for a day's R & R. Vickey had drawn Griff a quick map this morning before they'd broken camp.

Her heart beat strongly in her breast. She knew from BJS intel that there were no archeological excavation teams present at the complex right now. And there were no scheduled tourist hikes to this area, either. If they came upon anyone at Villecamba, it was more than likely to be Fierros.

Vickey had donned tourist attire—blue jeans, hiking boots and red tank top. The red baseball cap finished off her fashion statement. If Fierros spotted them, Vickey wanted him to think they were *turistas*. Griff wore tan chinos and a yellow T-shirt that said Planet Hollywood.

As she approached the corner of a wall with an arched stone entrance, she caught a whiff of smoke. Holding up her hand, she halted and crouched.

Griff knew that signal: it meant come up beside me but don't talk. He moved quickly to her side. Her eyes narrowed and seemed to focus on the corner of the temple. Crouching down next to her, holding his AK-47 ready, he leaned forward, close to her face.

"Smoke…" she whispered softly, gesturing ahead. "I smell smoke. That means someone's cooking a meal close by."

Nodding, Griff flipped off the safety on his rifle. So did Vickey. "Be careful," he warned her in a husky tone. When she turned, her face so close to his, he saw the beauty of her forest-green eyes for the first time that day. Thick sable lashes framed her wide, luminescent eyes. Once again he was captivated, and at that dangerous moment, he couldn't help but think how beautiful she was. Griff ached to say so, but now was not the time or place. Maybe never. He wasn't sure if telling her about his silver star had changed anything. It shouldn't have. He wanted Vickey to judge him on how he treated her daily. Right now. Not on his past behavior.

Her lips curved slightly. "Let's both be careful?"

Meeting her tight smile, he nodded. She turned and gave the signal to advance. Vickey walked like a ghost, almost floating as she made her way through the thick tangle of grass. She had a boneless grace as she crouched and crept forward. Griff found himself thinking she was more cat than human, and he was completely in awe. There was so much to her. Why the hell hadn't he appreciated that in flight school?

The fog thinned as Vickey reached the end of the stone wall. Peeking around it, she saw a long, grassy slope flowing down toward the jungle. The area had been cleared by archeologists a year ago, but without constant upkeep, the jungle would quickly reclaim this temple so important to the Incan people.

Birds called, high and piercing, warning of their approach.

Vickey froze. *Damn!* Would Fierros notice and understand? She wasn't sure. She felt Griff come up behind her again, close to where she crouched. Senses heightened, she took note of her surroundings. She inhaled deeply, and this time, she didn't smell the smoke from the wood fire. The ceiling of clouds was a light gray with dawn light coming through in slats. There was plenty of light, which was good. And it wasn't raining, also good. They'd had thunderstorms twice last night and she hadn't gotten much sleep. But that wasn't what had kept her awake.

Tearing that confession out of Griff had made her restless. Like so many military people, he didn't see himself as heroic; he was merely doing the job to save friends and comrades in a battle. Griff had had several options after his Apache had been forced to land. He could have stayed with his friend at the bird. Instead, he'd opted to help the Special Forces A team, which took guts. And then to think outside the box, sneak through that ravine and come up behind the Taliban—well, in her book, that was not only creative but damn brave of Griff. And the fact that she'd had to tear the story out of him one sentence at a time told her he wasn't using his medal to impress her. But she couldn't think about Griff or the future of their relationship right then. They had a job to do.

She crept toward the opening to the temple and peered inside. The smell of smoke permeated the air again. Where was it coming from? She eyed the square room in front of her. It had two other exits, stone doorways with no arch above them, for the stones had been pulled off by aggressive vines over time and lay in heaps around the entrances.

Her AK-47 held ready, Vickey moved quietly into the room and headed for the next entrance point. She could hear Griff right behind her. More birds were calling—this time melodically. Monkeys screamed nearby, fighting loudly with one another. As Vickey and Griff advanced, the wet grass slapped against their boots.

The smell of smoke was stronger now. Vickey's gut told her Fierros could be on the other side of this broken wall. She froze. *There!* She heard the distinct clink of metal. It sounded like someone putting a tin pot on a grate over a fire. With a hand signal, she told Griff that Fierros was to their right. Vickey knew the layout of this ruin. If he was in the second room over, there was a scaleable wall on one side and another broken wall on the opposite side. With two doorways, they'd have to circle around in order to trap him.

Crouching, Vickey made several gestures to Griff, who watched her hand signals intently, then nodded in understanding. She elected to do the circling. Griff would stay here to guard the entrance. All he had to do was move to the right, go through one room and be at the door where she suspected Roka Fierros was eating his breakfast.

Vickey got up and moved away from the wall. Looking skyward, she searched for a sign that she was right. There! Lifting her left hand, she pointed her index finger. Griff looked up. A thin wisp of smoke rose two rooms down from where they stood.

Vickey grinned savagely, and so did Griff. He gave her a thumbs-up. She nodded and quietly took off, to circle around to the other exit point.

Her heart started pounding as she approached the door. She could hear someone clinking tin pots. The man wasn't being too careful, which was fine with her. She glanced at her watch: five minutes had elapsed. By now, Griff should be in position at the other door.

Peeking around the corner, rifle ready, she saw what had to be Fierros. He'd built a fire in the corner near the tallest wall and stood facing it. For someone who had stolen a million-dollar world-class artifact, it was strange that he didn't know enough to remain on guard. Vickey would sure as hell have built the fire in the middle of the room so she could keep her eye on both exits points in case someone tried to jump her.

Roka Fierros was young. He looked to be in his early twenties. Vickey watched him and mentally recorded his physical details. She suspected he was Quero. Short and compactly built, the man wore cut-off breeches reaching just above his knotty calves. The rubber flip-flops on his feet were typical footgear for Indians of Peru. Hunkered over the fire, he was frying eggs in a skillet, completely immersed in what he was doing. The bright red-yellow-and-green-striped llama wool poncho he wore would keep his lean body warm in the fifty-degree temperature and dampness. On his head of thick, black hair, he wore a beat-up brown felt hat. She saw his gun nearby, an AK-47, but it was out of his reach. The man's pack sat in the other corner. Vickey itched to know if the crystal star was in it.

Taking a gulping breath, she rounded the corner.

"Freeze, Fierros!" She quickly moved toward him. Out of the corner of her eye, she saw Griff come through the other door, his rifle aimed at the startled Indian.

Giving a cry of surprise, Fierros leaped up, and the skillet and eggs went flying through the air.

Vickey snarled, "Get down on your belly now or I'll blow your head off!"

Instantly, he dropped to the grassy, damp earth. "Don't shoot me! Don't shoot me!" he cried.

"Hands behind your head," Griff growled, kneeling down and shouldering his rifle. He pulled out a pair of plastic handcuffs and soon bound Fierros's wrists behind him. "Okay," he ordered, "get up!" He hauled the young Indian to a sitting position.

Vickey kept vigilant. "You got friends here, Roka?" She kept her eyes and ears alert. Roka Fierros could have hooked up with others for all she knew.

"N-no, no one else is here.... Who are you? Did Balcazar send you?" He looked at each of them, his face filled with fear.

"We're not associated with Balcazar, although he *is* hunting you," Vickey said. She kept her rifle ready. Thieves were known to lie, and Fierros could be doing so.

"Aiyee," Roka whined, as Vickey pulled him by the shoulder of his poncho.

"Where's the crystal star?" she breathed savagely, giving him a shake that made his hat fly off. "Where is it? We know you have it."

Griff watched the Indian youth wince and cry out. He admired how Vickey could be a jaguar when she wanted to be. Her fierce countenance seemed to convince Fierros she was serious. She was a woman warrior. Bold. Aggressive. Griff liked what he saw.

"I—it's in my pack—over there! Don't hurt me! Don't hurt me!" Fierros leaned away from Vickey, but she hauled him back toward her.

"You'd better be telling the truth, Fierros. Which pocket of your pack is it in?"

Their prisoner stammered, "It's in the t-top of my pack. On the left-hand side. I—I have it wrapped in soft alpaca wool to protect it." He looked at Griff, who held a gun to his chest. "Don't kill me!" he sobbed.

"Shut up!" Vickey growled. She shouldered the AK-47 and went over to the dark green canvas pack, which was threadbare. She worked the stubborn zipper twice before it released. Immediately, she reached into the corner and came into contact with alpaca fabric. Sliding her hands around it, she felt an incredible shock and then warmth flow up her arm as she curled her fingers around a large object. The warmth continued, the tingling increased when she pulled it gently out of the pack and set it on the ground before her. Vickey unfolded dark blue alpaca wool with trembling fingers. She gasped. There it was.

Griff divided his attention between Fierros and the incredible beauty of the seven-pointed crystal star. It seemed alive, as if a light glowed from within. He could see that Vickey felt the same awe that he did.

Vickey reached down, scooped up the star and stood. "This is incredible," she whispered, gazing at the crystal. The artifact was two-sided, the seven points having been painstakingly created with perfect symmetry. Mesmerized, she whispered, "Griff, this thing's alive. I feel heat in my hand, and tingling up my arm. This is alive. My God, no wonder they wanted it...."

"What's that?" Griff said sharply. A dull, thudding sound grew louder.

Vickey lifted her head and suddenly felt woozy. Holding the sacred Eastern Cherokee totem was having a strange effect on her. It was as if she was out of her body and not here at all. She had the sense that if she continued to hold the crystal totem, she really would go elsewhere. But Griff's repeated warning slammed her back to the present, and Vickey scanned the sky. The whapping sound came closer and closer. She could feel faint reverberations as if the chopper were puncturing the humid jungle air.

"A helicopter?"

"Yeah, I'm sure it is." Griff's eyes narrowed and he glared down at Fierros. "You expecting company?"

"Uh, no," he whimpered, his eyes showing white as he looked at the sky. The chopper was approaching quickly. Whoever it was would be here within two minutes!

Vickey hurriedly wrapped up the star and tucked it inside her vest pocket. "Could be Balcazar. Remember he said he was going to fly his guards out here to find this guy today?"

Roka Fierros gave a cry. "No! Let me go! Please? You have the star! Let me go! Cut my bonds! Let me escape into the jungle! He'll kill me. Please..." he wept.

"BJS?" Griff wondered.

"Not a chance." Vickey strode quickly over to Fierros. She took his gun, an old model with a scarred stock. Leaning down, she pulled the knife from her ankle sheath and cut Fierros's bonds.

"Now vamoose, Fierros! Get out of here!"

Instantly, the Peruvian leaped to his feet. He raced out the doorway that led deeper into the temple complex.

"Why release him?" Griff asked.

Vickey shoved the knife back into its sheath. Straightening, she said, "Because if that's Balcazar, it gives them someone to chase rather than us. Come on! We gotta make a run for the river! It's our only chance of escape!"

Vickey's mind raced as she searched for ways out of the danger they would soon encounter. As far as she could tell, there was only one way out—crossing the river on the vine footbridge that spanned the violent, boulder filled Urubamba. The river was rated by kayakers as a number five—one of the fiercest and most violent. One that could easily kill any fool stupid enough to try to ride the waters in any kind of boat. The river flowed down from the Andes, its greenish white water as cold as the glaciers it came from. No one could survive in it for more than fifteen minutes before hypothermia set in and killed the person. No one.

Zipping up her vest, she snapped, "Let's get out of here!" They could take one of three paths down to the river, which was five miles away. If they could cross the bridge, they could reach the secondary extraction point they'd decided on with BJS.

Vickey ran down the slippery, grassy slope, surging ahead of Griff. "Let's take this path!" she yelled. The helicopter was nearly on top of them. She couldn't see it, but she sure as hell could feel it. The pounding of the blades shattered the jungle stillness. Looking up as she ran, she saw ropes tumbling down out of the clouds. They were going to rappel out of the helo down into the ruins! Vickey saw the first man sliding down the rope. Yes! She recognized the bastard. It was the guard called Manuel.

She and Griff raced into the jungle. The path was narrow, wet and tricky. Vickey didn't see an exposed root, and she hit it at full speed, the toe of her boot jamming underneath. She went tumbling end over end and landed with a grunt, slamming into a rubber tree. Stunned, Vickey felt something shatter in her back pocket. Oh, no! It was the Iridium satellite phone! Their only way to call BJS and get help.

Griff leaned down, gasping, and hauled her to her feet.

"You okay?"

"Yeah, yeah." She felt in her back pocket and discovered the phone was in several pieces, as she'd feared. Gunfire erupted behind them. Bullets whined past them. Limbs cracked and exploded around where they stood. They'd been spotted! Vickey gave a cry, turned around and sprinted away, her boots digging into the red mud. The path was narrow, straight and the fastest way to the river.

She heard shouts of Balcazar's men behind them. They were coming after them and not Fierros! *Damn!*

Vickey had seen six ropes dangling from that helo. Six against two. Was there another copter coming? Balcazar wanted that star. Had he sent two teams in? Breathing hard, her lungs pumping, she pounded on. Leaves and branches swatted against her body, making her skin sting. She heard Griff thundering down the trail, hot on her heels.

More bullets penetrated the jungle. *Damn! They were close!* She heard the men screaming and yelling. Now it was a race to the bridge.

"They're onto us!" Griff yelled, breathing hard. He ran as hard as he could. But he, too, hit an exposed root and went tumbling. The AK-47 flew off to one side of the trail. After landing with an *oomph,* Griff scrambled back to his feet, his jeans covered in mud.

Vickey picked up his rifle and handed it back to him. "Hurry! Hurry!" she rasped, spinning around.

More gunfire.

As she sprinted away down the path, she heard Griff grunt. Sliding to a stop, she twisted back and saw him stagger, the rifle dropping from his hands. Eyes widening, she saw blood smearing his left shoulder. He'd been hit! *No!* Whirling, she grabbed his rifle and threw the strap over her shoulder. His face white with pain, he clasped his right hand over his wound.

Gripping him by his uninjured arm, she barked, "Get ahead of me! Run to the river! Jump in! We aren't gonna make it to that bridge in time. We're gonna have to take our chances in the river! We have to get away from these guys! It's our only chance!"

Giving her a shocked look, Griff felt the warmth of

blood flowing down his chest and across his ribs. "Yeah, okay." He stumbled forward, his mind whirling with shock. He felt no pain—not yet. He'd heard that when hit by a bullet, one felt shock before the pain set in. Running awkwardly down the path, he could hear the roar of the rapids ahead.

Vickey waited, making sure Griff was well ahead of her. Then she took out one of the grenades from her vest, pulled the pin and threw it back up the trail. That would slow those bastards down. She then spun around and sprinted down the trail. The grenade would explode six seconds after it was detonated. She hustled hard, racing down the slippery path. Ahead, she could see Griff hauling himself for all he was worth.

Just as she rounded the turn, the grenade went off. There was a huge explosion, and the jungle shook. She cringed but kept on running. She heard cries of anger and confusion. *Good!* Breathing harshly, she finally caught up with Griff.

"How bad is it?" she yelled, running at his heels. The path was too narrow for two people to run side by side.

"Shoulder wound," Griff cried.

"We got a mile to go! That grenade is going to slow them down, not stop them." Her breath was raspy. "We won't make the bridge, Griff! They're too close. They'd shoot us like ducks on a pond if we tried to cross it. We have to take our chances jumping into the river."

"I know!" he panted. Pumping his legs as hard as he could, Griff knew that he was losing blood. The more he lost, the weaker he'd get. "Did you use the Iridium phone and call for help?"

"I can't! I smashed it when I fell back there against the tree! We're alone, Griff! I can't call out for BJS to rescue us."

"Are you a strong swimmer?" he demanded, forcing himself to keep moving.

"Yeah. You?"

"Yeah. We can get killed in that river!"

"I know. But we don't stand a chance on the ground! They won't follow us down the Urubamba. It's too fast, and too rocky for them to run along the bank and shoot us. It's our only way out, Griff! We gotta take it!"

Branches and leaves smacked at his face and body. Griff held up his right hand as he ran so he could see where he was going. A half mile from the river the path canted steeply downward. Slipping and sliding, he landed several times on his butt. Each time, Vickey was there to help him up.

"Come on," she breathed raggedly. "The river's just ahead!"

Griff heard shouts behind them. Balcazar's men were closing fast. Gunfire started again, bullets raining around them. Griff felt suddenly light-headed. The loss of blood was getting to him. Faltering, he shoved ahead while Vickey remained behind. She was going to throw another grenade.

Griff made it to the river, which was over two hundred feet wide. The white, churning water roared like a jet engine, pouring and tumbling over a continuous carpet of rocks and boulders, thousands of stones in all sizes and colors. For as far as Griff could see, the bank on either side was lined with river rock. It was hell trying to pick his way across them.

Vickey raced out of the jungle. "Jump in!" she yelled, gesturing toward the river.

Griff had dropped his pack when he'd been hit; it would only drag him down, anyway. He didn't have time to get rid of his boots now. Wading into the water, he felt his legs instantly grow numb.

The grenade exploded, the resulting blast pounding against his eardrums. Momentarily deafened, he saw Vickey coming up fast, charging across the rocks toward him, her eyes wide with terror. Yeah, he was scared as hell, too.

"Come on!" Vickey cried. She leaped in, the water splashing around her knees. Grabbing Griff by the arm, she headed toward the deep water in the middle of the river—their best chance of escape. Lunging forward, gasping for breath, she threw herself into the raging depths. Her hand remained tight on Griff's arm as she hauled him with her.

In an instant, the swift current snapped them up and sucked them at over thirty miles an hour into the center of the channel. Griff was thrown ahead of her, where boulders loomed.

Behind her, Vickey heard shouts. Gunfire erupted. Geysers of water danced up around them. Too late! The river curved sharply and they were swept away, together.

Chapter 17

There was only one way to survive the rapids of a river like the Urubamba. The military had trained them to float with their legs stretched out in front of them, facing downstream so they could see all rocks and boulders coming. They could then use their feet and legs to absorb the impact when they smashed into one at high speed.

Vickey quickly assumed the survival position after she'd lost her grip on Griff's arm. He drifted nearby, his face pale, his eyes dark with shock. Knowing he was losing blood from his shoulder wound, she flailed her arms, trying to reconnect with him. She stretched out her hand in Griff's direction and screamed at him over the roar of the river. They were being carried around the sharp bend at a frightening speed!

Griff heard Vickey cry out his name. She was bobbing along, a few feet away on his left. And it was his left arm that was wounded. It dragged like an anchor, so while he fought to keep the survival position, it was impossible. Boulders as big as small cars loomed in front of them. Vickey continued to reach out for him, to no avail.

Griff grunted as his wet, heavy boots struck a big rock directly before him. The jolt ran through his numb and frigid body like an earthquake. He felt raw, serrating pain ripping his shoulder.

The swift current dragged him to the left of the boulder after he'd hit it. Thrashing around, Griff became dizzy and disoriented. The blood loss was causing him to lose his bearings. Desperate to get into the survival position again, he swallowed a lot of freezing water as he sank momentarily beneath the waves. When he struggled back to the surface, he started vomiting. The power of the unrelenting river dragged him sideways. *No!*

Vickey saw that the river made a sudden snakelike turn ahead, the waves of the rapids boiling six to eight feet high. That meant a helluva lot of rocks just beneath the jade-green water! Seeing Griff flounder, Vickey made a decision that could either save them or cost them their lives. Aiming her feet at an approaching boulder, she pushed herself off it like a billiard ball, using the rock as a springboard to reach Griff. The impact was a shock to Vickey's system, jamming the bones in her legs and jarring her teeth. She felt as if she'd been hit by a car traveling fifty miles an hour.

Shaking off the whiplash effect, she flexed her knees to absorb the worst of the punishing blow. Water swirled around Vickey. She was completely numb, with no sense of pain or cold—a dangerous sign.

Pushing off with all the strength she had left, she threw her arms outward and leaped in Griff's direction, landing with a horrific splash just in front of him. Instantly, she felt the grip of the river pull her downward. *No way!* Thrusting and kicking, she surged out of the water just ahead of Griff.

His face was white, his eyes half-closed. He continued to be pummeled around, obviously weakened by the continuing loss of blood. Terror sizzled through Vickey as she grabbed for his shirt. Hauling him around, she screamed, "Kick! Kick hard, Griff! We're heading to shore!"

Not waiting for a response, Vickey saw another dark gray rock coming up fast. The roar of the river was deafening. Shaking the wet hair off her face, she looked back. No gunmen. They couldn't follow along that bank to fire at them. One enemy down. Now the river was their foe in a fight for their lives.

Clenching her teeth, Vickey hauled Griff to the left. She turned and straightened just in time to allow her boots to take the shattering impact of the boulder. This time, she pushed off to the left. The riverbank was only fifty feet away now, but it might as well have been ten miles. The thundering rapids, the deadly racing current, would keep them unwilling prisoners in the middle and not allow them to reach the safety of that bank. But they had to!

As she fought to keep Griff's head above water, his efforts weakening with each stroke, a plan formed in Vickey's mind. Huge car-size boulders dotted the river. She would choose specific targets and bounce off them, maneuvering slowly out of the main current into the shallows. It was their only chance, Vickey knew.

As she straightened her legs for the impact, Griff groaned. Jerking a glance toward him, she saw his head fall back. *No!* Agony slashed through Vickey. "Griff! Fight back! Dammit, fight back! I can't do this alone! I need you!" The scream tore out of her mouth and was instantly absorbed by the thunderous pounding of the waves. He barely opened his eyes, his dark lashes beaded with water, his mouth contorted in a silent cry.

Her agony turned to anguish. Griff couldn't die! He just couldn't! Each time her boots struck a boulder, Vickey maneuvered them a few feet closer to the left bank. Her teeth were chattering. She was freezing to death. How long had they been in the Urubamba? *Too long,* her shorting-out mind screamed back.

The jungle seemed so green and soft to her. A flock of colorful parrots flew over, heading to the shore. Knowing she had hypothermia, that her mind wasn't functioning fully, Vickey focused on the next boulder. She couldn't feel her hand gripping Griff's shoulder. He bobbed beside her, his body heavy, and it took every ounce of her strength to keep his head above the churning water.

There! She struck the next rock and pushed off with all her might, her legs like pistons. All that hiking, all those gym workouts at BJS were paying off. After one last mighty effort, Vickey felt the tug of the savage current begin to lessen. *Finally!* She guided Griff to the left, the bank a mere thirty feet away. The more she struggled toward shore, the more the river loosened its grip on her legs and booted feet.

Her toes struck the slippery bottom. *Yes!* Sobbing for breath, Vickey twisted around and grabbed Griff by the shoulders to steady him. He was unconscious. Sliding her numbed hands beneath his armpits, she began to haul him toward the bank. He was dead weight.

Terror for his life made her work even faster. Water dripped into her eyes, stinging them and blurring the world around her. Her wet hair was plastered against her neck and face. Gasping for breath, still knee-deep in water, she kept slipping and falling, the rocks too uneven for her to negotiate.

A new feeling kicked in, one that startled Vickey. It brought her to her knees emotionally. As she tugged relentlessly to get Griff out of the water and on to the rocky shore, Vickey realized that she liked him a lot. Somehow, over the past week, their ugly past miraculously started to dissolve. What took its place scared the hell out of her, and yet beckoned to her as nothing else ever had in her life.

Dragging in gulping breaths of air, teeth clattering, Vickey hauled Griff on to the rocky bank. She saw a small sand spit just ahead and dragged him onto it. Hands completely numb, she grabbed a piece of driftwood and lifted his feet enough to place it beneath his ankles. He was in shock. With his legs elevated slightly, the blood would begin to flow back into his head and help neutralize the reaction.

He could die. Sobbing, Vickey fell to his side, sending water droplets cascading across him as she did so. His clothes were dark and clung to his body. With trembling hands Vickey jerked and pulled at his vest to get it open. She had to see the extent of the bullet wound. Her gaze moved to his lifeless face, his chalkiness scaring her. She was so cold she felt as if she was moving in slow motion, but finally his vest gave way. She rolled the material of his shirt upward in order to see his wound, the fabric stained pink by his blood.

With a small cry, Vickey eyed the injury. The bullet had struck him in the left shoulder, just below his collarbone. Sliding her hand beneath his left shoulder blade, she felt for an exit wound. *Yes!* The bullet had gone clean through. In a way, that was good; in another way, it wasn't. When she pulled her hand out, her fingers were covered with fresh blood.

What to do? What to do? She looked around, a sob tearing from her lips. With the Iridium phone destroyed, she couldn't call for medical help. They were alone in the jungle, and the mighty Urubamba roared past them like a banshee. Looking down at Griff, Vickey touched his dark hair and pushed it away from his clean, broad brow. Oh, why had she been so stubborn? Why had she disregarded her feelings for him? She liked him. And that had frightened her.

Her mind revolved back to options. Kneeling over him, her knees against his body, Vickey tried to think.

Their packs were back at Villecamba. She had no medical supplies. Nothing. And then she felt warmth against her chest—a warm heat spreading across her, infusing her with a startling, blanketing comfort.

The crystal star! Yes! Frantic, Vickey unzipped her soaked vest and laid it on the ground. Trying to be careful, her hands trembling badly, she removed the crystal from the blue alpaca wool. Her eyes widened enormously. Even now in her bloody hands she could see a light emanating from within the treasure. She felt that rush of tingles from her numbed hands into her arms. The heat was there, warming her fingers so that the numbness dissolved. In its place, she had feeling.

Something told her to place the crystal totem directly on Griff's wound. That was crazy! But she had nothing else to work with. The blood of her father, her Navajo heritage, kicked in. He worked with the unseen world, the world of spirit, and Vickey knew it was real. She'd seen him create miracles with the help of the spirits too many times to say it was her imagination.

"Okay, okay..." she rasped. "I'll do it! I'll do it. Just guide me. Guide me..." she whispered to the spirit within the star. Gently, Vickey set the glowing crystal directly over Griff's wound, which was still leaking red blood. Her father had taught her some things, important things. She settled the sacred object in place with her left hand and held it there. Closing her eyes, still sobbing for breath, Vickey imagined the roots of a tree winding around her ankles and then delving deeply into the sand and rock where she knelt. She knew that when her father laid his left hand on someone to heal them, he always grounded himself first. He'd told her that if she didn't do that, she would take on the energy of the sickness or wound and possibly die herself. By grounding herself into Mother Earth, whatever energy was picked up with the left hand would flow through her body and back to the Mother, who would eagerly absorb the deadly energy and transform it into something good. He referred to this method as "energy composting."

Trying to concentrate, Vickey pressed her free hand against her face. *Please, please, spirit of the star, help Griff! Help him! I don't want him to die! Please heal him. Stop the bleeding, just stop the bleeding!* She continued to say the prayer over and over, her lips moving silently.

And then Vickey began to feel heat throb in her left palm—the one holding the star. It startled her, scared her, but she continued on with her prayer, which flowed straight from her heart. Vickey knew that earnest prayer could move mountains. The star felt so hot in her hand now. At the same time it had a freezing sensation, as if she was touching a block of dry ice. All the numbness fled from her hand, and her skin throbbed with energy. Holding her focus, repeating the prayer, she felt heat shoot into all her fingers and up her arm. Within moments, the deafening roar of the river seemed to decrease in volume. Vickey no longer felt dragged down by the wet clothes she wore. Instead of feeling like a heavy lump on the sand, she began to feel lighter and lighter, as if she were leaving her body.

Understanding it was due to the energy throbbing from the crystal star, she didn't fight the sensation. The spirit within the crystal was thousands of years old and incredibly powerful. She would step out of the way and allow the healing process to continue.

Everything in her told her the star was capable of healing. After all, it was a clan totem. That meant it had the power of thousands of people behind it. Good people. People who walked the Red Road, the road of the heart. Her own heart was pounding in her chest. Everything became light behind her tightly closed eyelids. It was as if she were floating. The warmth snaked up her arm, across her shoulder and down her spinal column, then into her legs. She understood that the crystal star was removing the unhealthy energy from Griff's wound. Oh! If only it would stop the bleeding! She didn't want him to die! Crying helplessly, Vickey pressed her face more deeply into her hand, desperate sounds torn from her opened mouth.

Nothing mattered at this moment except Griff surviving. If only the Great Spirit would give her another chance with him. Why had she been so cruel to him? Stinging him with her Scorpian mouth? Never letting him live down his past with her? Hadn't he shown her in so many ways that he truly *had* changed? That he wasn't the youth in flight school anymore? That he was a man who was responsible, caring, sensitive and loyal?

Weakened by her trial in the river, Vickey slowly bent over, her brow pressed against Griff's chest. One hand covered her eyes and tears leaked through her fingers as the star continued its healing. She could feel the slow beat of Griff's heart beneath her ear. *Life. He had to live!* Her heart opened wide, just as powerful and strong as the river that thundered nearby. Strong emotion flowed through her shaking, trembling body as she prayed for Griff's life to be spared. Her left hand grew hotter and hotter until she thought for sure it was burning up. When she lifted her head from Griff's chest to look at her hand, she saw the skin had reddened as if sunburned. It didn't matter if she was scalded by the energy pulsing out of the star. If that would help stabilize Griff, stop the bleeding, it was worth it.

Vickey lost track of time as she knelt there. Minutes and hours seemed meaningless. Slowly, very slowly, she felt as if she were sliding back into her body. She was familiar with the sensation from when she meditated at BJS on days off between missions. It was a good feeling, this coming home to her body, the feeling of becoming heavy once more. Little by little, she felt herself returning. The heat of the star was diminishing. Vickey raised her head, sniffed and wiped away the tears beading on her lashes.

She was much warmer than she should be at this time of day in cold, soaked clothing. It had to be due to the crystal star. Looking up at Griff, she gasped. His once chalky appearance had changed dramatically. Ruddiness had returned to his cheeks. His face looked as if he'd never been wounded or lost so much blood. She watched as life flooded back into him. Purple shadows remained beneath his eyes, attesting to the brutal wound he carried, and his lips remained parted and slack. But when she pressed her fingers against his neck, feeling for a pulse, his heart was beating strongly once more. Shakily, she removed her fingers and glanced at her left hand.

The crystal star was no longer hot or burning. Something told her to lift it away. As she removed it, she saw that Griff's wound had stopped bleeding. It looked raw, the skin torn and heavily bruised, but no more blood oozed out. Maybe from the exit wound? Vickey had to make sure. She slid the star back into the protective blue fabric. Then, carefully lifting Griff's shoulder, she felt for where the bullet had exited.

He was no longer bleeding! Sobbing once, she removed her hand and quickly pulled his damp shirt across his chest. He had to be freezing cold.

A sound caught her attention above the roar of the Urubamba. What was it? Vickey twisted to look upward. The clouds lifted and she could see powder-blue patches of sky here and there. What was that sound? And then her heart plunged with terror.

It was a helicopter!

Gulping, she realized it was probably Balcazar's helo returning to retrieve his men, in order to find Griff and her. *Oh, no!* Scrambling to her feet, dizzy once more, Vickey nearly fell over. The power of the star had made her so light-headed. Staggering, she finally got her feet under her. Wrapping the fabric firmly around the crystal, she slid it back into her vest and put the garment back on.

She knew she had to drag Griff to the jungle, which was forty feet away. The helicopter was approaching rapidly, coming in fast and low. Panic set in, but Vickey remained clearheaded. She leaned down, bracing herself as she slid her arms beneath Griff's armpits and started to haul back with all her weight. Would moving him start the bleeding again? Desperate, she threw a glance upward, because the blades of the approaching copter punctured the air and shook the whole area around them. It felt as if someone were physically pummeling her with unseen fists—as if this helo pilot knew exactly where they were and was diving down to get them. Vickey had no time to flee, no weapon to fight with.

Gulping, she searched the sky. There! Between rifts of white clouds, against a light blue sky, she saw the dark shape.

Gasping, she felt her eyes widen. It was the BJS Blackhawk! With a cry of surprise, she knelt and released Griff. Who at BJS could know where they were? Or the trouble they were in? Questions careened through Vickey's mind as she watched the Blackhawk, with Wild Woman at the controls and Lieutenant Ana Cortina as copilot, land less than a hundred feet away from them on the rocky bank of the river.

The air whipped around Vickey, and she saw the door slide open. Out jumped the Angel of Death, Sergeant Angel Paredes, and her husband, Burke Gifford. They jogged toward Vickey, carrying a paramedic bag and a portable stretcher between them. Relief drenched her. Angel was the best paramedic in the world and had saved countless lives.

The noise of the river combined with the whirling blades of the Blackhawk drowned out all but essential conversation. Vickey stood on shaky legs as Angel ran up to her.

"How bad is he?" she yelled.

"Bullet wound to the shoulder. He's lost a *lot* of blood, Angel."

"Okay, get to the helo. Burke and I will get this stretcher set up and Griff on board pronto. Hurry! There're bad guys coming just around the corner of the river on the opposite bank. We've called in two Apaches to fire at them, but right now we're unarmed."

Nodding, Vickey glanced down at Griff, not wanting to leave his side. Angel waved at her to proceed to the helicopter, and reluctantly, she did. Running unsteadily across the rocky ground toward the black chopper, Vickey saw Wild Woman grin and raise her hand. Halting at the opening, Vickey looked over her shoulder. They'd lifted Griff onto the stretcher and were carrying him toward her.

Wanting to cry, but forcing down the reaction, Vickey turned back to the Blackhawk. Wild Woman stood just inside, holding out her gloved hand, which Vickey grasped. Her friend was small but strong. She pulled Vickey easily across the lip and into the main cargo area of the large helicopter. Then she handed her a helmet and plugged in the communication jack so they could talk to one another.

"You okay?" she asked as Vickey strapped on the helmet and moved the mouthpiece to her lips.

Nodding, Vickey said, "I'll live. I'm more worried

about Griff. He took a bullet in the shoulder and he's lost a lot of blood."

Angel expertly guided the stretcher into the cabin. Vickey stepped aside so the two paramedics could work on Griff. Burke leaped in and slammed the door. He gave Wild Woman a thumbs-up for takeoff. The pilot quickly moved back to the cockpit and trussed herself up in the harness, getting ready to lift off.

"Hold on, then! We're gonna redline this Blackhawk to Cuzco to get Griff medical help," Wild Woman announced.

Vickey knelt by Griff's head as Angel settled on one side of him, Burke on the other.

"Push this bird to its limits, Wild Woman," she muttered, worry almost choking her.

"Roger, read you loud and clear, Snake. Let's boogie!" The Blackhawk powered up and shook, the blades pounding. Everything rattled as the copter broke gravity with the earth and headed skyward. Vickey felt more relief pour through her. They were safe! *Safe!* She watched anxiously as Burke slid an IV needle into Griff's arm. Angel rapidly cleaned his wound and dressed it.

"How did you know where we were?" Vickey asked her pilot friend.

Wild Woman laughed. "Oh, those idiots were calling to one another on their walkie-talkies. We picked up their radio comms at BJS. When we realized they were rappelling down into Villecamba and going after *you,* we mounted this rescue effort. On the way here we heard them say you'd jumped into the river. So I knew we'd find you downstream...somewhere. I just followed my gut instincts as to where we'd spot you."

"Yeah, we damn near drowned in that river."

"That's what had me worried, Snake. You okay? Really?"

"Bruised, sore and tired. I'm worried sick about Griff." Vickey reached out and ran her trembling fingers over his drying hair. How badly she wanted to lie next to him and just hold him. Hold him, love him and let him know how much she cared for him. Oh, if only the Great Spirit would give her a second chance with him! She looked back and forth between Angel, who was now taking his blood pressure, and Burke, who was hooking up the IV bag. Griff had to be okay. Neither medic had on a helmet, so they couldn't hear her above the roar of the noisy Blackhawk.

"Thanks for coming. The Iridium phone I was carrying got busted all to hell," Vickey said.

Wild Woman laughed. "Listen, we weren't gonna let you fry your bacon out there with a bunch of grave robbers. Hey, did you find the star?"

"Yeah...we found Roka and we got the star. I have it here in my vest and it's okay." Touching her vest, which felt warmer than normal, Vickey smiled. She gazed at Griff, who looked healthier with each passing moment.

"Oh, good! Major Stevenson and Mike Houston will be happy to hear that."

"All I want right now is to get home," Vickey said, her voice trembling. "I want to know that Griff is going to make it because..."

She couldn't force the rest of the sentence out of her mouth. Vickey wanted to admit that if Griff died, a huge part of her would die along with him.

Chapter 18

When Griff regained consciousness, he felt as if he was emerging from a long tube of brilliant white light. Fatigued from walking what seemed like miles, his body became heavier and heavier with each step. He sensed warm fingers wrapped firmly around his right hand. It sent an incredible wash of relief through him. He struggled to open his eyes, the effort taking every ounce of energy he had left.

A blurred face met his gaze. Mouth dry, he parted his cracked lips, and a croak issued forth.

Instantly, the person holding his hand squeezed it gently.

"Don't fight so hard, Griff. It's okay. You're going to be fine. Just lie there and try to come back to me."

Vickey. It was Vickey's low, tearful voice. It was her hand wrapped around his fingers. Griff closed his eyes and took in several deep, ragged breaths. Vickey sounded wonderful to him. For whatever reason, he felt as if he'd been gone a long, long time—years, maybe. It was an odd feeling and he didn't like it. Just the touch of her fingertips brushing his hand assuaged some of his anxiety.

"Stop fighting," Vickey whispered near his ear. "You're alive. You've just come out of surgery and you're in Cuzco, at the main hospital."

The caress of her hand across his hair soothed Griff. It was simply too much of a struggle to open his eyes, so he stopped fighting. His body felt like a lead weight right now. Ragged pain floated around his left shoulder, and he realized his left arm was in a tight sling across his chest.

He was far more aware of Vickey's closeness. Flaring his nostrils, he drank in her feminine scent. She had always smelled so good to him. The corners of his mouth eased up slightly.

"What's so funny?" Vickey asked, watching Griff's lips curve just a bit.

"...You...smell good...."

Tears flooded Vickey's eyes. His voice was rough from disuse. "Thanks...and you look great to me." He did. Vickey sat at Griff's bedside in ICU. He'd come out of surgery two hours earlier. The nurses had said it would take one to two hours for the anesthetic to wear off. His face was pasty looking again. She wished she had the star, but Wild Woman had carried it back with her to BJS once they'd flown them here to the hospital grounds.

The crystal star had stopped the bleeding. Both Angel and her husband had said that if the sacred object hadn't stopped the hemorrhaging, Griff would have died on the stony riverbank, no question.

It scared Vickey deeply to think that he could have died. Nothing had shaken her as much as this had. Not even combat missions when she had to face off with a Black Shark. Tears blurred her vision. She lifted her hand from Griff's recently washed hair and quickly wiped the tears away, then settled her palm against his temple. When she touched him, she saw him visibly relax. He was fighting the anesthesia, the struggle evident in the wrinkling of his brow. Instinctively, Vickey wanted to ease his transition back to the living.

The beeping of instruments caught Griff's limited attention only momentarily. He could feel Vickey, her closeness, her warmth. Right now, he was chilled, and she made all the difference. The heaviness of his body began to ease and he found himself with a little strength as a result. After forcing his eyes open, he rested his gaze on Vickey, who was sitting in a chair and leaning toward him. For a while, her features remained blurry. Griff saw white walls behind her, but they, too, appeared gauzy and unreal. He honed in on her green eyes. As his vision sharpened and cleared, Griff saw that her hair was tangled and loose. There was tension in the set of her mouth, worry glittering in her eyes and a frown creasing her brow. Little by little, it all began to come back to Griff. He was no longer wet. No longer shivering and feeling as if he was going to die. The roar of the river was gone. His mind cartwheeled, recalling bits of memories.

Licking his lips slowly, he rasped, "Are you okay?"

She wanted to laugh. Hysterically. Vickey knew she was having an adrenaline letdown. Sometimes after a tough flight and a harrowing meeting with a Russian Black Shark, they would land back at the cave giggling hysterically. It was a way of releasing the terror and fear. "Yeah...I'm fine. No wounds. Just a lot of bruises and cuts from being slammed around like a Ping-Pong ball in that river." Vickey grazed his unshaved, bristly cheek. "Do you remember what happened, Griff? Getting shot in the left shoulder? Jumping into the Urubamba to get away from Balcazar's men? The crystal star?"

Closing his eyes, Griff saw fragments of every one of those scenes as she whispered to him. "Yeah, it's coming back to me in bits and pieces," he croaked.

"Are you thirsty? Warm enough? What can I do to help you?" Vickey didn't try to fight her heart where he was concerned. The words begged to be spoken: that she liked Griff, wanted a relationship of substance with him. What would he think or do? Vickey was unsure.

Opening his eyes, he whispered, "It would be real nice if you could just lie down beside me here and hold me. I'm feeling cold...."

She grinned. "Well, I think I can do that." She stood up and moved the chair away. After easing her hip onto the bed, she carefully lay down along his right side.

Griff was covered with a sheet and two blue cotton blankets, but it wasn't enough. Vickey knew that coming out of anesthesia made people feel very, very cold.

"Hold on," she whispered, placing a soft kiss to his brow, "I'm going to slide like a snake right next to you." She was very careful not to jolt his body or move quickly for fear of causing his shoulder more pain. His left arm was wrapped against his chest so he couldn't move it.

Sliding her arm beneath his neck, she settled her head on the pillow next to his. Feeling him sigh deeply, she draped her other arm across his torso, below the sling. She pressed her body fully against his right side and felt him begin to relax.

"There," Vickey whispered, her lips against his temple, "how's that?"

"Better...much better. I'm warmer already." She nurtured him, Griff realized, hungrily absorbing her warmth, the feel of her arm across his belly.

"Helluva way for you to get me to hold you," she laughed softly, closing her eyes and allowing Griff into her heart.

A smile pulled at his mouth. "I should get shot more often...."

"You're crazy, dude."

It hurt to talk, his throat was so sore. "Crazy...for you."

Lifting her head, her heart pounding at his roughly spoken words, Vickey looked down at Griff. His eyes were closed. She wasn't sure what that meant.

"We haven't exactly had a peaceful relationship,"

she reminded him, laying her head down again. What would it be like to be lying with Griff like this when he was well? Her body answered that question. She wanted to explore this man, his head, heart and soul. Vickey wanted the time to get to know him, but she knew that wasn't going to be possible. Because Griff had been wounded, he wouldn't be able to remain at BJS. No, as soon as he was medically stable and able to walk, she was sure the military would send him north to a U.S. base hospital to recover. Then, and only then, might he be sent back down here. It was a depressing thought. And it made this moment even more exquisite and important to her.

Stroking her hand against his ribs, she whispered into his ear, "Go to sleep, Griff. You're tired."

"Will you be here when I wake up?"

"Yeah, I'm not leaving you." He sighed again, and she felt him let go fully. A sense of contentment washed over Vickey.

"Good. I like having you as a blanket. I'm warm now. Thanks…"

Chuckling quietly, Vickey pressed a kiss to his temple. "You're incorrigible, Griff."

"But you like me a little, anyway?"

Choking back tears, Vickey closed her eyes and gently squeezed him. "Yeah, I like you a little, anyway."

The next time Griff awoke, he realized two things right off the bat. First, Vickey was gone, no longer warmly pressed against him. He missed her strong, comforting presence, her soft touch. Secondly, he was in a private room instead of the ICU. It was quiet, though he could hear people in the hall speaking in Spanish. Looking to his left, he saw that the blinds were open. The sky was a bright turquoise with a few puffy white clouds drifting here and there. Griff could see the red tile roofs of Cuzco and the brown, naked hills that surrounded the Peruvian city.

This time, he felt stronger. His bed tilted at a slight angle, the pillows behind his head fluffy and supportive. He glanced down at his left arm and saw that it was in a sling. There was no pain. An IV tube ran into his right arm and Griff was sure he was receiving some kind of pain drug to keep him comfortable.

The room was painted a light green, with several large pictures of the Andes and of orchids in the jungle. Another framed poster depicted two jaguars—one black, another gold with black spots on its sleek coat—sitting side by side. The graceful animals made him think of Vickey. When had she left? Where was she now? Back at BJS, most likely.

Stretching slowly, he realized he felt more like his old self. What time was it? There was no watch on his wrist, and no clock on the walls. What day was it? How much time had passed?

His memory returned full force and Griff was grateful for that. A little dizzy as he sat up, he pushed the bed covers aside and eased his legs off the mattress. As his bare feet touched the cool tile of the floor, he looked toward the closed door. For the next few minutes, Griff oriented himself. Despite his shoulder wound, he felt good. His stomach grumbled loudly. Grinning a little, he slid his hand across his torso. Yeah, he was starving to death. Memories of the delicious steak and baked potatoes slathered with sour cream and butter that he'd enjoyed with Vickey at the Liberator Hotel made his mouth water.

Damn, he missed her. Acutely. Where was she? Had he been unconscious for days? Griff knew she had duties at BJS and would have had to fly back to the cave complex to assume the combat missions. Frowning, he sat there, legs dangling over the bed.

Griff noticed a wheelchair in the corner. Could he get up and walk over to it? Would he fall flat on his face trying? Not wanting to jar his healing wound, he decided he'd better just sit there and hope a nurse or orderly would drop by to check on him.

He didn't have long to wait. To his surprise, it was Vickey who arrived. She halted in the doorway, her eyes growing huge when she saw him sitting there.

"Griff!"

"Hi, stranger. Come on in. I'm sitting here all alone and wondering what time and what day it is."

Her full mouth curved into a warm, welcoming smile, and his heart thundered in response. She looked gorgeous in a pair of form-fitting blue jeans, a white tank top that outlined the curves of her sweet body, her loose hair framing her face. A white leather purse was slung across her left shoulder, and she held a brown paper bag in her right hand.

Delighted that Griff was awake and sitting up, Vickey grinned and closed the door behind her. She held up the sack. "The docs said you'd be a starving guy when you woke up today. This is a hamburger and french fries from the Liberator Hotel. I thought you might like to chow down on some real food instead of IV drips." Vickey eagerly looked Griff over. His hair was mussed and she wanted badly to tame the dark, short strands into place. The look in his gray eyes made her heart sing. They were clear and no longer murky. And Griff was very alert and present. No more drugged drowsiness.

Reaching out, Griff took the proffered sack from Vickey. Their fingers touched. And lingered. He saw Vickey avoid his gaze after a moment. She released the bag and placed her purse on the end of his bed.

"Well, let's see." She looked at the watch on her left wrist. "The time is noon. The day is Wednesday." Looking up, she said, "You got out of surgery two days ago. The docs said it would take three days for you to get back to your old self. They were right."

"Three days..." Griff muttered disbelievingly. Vickey puttered around. She made sure the IV was out of the way and then pulled the blankets across his lower body to keep him snug and warm.

"Want me to open the sack?"

"Yeah. Being one-armed isn't great," he muttered. Her closeness intoxicated him. "You smell really good. Are you wearing perfume?"

Vickey smiled, opened the bag and unwrapped the hamburger. "I washed my hair a couple of hours ago." She kept half the burger in paper so it wouldn't leak all over Griff when he bit into it. She was more than a little aware of his maleness, his nearness. "I use a lilac fragrance shampoo. That's what you smell."

"Thanks," he said as she gave him the food. The hamburger smelled wonderful, too, and Griff eagerly devoured it. Closing his eyes, he savored every bite.

"Mmm, this is good," he said, his mouth full.

Laughing, Vickey placed the carton of french fries on his lap with a napkin beneath it. Opening several packets of salt, she shook it across them. "Spoken like a true *norteamericano.* I might be dying, but give me a hamburger."

Chuckling, Griff watched as she plucked up a french fry and held it up for him to eat. "Thanks. Being one-handed does have its positive side."

Heat flooded her neck and face. Vickey lowered her lashes and avoided his burning gaze. "Don't get used to it. This is a one-time deal. I'm due back at BJS in two hours. I've got to catch a taxi and get out to the airport by 1500."

Devastated, Griff tried not to show it. "I wish you could stay, but I know they need you back there."

Vickey nodded and eased up on the bed, her hip brushing against his leg. She ate a few of the warm french fries and contented herself by watching Griff wolf down the hamburger. How handsome he was! Why hadn't she realized that before? Knowing why, Vickey felt torn inside.

"Yeah, I'm back on the flight schedule as of today," she told him quietly. Crossing her legs, her hands clasped in her lap, she absorbed Griff's presence like sunlight into her heart.

Griff lost some of his appetite as he considered her departure. "What's happened since I was shot? Is the crystal star okay? It didn't break, did it?"

"It's fine. Kai Alseoun is flying in tomorrow to pick it up and take it back to her nation. Jake Carter is going to be accompanying her." Vickey gazed warmly up at Griff. Right now he looked like a little boy, his hair mussed and a dab of ketchup at one corner of his mouth. She took a paper napkin and wiped it away. The unexpected touch made his gray eyes darken instantly. Hesitantly, Vickey withdrew the napkin from his mouth.

"Ketchup," she whispered.

His mouth tingled where she'd grazed him. What would it be like to kiss her? How many times had Griff wanted that to happen? A million, maybe?

"You had ketchup on the corner of your mouth."

"Oh. Thanks…"

"Don't mention it." Vickey leaned back, nervously knotting the napkin between her fingers. She was shaken by the look he'd given her and feeling terribly unsure of herself. What was happening? She had never felt like this in her life! How could one look send her heart skittering, her blood pressure shooting through the roof and her lower body aching for his nearness?

Trying to gather his scattered thoughts after her unexpected touch, Griff finished off the burger and picked at the fries in his lap. Vickey seemed distant all of a sudden. Why? "What's going to happen now?"

"To you?" She lifted her lashes and held his burning look, which was etched with desire—for her. "I—

well, Dr. Elizabeth Cornell, our medical doctor at BJS, said that as soon as you were stable, you'd get flown back stateside. She said you'd need time to heal and strengthen your shoulder. There's no nerve damage, so that means you'll probably be able to resume your flight status down at BJS as soon as you're better. She said you'd go through a lot of tests first, but she has every reason to feel you'll be flying the Apache within the next six months."

Griff should have been elated. "But that means I'm leaving here." *And leaving you.* The words stuck in his throat. Scowling, he put down the french fry he held.

"Yes, it does…." Tearing the napkin into little pieces in her lap, Vickey discovered that she was a coward when it really counted. She wanted desperately to talk to Griff, to share with him how her feelings had changed. But how? *How?* There was no guarantee he would forgive her for holding such a long grudge. He might not be able to let go of the past. Nervously, she continued to shred the napkin. Though unable to meet his gaze, she could feel Griff looking at her. Her body ached for his touch.

"Yes, Lieutenant Klein already has your new orders and travel documents prepared." It hurt her to say those words. *Damn.*

Putting the fries to one side, Griff stared at Vickey. Her mouth was set in an unhappy line. Was she going to miss him? How desperately he wanted to ask, and the silence in the room became oppressive. So many questions, and he was too chicken to ask a single one. What a monumental coward he was at heart!

"I had a dream last night...or maybe it wasn't. I'm not sure," Griff began quietly. Vickey lifted her face, and he met and held her warm green eyes. "Maybe it was post-traumatic stress coming to haunt me. I remember being in the river and how damn cold I was. And you were hauling my ass toward the bank. I didn't realize just how strong you are, Vickey."

Her heart opened. She saw the respect in Griff's eyes and heard the admiration in his tone. "Adrenaline," she said. "It kicked in. I was scared for both of us. That's how I was able to do it."

"Maybe. The next scene I saw in the dream was you leaning over me. You were crying. I saw you pull the crystal star from your vest and lay it over my wound. I was so cold that I didn't feel the pain, but I sure felt that burning sensation when you pressed it there." He gestured toward his shoulder.

Griff measured his words carefully now, his gaze locked on her widening eyes. Eyes he wanted to see shine with that same look he'd seen in his dream. "If I read the dream correctly, you really *cared* about me. I know we've had a lot of bad blood between us and I was shocked at what I saw in your face, your eyes...and what I heard in your voice. You really cared for me, Vickey. And it was more than just a casual friendship kind of thing." Griff released a ragged sigh. Fingers curling on his thigh, he asked in a low, unsteady tone, "Did that really happen, Vickey? Or was it all a dream?"

"How about I answer that before you leave?" Vickey told him. She knew from speaking to Dr. Cornell that in all likelihood, Griff would be shipped stateside in a week or less. And that's how much time she had to craft an answer to his innocent question that could mean a turning point in her life—and his.

Chapter 19

"You're leaving," Vickey said as she allowed the hospital room door to close behind her. She stood uncertainly in Griff's room. It had been seven days since he'd asked that question: *was it a dream?* She hadn't had the guts to answer him, and had fled back to BJS, promising him she would tell him before he left for the States. That time had come.

Griff was casually dressed in a pair of jeans, a lime-green polo shirt and a pair of tennis shoes—a far cry from his hospital gown. His left arm was in a sling, and she could see the frustration etched on his face as he tried to pack his suitcase.

How handsome he looked! Why hadn't Vickey savored his good looks long ago? Or the quality of his heart? Why hadn't she appreciated the changes he'd made? Now it was too late. Gulping, her throat tight with unshed tears, Vickey forced herself to walk toward Griff. She saw surprise flare in his eyes as she quietly spoke those husky words. And then she saw his gray gaze warm with pleasure at her arrival.

Griff straightened. "I've...got an hour before the taxi takes me to the airport and I fly home." Swallowing hard, he couldn't tear his gaze from hers. She was dressed in a flattering white blouse with a lace-edged boat neckline, and a burgundy silk blazer. White silk slacks enhanced her summery appearance. As stylish and feminine as she appeared, he couldn't help sensing the wild and natural side of her, the lithe, powerful jaguar within, mystical and sleek.

Vickey nervously adjusted the white leather purse strap on her shoulder. "You having trouble packing?" That was a safe topic compared to what she really wanted to say. But the past shadowed her. Was the old Griff gone for good? Was this new one, a much better version, for real? Vickey halted on the opposite side of the bed and avoided the burning question she saw in his eyes. "You got a mess in there, Lone Ranger."

"With only one hand I can't fold anything, Tonto," he told her with a grin.

"Want some help?" She held up her hands.

Griff stared at her long, lovely fingers. Flight hands. Hands that were strong and yet incredibly feminine. Hands he wanted on his body, touching him, loving him... At odds with his pounding heart, he tried to convey lightness in his expression. "The Lone Ranger definitely needs all the help he can get."

Her mouth quirked, and she placed her purse on the bed. "This would never pass inspection at Fort Rucker," she murmured, quickly beginning to separate and fold his polo shirts, boxer shorts, T-shirts and jeans. "That's the scuttlebutt—that you've got orders to go there?"

Sitting on the bed, absorbing her quiet voice and watching her work with her usual efficiency, Griff said, "Yes, they have me flying a desk at the flight school for about a month and a half."

"To let your shoulder heal?" Vickey didn't want to look up. Her fingers trembled slightly as she quickly continued to fold clothes and organize his suitcase.

"That's right. Dr. Cornell at BJS said the hospital at Fort Rucker was the best place for my recovery." Griff wiggled the fingers of his left hand. The movement hurt a little. "No nerve damage, thank God. She said it would take eight weeks for me to heal before I'm ready to fly again. I figure three months stateside is all I'll need, and then I can get rotated back down here."

"So they're looking for you to sit in the Apache again, for sure?" Her heart pounded briefly at the news.

"That's what Dr. Cornell told me," Griff said. He watched Vickey's soft, shining dark brown hair frame her face, emphasizing her large green eyes. Studying her features, he saw that her cheeks had reddened considerably. He admired the tasteful pearl earrings and single strand of pearls around her neck. "You look really pretty today." The words came out unbidden, and he couldn't take them back. Vickey's hands stilled over his clothing. Her brows knitted momentarily, and she lifted her head. He saw confusion in her eyes and didn't know why. Her lips lifted slightly—lips he badly wanted to kiss.

"Why, thanks. You don't look too bad yourself, Griff."

"My heart be still." He pressed his hand over his chest. "A compliment! Finally!"

Laughing softly, Vickey shook her head. "You know Scorpios—we don't say much but what we do say, we mean."

Chuckling, he watched her rummage deeper in his suitcase.

"What's this?" Vickey pulled out a large fuzzy toy. It was a small llama covered with white fur and embellished with a red woven blanket and halter.

"That, oh..." Griff lost his smile. He looked away for a moment and then met her inquiring gaze. "That's a toy for Roger."

"Who's Roger?" Vickey gently handled the toy. She saw Griff's face go dark, his gaze dropping to the floor. Instinctively, she felt his pain and sobered instantly.

"Remember I told you about the day I was shot down? Landing on the hilltop with that Special Forces group?"

"Yes," she said softly, hearing the hesitation, the rawness in his tone.

"Well, like I said, my copilot, Frank Johnson, was

hit and wounded. He was my best friend." Giving a one-shouldered shrug, Griff looked down at his fingers. "He died in my arms. He has a wife and a child. Roger is his son. He's five. I thought, well, since I'm going back to Fort Rucker where his wife, Addy, still lives outside the base, I wanted to bring Roger a little something. Maybe cheer him up." Griff shook his head and gave Vickey a sad look. "This happened six months ago, and I know they're struggling. Frank and Addy had a great marriage and they loved each other deeply. It hurts me even to think about it."

Gently squeezing the llama toy in her hands, Vickey said, "This is such a thoughtful gift to give that little boy. I know he'll love it." She stared at Griff's set profile, the way his mouth curved. Silence settled around them until she couldn't stand it anymore. "You really have changed since I knew you in training." Picking up one of his shirts, she carefully wrapped the toy in it so it wouldn't be damaged by careless baggage handlers.

A painful sigh escaped Griff's pursed lips. Hearing the puzzlement in her husky tone, he glanced at Vickey. She rested her hands on the suitcase and watched him with those intense eyes of hers. "War changes people, Vickey. It changed me. When Frank died in my arms, I realized that life was precious and fleeting. We could die any day and that would be it." He opened his right hand. "Roger doesn't have a father now, Addy doesn't have a husband. War tears the hell out of everything and everyone. I can't find anything good about it."

Snorting softly, Vickey said, "I know."

"You do know. You're at war down here." His mouth flexed in a grimace. "A quiet battle, but war nonetheless."

"We live daily with the fear that one of our Apaches will be shot down by Black Sharks. Every day I see Wild Woman and we're flying apart rather than together, I think to myself it might be the last time. The last time I experience her crazy wild humor, her independence, that look of trouble that's always dancing in her eyes. Being down here for four years has taught me to really savor the relationships I have. I take every day and try to live it to the fullest, realizing I might be dead tomorrow."

"I understand."

Vickey carefully placed the polo shirt and stuffed animal in the center of the suitcase where it would be best protected. "You really are a knight in shining armor," she murmured, a soft smile coming to her lips.

"Not with you," Griff said, lifting his head and holding her startled gaze. "I screwed up with you. And you were the last person I wanted to do that with. But I did it and I can't change the past."

"Scorpios aren't known for forgetting or forgiving," she said, shrugging.

"I know that."

"Maybe that's wrong," Vickey whispered, placing the jeans gently on top of the llama to protect it.

His heart pounded once to underscore her softly spoken words. "What do you mean?"

"When I found out you were coming down here, and even worse, being assigned to me to be checked out in the cockpit, I threw a fit." Vickey stopped packing, walked around the bed and stood in front of Griff. He deserved her courage, not the fear that was eating her alive.

"I'm sure you did," he told her, meeting her narrowed green eyes. She had clasped her hands together, and he could feel the tension radiating from her. "So what's changed?"

"A lot of things." Fear tightened her throat and the next words came out sounding strangled. "I didn't want to admit you'd changed for the better, because I had so much old, built-up rage over what you'd done to us."

She was so close…so close Griff could reach out and touch her. How badly he wanted to, and yet he didn't dare. Vickey had to give him permission, otherwise it would be just as before, where he'd bulldozed her into something. He wouldn't go there again, ever. Anguish moved through him as he saw tears glimmer in her eyes.

"You've more than proved you've changed. You've shown me how courageous you are. You're someone I can count on, Griff. And you were there in the thick of things when we got nailed in that warehouse."

The tension mounted, and Griff didn't move. He could tell she was fighting back tears. "We haven't had time to talk about that whole thing," he said. "When we got caught, I was more scared and worried for you than myself. When that gunfire went off near the door, I thought they'd killed you."

"Just the other way around," she said wryly. "I shot

the guard and escaped." Opening her hands, she muttered, "But I couldn't help you. I felt horrible, Griff. And scared…"

"Listen," he told her quietly, "there were a lot of bad guys in there with AK-47s, and only one of you. If you'd tried to rescue me, we'd both be dead now and you know that. So do I. You did what you had to do to survive."

Vickey drank in his wide gray gaze, so tender and filled with understanding. "I know, but it tore me up inside. I didn't know what to do. I was so afraid they'd kill you." She sniffed and wiped the tears from her eyes with trembling fingers.

Griff reached over to the bed stand for the tissue box.

"Thanks." Vickey blew her nose and blotted her eyes. "I don't normally cry in front of people."

"I know. Scorpios are good at hiding in the nearest closet and crying quietly and alone. They aren't ones to cry in front of others."

"How do you know that?" she asked, amazed.

"I'm a Scorpio just like you."

Stunned, she stared. "You are?" She watched a little-boy smile tug at his mouth. And she wanted to throw her arms around him and kiss him breathless.

"My birthday is November 6. When's yours?"

Her mouth dropped open. "November 7. This is incredible!" She saw Griff in a whole new light—they were both Scorpios! That meant he was very much like her in every respect.

"Is that good, then?" Griff teased.

"Yeah, it's a good thing."

"I know enough about astrology to shoot myself in the foot with it," Griff added. "I understand from Wild Woman that you're a bit of a professional."

"Yeah, I'm learning in my spare time. It doesn't hurt to know when there's a bad day coming up for me. I fly real careful and stay alert."

"Listen, I'm for anything that will keep us safe," Griff exclaimed with a chuckle.

Sobering, Vickey said, "Do you remember what happened after I dragged you out of the river, Griff? The crystal star? Do you recall me placing it over your bleeding shoulder?"

"Yes. I wanted to share that with you when you were ready." Looking at the clock on the wall, he saw time was slipping away. He didn't want to leave. This conversation had been a long time in coming and he didn't want to rush it. Vickey was open to him. Her guard was down. She was talking to him, woman to man, for the first time. God knew how much he'd wanted that to happen.

"I was semiconscious at that point and in a lot of pain. I heard you sobbing my name and I felt you pulling my shirt away from my wound." He pointed to the sling. "When you placed that crystal on it, I felt a white-hot heat shoot into me. For a while there, I thought I was going to burn up. That fire, or whatever it was, went through me like a bolt of lightning and then intensified. I felt like I'd been ripped out of my body, like I was floating somewhere. I saw a lot of rainbow colors around me—soft, pastel ones." Shaking his head, Griff held her fascinated gaze. "I didn't hear the river anymore. All I could hear was the slowing beat of my heart. It was beautiful where I was. I did feel you, though, and I could hear you. You were crying and talking to me, but I couldn't answer."

"Y-you heard me?"

"Yeah." Griff tapped his temple and smiled a little. "Every word. Did you mean it, Vickey?" He wanted nothing more than for her to say yes. Seeing fresh tears flood her eyes, he pulled another tissue from the box and held it out to her.

"I didn't say anything out loud, Griff. I remember thinking a lot of things as I tried to help you on that riverbank."

"I heard what was inside your head. I *felt* what was in your heart toward me." He searched her eyes and then reached out and wrapped his hand around hers. "It's crazy, I know. Wherever I was suspended, I could hear your thoughts and feel your feelings. All of them."

"Oh..." Wiping her eyes, she squeezed his fingers gently. "I believe you. My father said that things like this happen to people when they are pulled out of their body. They see everything and everyone. They not only hear what we say, but what we think and how we feel."

"Well, that's what happened to me. It was the damnedest experience I've ever had, Vickey. It's never happened before but—" Griff met and held her green eyes "—it rallied me. I started fighting back when I realized that you cared for me. I felt as if you had forgiven me for the past. Maybe I'm wrong about that."

Shaking her head, Vickey whispered unsteadily, "No...you're not wrong, Griff. I know forgiving is the right thing to do, but as a Scorpio, I really hold on to the hurt someone has inflicted on me. And I want to hurt them back, to sting them like they've stung me."

"Yeah," he chuckled. "I'm the same way."

"I have forgiven you." There, the words were out. His fingers were warm and caring around hers. Choking, Vickey said in a strained voice, "Damn, this is so hard, Griff! I have so much I want to say, so much to explore with you, and you have to leave in fifteen minutes."

"I know," Griff said, holding up her hand and kissing her gently. Her flesh was soft and scented with lilacs. "I like discovering you, Vickey. I want the time to do that. With your permission." He held her shocked stare. "I might have to leave for Fort Rucker and earn back my right to fly the Apache in combat. But unless you tell me otherwise, I'll be fighting to get down here for a year's rotation—with you. What do you say? Are you game?

"In the meantime we could e-mail each other and talk that way. Or writing in letter form is okay, too. It might give me time to think things through instead of inserting my foot in my mouth, which I'm known for doing." That boyish smile crept across his mouth. "And I want you to know I'm sitting here sweating like a pig, afraid that you'll tell me no..."

Vickey felt the dampness of his fingers around hers

as she allowed him to draw her next to him. He sat down on the edge of the bed, and her body brushed lightly against his.

"Maybe one of the lessons I have to learn is letting go of the darkness of the past," she told him, lifting her hand and smoothing his hair into place. "You've made me grow, Griff. You've shown me that a person can change, can come out of something bad and struggle to become good, instead." Leaning down, she framed his face, holding it in a position where she could kiss that very male mouth of his.

"And unless you tell me no, I want a hello-goodbye kiss from you right now," she said.

Shock bolted through Griff as her warm, strong hands bracketed his face. Vickey was so close, her eyes a dazzling green flecked with gold. Drowning in them, he slid his hand around her neck and pulled her forward.

"We both want this," he told her raggedly, and brought her mouth against his own with a crushing, searching force. The world tilted. As Griff closed his eyes and focused entirely on the warm feminine softness of her lush mouth blossoming eagerly beneath his, he understood what heaven felt like for the first time in his life.

Vickey's hair grazed his cheek. Her breath quickened in cadence with his. Griff couldn't get enough of her. He felt her hands tighten around him, her lips questing, searching, starving. So was he! Claiming her mouth firmly, Griff let Vickey know just how much she meant to him. If he had only one chance to convince her that he cared deeply for her, and wanted to have a relationship with her that could lead to marriage, it was this one indelible, life-giving kiss.

Vickey's careful world of control dissolved heatedly beneath the scorching exploration of Griff's mouth. Tasting him and inhaling the fragrance of his spicy aftershave set off rockets deep inside her melting body. Nipping at his lower lip, she ran her tongue across it and heard him groan. The sound reverberated like thunder on a hot summer day. *Yes!* This was what she wanted! Him. The ache in her body exploded. *Oh! To have him. All of Griff!*

Why had she waited so long? Why had she been so damn stubborn and slow to forgive him? Griff was a hero of the first order. Giving candy to the poor children of Lima, trying to save his friend's life in Afghanistan, saving the Special Forces team with his courage and intelligence, and then to give that llama toy to little Roger…

What a fool she'd been to hang on to the past! As her mouth slid wetly across his, she felt the carefully monitored strength of his hand around her neck. She could barely restrain her desire. His kiss told her how much he wanted her.

Gradually, oh so gradually, Vickey eased away from Griff's mouth. His strong and giving mouth. As much as he'd taken from her, he'd given twice as much in return. Breathing hard, their breaths mingling, she lifted her lashes and drowned in his blazing silver-gray gaze. His eyes focused on her like a hunter. She was the target, but in the best of ways. Aching deeply for him, as only a woman can for her man, she eased her hands from his face, her fingers grazing his cheek and his mussed hair.

"You have to leave," she said.

"I don't want to."

"I know. I don't want you to leave, either."

Griff slid his palm against her flaming cheek. Vickey closed her eyes and pressed her face into it. That one gesture of surrender broke his heart. Gulping unsteadily, Griff rasped, "Three months, sweetheart. Only three months. We can hang on until then."

Vickey chuckled softly and kissed him again, swiftly and hotly. As she eased away, her hand on his uninjured shoulder, she said in an unsteady tone, "It's going to be three months of hell, Griff. Three of the longest months of my life."

He gave her a wry smile, trying to make her feel a little better because the tears were back in her eyes. It hurt him to see her upset. All he wanted was to hold Vickey and make her feel loved and safe. Griff knew he could give her love and security. "They will be, but we're old enough, mature enough to make the best of it. We have e-mail."

"I'll call you on the satellite phone. Other BJS personnel call their husbands and significant others from it. I'll get on the list to have a weekly call with you." Her heart ached. "I was so slow to realize everything."

"We're Scorpios," Griff murmured, standing up. "We're like that and it's okay." He placed his arm around her shoulder and drew her gently against him.

When Vickey nestled her head against his shoulder, nothing felt more right to him.

"Listen, we've found one another. We're lucky. We'll work through our past and lay a solid foundation for the present and the future." He pressed a kiss to her soft, lilac-scented hair. "And we're strong people, sweetheart. We'll make this being apart work for us, not against us."

Easing away, Vickey said, "I've just lost Wild Woman today, too. And now you."

He heard the forlorn tone in her voice. "What?" He knew Wild Woman was Vickey's best friend. It made their own parting worse for her, and that hurt Griff.

"Yeah," Vickey muttered, wiping the tears from her eyes, "Kai Alseoun and her partner, Jake Carter, were down here last week to pick up the crystal star and take it back to the Cherokee nation. She told Major Stevenson that the woman in her dreams who's meant to find the Wolf Clan crystal was Wild Woman…Jessica."

Frowning, Griff asked, "And she's TDY, to where?"

"Washington, D.C. She's flying out from Lima this morning to meet a CIA undercover agent there. Apparently because of information from cell phone messages, they think the wolf's head crystal is at Marston's Hong Kong mansion. Wild Woman is flying there with this guy who speaks fluent Chinese. They are going undercover together to retrieve the last artifact."

Squeezing her gently, Griff whispered, "Losing two friends in one day is rough."

Nodding, Vickey said, "Yeah, I feel really abandoned." She stepped out of his arms. "Come on, it's time. I'll carry your suitcase down to the lobby for you."

Griff didn't want to go but knew he had to. Picking up his wallet, he stuffed it into his back pocket. His airline tickets were on the bed stand. Scooping them up, he heard Vickey snapping his blue canvas suitcase shut. He turned and watched her pull it off the bed. She was so strong and capable. His body burned with an ache to love her, satisfy her and take her to the edge of the stars with him.

"Come on," she urged, opening the door for him, "you've got a plane to catch, Lone Ranger."

As he walked with his arm around her shoulders, Griff tried to deal with the gamut of emotions in his heart. "I'm serious about you, Vickey," he told her, giving her a sideways glance. "About us."

"I am, too."

"I'm not a one-night stand kind of guy."

"What Scorpio ever is? We're long-term people."

"I'm in for the long haul with you. Okay?" He felt that touch of anxiety again, but when Vickey raised her head and fearlessly looked him in the eyes, it instantly dissolved.

"Scorpios play for keeps. I thought you knew that." She tried to smile.

The elevator opened and they stepped in. As the doors whooshed closed, Griff drew her close as soon as she'd put the suitcase down. "I like what we have, sweetheart."

Vickey slid her arms around his waist and laid her head on his shoulder. "So do I. And we're going to explore it. All of it."

"And then," Griff whispered, kissing her temple, "I'm going to be back here, taking you in my arms, shutting the hotel door, locking it behind us and throwing away the key."

Laughing, she felt her aching heart lift and soar beneath his blazing gray eyes. Griff meant every word. "Maybe it won't be three months. Maybe if I get lucky, I can wrangle five days off to fly north for a visit. No promises, but the major owes me a lot of accumulated R & R."

"Anytime, sweetheart, anytime. The sooner, the better."

As Vickey picked up the suitcase and walked into the busy lobby, she knew that somehow she'd get to see Griff a lot sooner than he expected. Three months was too long to wait. Now that she had discovered what she'd nearly lost, there was no way she was going to lose it again.

As they moved out the glass doors and into the bright sunshine, Vickey saw a green taxi waiting for them at the end of the walk. Sliding her hand into his, she said, "One thing, Griff. I don't want you to ever forget that in my eyes, you are and always will be my knight in shining armor. Forever…"

* * * * *

Books by Lindsay McKenna

Silhouette Bombshell

°°*Daughter of Destiny* #1
°°*Sister of Fortune* #21

Silhouette Intimate Moments

Love Me Before Dawn #44
ΔΔ*Protecting His Own* #1184

Silhouette Shadows

Hangar 13 #27

Silhouette Desire

ΔΔ*Ride the Thunder* #1459

Silhouette Romance

ΔΔ*The Will To Love* #1618

Silhouette Special Edition

†*A Question of Honor* #529
†*No Surrender* #535
†*Return of a Hero* #541
†*Dawn of Valor* #649
‡*Heart of the Wolf* #818
‡*The Rogue* #824
‡*Commando* #830
‡‡*Morgan's Wife* #986
‡‡*Morgan's Son* #992
‡‡*Morgan's Rescue* #998
‡‡*Morgan's Marriage* #1005
Δ*Heart of the Hunter* #1214
Δ*Hunter's Woman* #1255
Δ*Hunter's Pride* #1274
§*Man of Passion* #1334
§*A Man Alone* #1357
§*Man with a Mission* #1376
◊◊*Woman of Innocence* #1442
ΔΔ*The Heart Beneath* #1486
◊◊*Her Healing Touch* #1519

Silhouette Books

Silhouette Christmas Stories
"Always and Forever"

Lovers Dark and Dangerous
"Seeing Is Believing"

Midnight Clear
"The Five Days of Christmas"

The Heart's Command
"To Love and Protect"

**Morgan's Mercenaries: Heart of the Jaguar*

**Morgan's Mercenaries: Heart of the Warrior*

**Morgan's Mercenaries: Heart of Stone*

Destiny's Woman

To Love and Protect

An Honorable Woman

In Love and War
"Comrades in Arms"

Snowy Nights
"Always and Forever"

**Morgan's Honor*

**Morgan's Legacy*

Firstborn

*Morgan's Mercenaries
†Love and Glory
‡‡Morgan's Mercenaries: Love and Danger
ΔMorgan's Mercenaries: The Hunters
§Morgan's Mercenaries: Maverick Hearts
◊◊Morgan's Mercenaries: Destiny's Women
ΔΔMorgan's Mercenaries: Ultimate Rescue
°°Sisters of the Ark